Too many thoughts whirled through Claire's head

Too many jumbled emotions. She felt sick at the discovery that the man she loved—*thought* she loved—was a murder suspect.

"I *trusted* you," she finally managed. "I trusted you, and you lied to me."

"All right, Claire," Michael said wearily. "I wasn't completely straight with you. I *needed* to have access to your house so I could try to find your aunt's journals—so I could prove my innocence."

"Then all our lovemaking was a farce, right? A way for you to gain entry into the house?"

"You have to believe me, Claire. Our lovemak-ing—"

"I don't know what to believe anymore."

Morgan Hayes

Twilight Whispers

Harlequin Books

TORONTO • NEW YORK • LONDON
AMSTERDAM • PARIS • SYDNEY • HAMBURG
STOCKHOLM • ATHENS • TOKYO • MILAN
MADRID • WARSAW • BUDAPEST • AUCKLAND

ISBN 0-373-70591-3

TWILIGHT WHISPERS

Copyright © 1994 by Illona Haus.

Printed in U.S.A.

ABOUT THE AUTHOR

The impulse to write came to Morgan Hayes during a visit to her family's lakeside home. The desire to create—and experience—other lives through her characters resulted in a number of stories in various stages of completion. She quickly realized that all the novels she'd written were romances and thought—correctly—that they might appeal to Harlequin readers.

Morgan is already hard at work on her second Superromance title. She lives in Kitchener, Ontario. She loves her cat, but wishes it were a dog.

To David, for the encouragement, the support
and the wisdom

PROLOGUE

SHERIFF RAYMOND BANNON raised the fake-sheepskin collar of his parka against the bitter wind. An early February gale lifting off of the rocky shores of Somerset Bay swirled the freshly fallen snow into miniature whirlwinds. His fingers had numbed from the cold and even his toes were beginning to feel as though they might freeze as he paced the distance between his cruiser and the ambulance.

He paused, stamping his feet and burying his gloved hands deep into the pockets of the heavy uniform coat, as he watched the medics carry the stretcher down the back steps and across to the ambulance. They had been careful to tuck in the edges of the sheet, he noted thankfully, as the wind battered the thin cloth against the contours of the body it shrouded.

He dragged hard on the end of his cigar, without success. It had fizzled out long ago. Bannon shook his head. There were better ways to start the week—like a hot coffee and an apple fritter down at the One Stop Donut Shop, for one.

His deputy, Frank Turner, didn't seem overly impressed with the events of the morning either, he noted, watching Frank saunter across the snow-packed drive toward him. He'd had a scowl on his tired face from the moment he'd stepped out of the patrol car, blowing into his bare hands and muttering about the weather. Even now, he didn't look as though he was fully awake. His hair was tousled and his cap missing. His parka hung open and the yellow piping on the cuffs of his uniform trousers was beginning to fray.

Bannon made a mental note to warn Frank about his uniform when they got back into town.

"So, what d'you think?" he asked as Frank joined him, watching one attendant close the rear doors while the other gunned the motor.

"What do you mean?" Frank turned to catch the sheriff's nod toward the crumbling Victorian house. "The old lady finally quit. What else is there?"

Bannon remained silent. He stared at his boots as he kicked a chunk of ice that had fallen off the fender of one of the vehicles. Eventually he turned and crossed the snow-packed drive to the back door.

"What? You think someone did her in? Come on, Ray. She died in bed, in her sleep," said Frank, following the sheriff up the steps and into the house. Instinctively, he knocked the snow from his boots when he stepped into the kitchen. "You're not trying to tell me that we're going to have to investigate this? She was in her eighties, for Christ's sake. What are you getting at?"

"I'm not getting at anything."

From the chill in the house, Bannon guessed that the furnace must have shut down several hours ago. Even so, the old stone walls were shelter from the frigid wind outside. He walked through the kitchen and into the cluttered sitting room. Having had many of the rooms boarded up years ago, she had lived primarily on the first floor. Here he found all the evidence of the secluded existence she had led in this house on the bluffs overlooking Somerset Bay and the town of Westport.

He removed his gloves and blew on his fingers before leafing through the top layer of papers that buried an antique desk. There was nothing revealing here—nothing but receipts, notes, unpaid bills. Henry Lubinsky had told him that he would be up in a couple of days to settle the old woman's affairs, and he could wait for the Westport lawyer to deal with the mess of paperwork.

The sheriff scanned the room again.

He had heard about the work being done on the house, but only now could he actually see what had been completed—the carpentry, the molding, the new fixtures. And he had to admit, it was starting to look more than livable.

Estelle Bramley had occupied the towering house that stood as a permanent sentinel to the Maine coastal town for as long as Raymond Bannon could remember. Even today he could recall the childhood rumors about the woman in the house on top of the bluffs. She could see everything, the people of Westport claimed, from her third-story turret.

He turned to the impressive winding staircase now, his boyhood curiosity beckoning him. He had to see the turret for himself.

His boots echoed on the old stairs and he wasn't surprised to hear the creak of every other step as he climbed past the second floor.

Frank was right behind him. "You're serious, aren't you, Ray?" he asked, bounding up the last two steps. "You really want this thing investigated?"

"Yes, I'm serious. And since I'm already behind with the paperwork on the Hobson case, I want you to handle it."

"You're kidding me, right?"

"We have to be sure—you know that."

"So what are you saying? Someone came in here and iced the woman? Come on, Ray, what would they have to gain by that?"

Bannon gave him a noncommittal shrug. "All I'm saying, Frank, is that what we have here is the second dead body up on these bluffs in less than one week. I want you to look into it."

Having tried a couple of doors on the third floor and found them locked, Bannon at last reached the room he'd been seeking—the turret. Its six windows overlooked the fields and the town below the bluffs. The interior itself seemed huge, almost all out of proportion to the rest of the house, and even Bannon was surprised at the amount of space encircled by the curved wall of windows.

But the room was nearly empty. Some wood had been stacked beside the fireplace, with its cracked and smoke-stained brickwork. In spite of its appearance, Bannon guessed that it was probably still functional. A small desk was pressed up against the wall beneath one of the windows, and beside this, turned to face the same window, squatted a well-worn, oversize armchair.

For a fleeting moment, Bannon could actually picture Estelle Bramley sitting right there, observing the goings-on of the people in the community, watching the tourists scour the shops for souvenirs and surveying the boats that came in and out of the bay in the summer. He stood there now, his cold fingers gripping the back of the chair, and looked out to the snow-swept fields. In the distance, he recognized the ambiguous outline of the Dalton house hidden by the tall firs that seemed to threaten a takeover of the other mansion.

"I don't get it, Ray." Frank's voice ruptured the momentary silence of the room as he flicked a piece of lint from his uniform pants.

"What's to get, Frank?" Bannon tried to ignore the youthful impatience in his deputy's voice and watched the swirl of his breath curl into the cold air. "All I want is for you to look into a woman's death. Most likely routine, nothing more. Humor me, okay?"

"Yeah, but you think there's a connection, right? I just don't see the link between the old woman and the Hobson girl."

Bannon looked out at the drifting snow again. Frank was probably right. More than likely there was nothing behind Estelle Bramley's death. But after thirty-five years being sheriff in Westport, he was not about to run the risk of retiring with a blemish on his clean record.

It had happened only a week ago, here on the bluffs. It was the end of January and there had not been much snow since Christmas. But it was still cold—a bitter, bone-biting cold. Especially that night when they had finally found Annette Hobson. He could still remember the icy silence that had fallen over the last exhausted members of the search party as they circled the young girl's body on that rigid slope. The relentless wind had battered their numb faces and clutched at their breath as they stared down at her beaten body.

She had been missing for more than three days. Even with the aid of the villagers and some of their dogs, it had taken them that long to find her.

Bannon had initially harbored hopes that Estelle Bramley might have seen something. But the woman would speak to neither him nor Frank about it. She had invited him in for tea and had babbled restlessly about the community and the weather. But as hard as he tried, the sheriff had been unable to extract any information from the old woman regarding the Hobson murder. He would never know if she had seen anything.

So there had been nothing to go on. No witnesses, no evidence, not even any clues. And now the fields were deep in snow. Any trace of the girl's killer would have been covered. Perhaps in the spring they might be lucky enough to find something, but Bannon didn't hold much faith in that.

Still, he believed that Estelle Bramley had seen something out there in those bleak fields that afternoon. He believed she had known something the rest of the town didn't—something they now might never know.

"All right, then," Frank said, his voice quick with impatience, "can you at least fill me in on a few items? Seeing as I'm going to be doing the legwork on this one."

"There's not much to know." He didn't look at his deputy, but continued to stare out the window.

"Well, let's start with who found her."

Bannon squinted as the sun glared off a sparkling swirl of snow. "Michael Dalton," he replied eventually.

"Oh, great! So why isn't he here now? Why aren't we questioning him?"

"Relax, Frank. He's not going anywhere. He had a meeting to go to. I told him he could leave." He heard Frank mumble under his breath. It sounded like something about rich people getting away with murder. "You can question him later."

Frank shook his head as he buried his hands in the pockets of his parka. "Probably written up in the old lady's will."

"Who—Dalton?"

"Yeah, he's the only one she ever spent any time with. Fixing up this old place for her and all. Wouldn't be surprised if she left the entire estate to him."

Ray looked around again, noting Michael Dalton's handiwork in the intricate details of the room. "I have n idea, Frank. Henry Lubinsky will have to fill you in on that."

"Well, not that anyone would want this drafty old house, anyway." Frank huffed, drew his coat tighter around himself and looked out toward the cold fields himself. "Is her family being contacted?"

Bannon nodded. "Not much family to contact, according to Lubinsky. Estelle Bramley's closest remaining relative was a niece. She died a number of years ago, but her daughter is living in New York. I guess Lubinsky will be in touch with her."

"Yeah?" Frank made a sound somewhere between a sniff and a grunt. "Well, I'd be damned surprised if *she* wanted the house, either."

CHAPTER ONE

CLAIRE MADDEN SIGHED and dropped the paintbrush into a jar of water. She slumped back on her stool, coming dangerously close to tipping it, in order to gain a fuller view of the canvas she had been working on for the past four days.

With a deepening furrow between her brows, she studied the swirls of blues, greens and deep purples before her. The shapes and forms that seemed to swell from the surface of the canvas were somber, she had to admit. They looked black, almost—colors layered upon colors.

The paint had become thick. It glistened in the sunlight that poured into the warehouse apartment through the floor-to-ceiling windows lining its south side. Claire looked around the spacious main room that served as her living room, kitchen, dining room and studio, as if trying to find an answer to the widening abyss that had appeared on her canvas.

Why was it that she could find only shadows, even in the sunlight?

She had tried so hard for the past eight months—tried to forget the shadows, tried to forget the pain. But still her work had become menacingly dark. She knew that. She also knew that Alec would not approve.

Turning back to the painting, she stared at it awhile longer and finally swore. Just this morning she had emptied half a tube of crimson onto her palette in hopes of escaping the black hole that had threatened her canvas for the past four days. But even its bloodred brilliance was lost in the dark, writhing forms that dominated the painting. She wiped her hands with the rag draped over her shoulder.

"Damn," she swore to herself again. The golden retriever that had been lying half-asleep against the cupboards of the kitchen island looked up at her. He yawned, stretched and stared back through bleary eyes before cradling his head in his paws again. He whined once and Claire turned to him.

"Yeah? Well, you're not the one who has to deal with deadlines and a nagging agent."

She was answered by the lazy thump of the dog's tail, and this alone seemed enough to warrant a mild smile. She turned back to her canvas, taking up the paintbrush again.

It was the retriever's low growl that stopped Claire before her brush could reach the palette. She listened for the footsteps on the stairs, and as they grew louder, so did the dog's growl.

"Relax, Decker. It's only Alec." She heard the key in the lock and then the grating of the massive warehouse door sliding open.

Wiping her hands again on the rag over her shoulder, Claire watched Alec Thurston step into the apartment and heave the door shut behind him. As he crossed the room, he wore that characteristically glowing smile that had won over so many in the New York art world. His eyes held a mischievous sparkle that Claire had come to know and adore over the past ten years of their evolving friendship. Even now, in the midst of her frustration over the painting, she was able to return the smile that lit up his face.

"Good afternoon, Mr. Thurston. And to what do I owe this unexpected pleasure? Business or social?"

"Social," Alec claimed, even as his eyes strayed to the painting.

Claire followed his gaze for a moment, then, knowing he did not approve, slipped from her stool and pushed him away from the easel. "Well, if this is purely social—"

"I'm just looking, Claire." He stared at the canvas a second longer, squinting and angling his head, but made no comment. Instead, he looked back at Claire and kissed her lightly on the cheek. "So, how are you doing?"

"Fine. I'm doing fine."

"Really?"

"Alec, you worry too much."

"Only about you, darling."

She watched concern flicker behind his eyes and was comforted by its presence. "Well, thanks for worrying."

"No problem. That's what agents are for, right?" He placed another kiss on her forehead and immediately heard a quiet growl from the kitchen. He looked over to the retriever as it stood, bristling, next to the cupboards. It stared back coldly, lips quivering. "Hey, Decker. How's my favorite puppy?"

"Alec, don't tease him."

"I'm not teasing him, Claire. I'm just trying to be nice."

"You know better." She moved over to the retriever and placed a hand on its neck to quiet it.

Alec shook his head. "Why is it that dog never liked me? I bring him tidbits and toys, I treat him like royalty, and he still can't stand the sight of me."

"Decker doesn't like anyone, Alec. You know that. Don't take it personally. He just hasn't been the same since..." Her voice faded and Alec recognized the need for a comforting hand. He walked over to her and slung an arm over her shoulder, keeping an eye on the dog by her side.

"So," he asked, grinning, "how about a night on the town with your best friend, hmm?" But his attempt to break the bleak mood that hung over the apartment did not succeed.

Claire shook her head. When would Alec understand that she was not up to going out? When would he stop trying to change her life? And when would he stop believing that she even *needed* a change? "Alec, I can't. I've got too much work to do. You know that."

"Claire, I'm your agent—of all people, I know you have work to do. And so it stands to reason that, if I tell you to take a night off, you should jump at the chance. You know it doesn't happen often. Besides, it's Friday. All-you-can-eat spaghetti night at Vincenzo's. What do you say?"

"It's Friday already?" Claire looked to the calendar that hung on the wall beside her easel.

"Yeah, Claire, it's Friday. And it's also February." He reached for the calendar, turned the page and pinned it up again. "But, hey, you got the year right."

He stared at the calendar again and almost regretted having turned the month. February. He should have guessed that was the reason Claire hadn't flipped the calendar. He should have known that she might have left it there on January until March arrived.

He looked quickly around the apartment. The old warehouse loft had come a long way since last February, when Claire and Greg had finished the renovations and moved in together. It seemed a lifetime ago now.

Still, Claire had most of Greg's things around the apartment—things Alec wished she would have gotten rid of long ago. He knew about the boxes at the back of her closet filled with Greg's clothes. He knew about the bottles of after-shave that she still kept in the bathroom—he'd caught that distinctive scent on her several times. And then there was Greg's tennis racket hanging by the door, as if he would be heading out for a game at any moment, and the downhill skis propped in the corner next to Claire's, unused since their trip to Vermont last Christmas. Even his bright red ski jacket still hung on the clothes tree along with the faded Mets cap he had worn faithfully whenever the three of them went to a game.

They were hard memories to carry. Even for Alec. He had no idea how Claire lived with these constant reminders around her, day in and day out.

He turned to look at her again, and when her eyes lifted from the calendar to meet his, there was no mistaking the shudder of pain behind them. Those deep black-brown eyes that made you want to just keep on staring. Eyes that seemed to hold an innocence that belied Claire's twenty-nine years.

"I'm sorry, Claire. I didn't mean to—"

"It's all right." She dismissed the calendar with a wave of her hand.

But when Alec lifted a finger to her chin, she pulled away and looked down. She picked up a paintbrush and a rag and started cleaning.

"Claire?"

"Alec, I'm fine. Really."

"Dammit, Claire, you've got to stop this." He swallowed hard, knowing that he was about to step over the barrier she had pulled up around her pain. There was no backing out now. And he knew that soon enough, if he didn't tread very carefully, he would be facing the wrath of Claire Madden.

"Stop what, Alec?"

He could tell then that she was restraining herself. He could tell by the tension in her stance as she stood with her back to him, her hands working the brush into the rag she held. "This obsession of yours," he answered finally.

He waited for a response from her, but none came.

How many times had they been through this before? How many times would it take before Claire picked herself up and got on with her life?

"When are you going to stop blaming yourself, Claire?"

"Alec..." Her eyes flashed a warning before she turned angrily to the kitchen area. "I don't need this right now. Okay?"

He watched her open the refrigerator and take out a bottle of water. Tossing the cap onto the empty counter, she took a swig and began rolling up the sleeves of her shirt.

When he'd entered the studio apartment, Alec had noticed the faded denim shirt she wore loose over her jeans. He had known it was one of Greg's favorites. He'd even been with Claire when she had picked it out for her fiancé.

"Claire, you've got to stop this. There was nothing you could have done, you know that." He stared at her, but still she would not look up. "The bastards would have shot you, too, if you'd been here—"

"Alec, please!"

Even across the apartment, Alec saw the anger darken her face. He saw her hand clutching the water bottle and wondered for a moment if the plastic could withstand the pressure of her fury. And, for that same brief moment, he wondered if he should heed her warning—if he should back off now while he could still make a clean break, while he might still persuade her to join him for dinner.

But he cared too much. He always had. "Claire, listen to me. You know I'm right. You've got to get out. You've got to meet people. There's more to life than this apartment and that deranged dog of yours. You need people."

"I'm perfectly fine on my own, Alec. I don't need anyone in my life. I don't *want* anyone. Besides, I like my space." She threw up her hands in a gesture of exasperation and turned away from him. "God, I can't believe we're going through this again."

"You're obsessed, Claire. Still. For crying out loud, he's been dead for over eight months. When—"

"This has nothing to do with Greg."

"It has everything to do with Greg."

He watched her flip back her hair angrily, the sunlight catching its golden highlights. She gripped the edge of the counter now. As if attempting to sound calm, she lowered her voice. "I'm not obsessed, Alec, all right?"

"Oh, and I suppose that explains why you haven't done any new work in months, even though you have a show coming up in seven weeks."

"I'm working! What do you think all of this is?" She waved a hand at the stacks of finished canvases lining the far wall next to her easel.

"These?" Alec walked over to them and pulled one out. It was one of her most recent. The forms, like those rippling on the surface of the canvas on Claire's easel, were dark and heavy and ominously threatening. They moved in their own space, as though they wished to avoid all interaction with their viewers.

Alec tried to lighten his voice. "These, Claire? Come on, you know the gallery won't hang these. Their objective is to *sell* pieces to their clients, remember? Not turn them away."

He gave her that look—his tilted grin—that always, somehow, put a smile on her face. Even now, it worked to some extent.

A shrug accompanied her weak smile. "So, they're a little dark."

"Dark? Claire, they're pitch-black! They're depressing."

She screwed the cap back onto the water bottle. "What can I say? I'm going through my black period. It'll phase out. Just give me some time, Alec."

The smile on her lips tamed the anger that had clouded her face only moments ago, and Alec couldn't resist smiling back. He only hoped she understood that seven weeks was not much time at all. Despite his undying faith in Claire Madden, gained through years of friendship and now through their professional relationship, he was beginning to wonder if she was actually going to pull off this particular show. Still, he loved her. And all he could do now was maintain his faith in her a little while longer. Maintain his faith and pray that something might enter Claire's world to revive her former passion for life.

He watched her cross the kitchen and open the refrigerator. She'd lost more weight, he guessed. Even with Greg's oversize shirt on, he could tell that she hadn't been eating properly. She hadn't in eight months. But this time he wouldn't say anything. He really had pushed her further than he had intended. She would come around. Claire Madden always did. But he knew this blow would take her longer to get over.

"So." Alec took a breath and walked over to the couch, falling into the soft leather cushions. The coffee table had vanished under a mass of newspapers, unanswered mail and thumbnail sketches for possible paintings. Alec couldn't remember if the apartment had ever looked quite this chaotic. Claire had always been such a neatness freak. "So, you're not opening your mail these days either?"

"I haven't had a chance to look at it today."

"This one's postmarked the tenth of January. Guess it took a long time getting here," he teased, knowing that the pile had been mounting for well over two weeks. "Couple of bills here you might look at, Claire. And a letter from your father. Don't suppose there's anything urgent from Washington, hmm? Doesn't he call anymore?"

"He's been overseas a lot. Give the man a break, Alec."

"Probably got his secretary to write this one. What do you think?" Out of the corner of his eye he could see Claire shake her head.

Alec turned his attention back to the pile of mail, shuffling through the unpaid bills and invoices until his hand found an official-looking, buff-colored envelope. He flipped it over in his hand. The return address bore a faded emblem of a lion and carried the name Lubinsky and Ames, Attorneys-at-Law. He lifted it to the light. "Who do you know in Westport?"

"Where?"

"Westport. You got a letter from some law office there."

"Never heard of it."

"Up in Maine. Somerset Bay area, I think. One of those tourist traps. Want me to open it?"

"Sure, go ahead." She'd started cleaning up her paints, and Alec half hoped that she had at last decided to go out with him for the evening.

He unfolded the crisp paper and began to read. He scanned through it twice before Claire finally interrupted him.

"So, are you going to read it to me or not?"

He shook his head a couple of times before looking up at her. "Your great-aunt died."

Claire turned from her stool across the room. There was that deep furrow on her brow that she always got when she was either thinking or worried. "I don't have a great-aunt. What are you talking about, Alec?"

"It says here, your great-aunt Estelle Bramley."

"I don't have the faintest idea who you're talking about. Estelle Bramley?"

"Maybe she's from your mother's side." Alec silently read through the last paragraph of the letter again.

"I've never heard of her. I guess Dad didn't know her."

"It doesn't matter, Claire. She certainly knew about you. She's just died and left her entire estate to you."

He heard Claire's paintbrush hit the floor and looked up to see her cross the room toward him. "Alec, what the hell are you talking about? I don't even know this woman. What—"

"I'm just telling you what's in the letter, darling. Here. Read it yourself." He handed the paper to her as she sat down on the couch next to him. "This lawyer Lubinsky says she left everything to you. Sixty acres of land and some reconditioned Victorian house. It's right there in black and white."

He watched Claire read through the letter herself before she looked at him. "So what do you think, Claire? Wanna run away to Maine together?" He grinned.

"Right, Alec. Don't you think I should at least make some phone calls before we go packing our bags?"

"What more is there to know? Lubinsky says it all in his letter. Renovations on the house are almost finished—it's all paid for, apparently. There was enough money in the estate to cover the taxes, and the woman's savings take care of the place itself. It's yours. All you have to do is get together with this lawyer to sign the papers."

Claire stared at the letter as if she had missed something in the initial reading. As if there was something there that might answer her mounting questions. "I'll sell it, of course," she said eventually.

"Claire, you've got to be kidding. An old Victorian? Upper Maine? I wouldn't be so hasty. Just imagine all the work you could get done out there. You could even finish the pieces for your show."

"Alec, I'm not going anywhere. I like this studio. I *need* to be here." But she was still staring at the letter.

"Yeah, but this could be your getaway. Think for a minute, Claire." He didn't get a response. "Okay, let's at least talk to this Henry Lubinsky, find out what the house is like. He says he's coming to New York on other business. He'll meet with us if you want and then you can find out what this is really about. What do you say, darling? It could be the change you need to finish your work. Get some of that sea air, a fresh perspective. After the show is over, you'll have plenty of time to think about selling it."

He could see the wheels turning in her head. He could see her toy with the possibilities and then, just as quickly, dismiss them. "I don't know, Alec. Westport—it sounds so remote."

"Let's just talk to the guy, all right? His number's on the letter there. Why don't you at least give him a call and see if you can arrange a meeting with him?"

After a moment's thought, she nodded, smiling tentatively, as if uncertain of this newfound wealth.

But Alec was already planning.

CHAPTER TWO

THE SPEED with which Alec had made the arrangements for Claire's temporary move to Westport amazed even her. In her years of knowing him, Claire had always admired the organizer within Alec and now, with his star artist falling behind schedule, there was no slowing him down.

Within a matter of days after opening the letter from the law offices of Lubinsky and Ames, Alec had not only contacted Henry Lubinsky to schedule a meeting, but had arranged for his own lawyer to advise in the signing of the estate's transfer. By late Wednesday afternoon, the negotiations had been finalized.

That night, over another dinner at Vincenzo's, Alec had at last convinced Claire that the move to the Bramley house was the best plan with respect to her work. With a familiar spark of enthusiasm, Claire eventually took over the conversation, outlining what still had to be done before the move. And, by Thursday afternoon, Alec had arrived with a delivery of art supplies that was to last her for the next six weeks.

Thursday and Friday were spent packing, and by early Saturday morning, Alec's minivan was loaded with empty stretchers and canvases, paints and Claire's studio supplies. Her own car was packed with suitcases, boxes and two small trunks.

And now, after ten long hours of driving, Claire was exhausted yet grateful to be following Alec's van through Bangor and finally east toward the northern Maine coast. She ran through her mental list of everything she had packed. There was nothing she had forgotten, including Decker's kibble. She glanced over at the golden retriever in the passenger seat of the Volvo station wagon and gave him a smile. He seemed to have had a fixed grin on his canine lips from the moment they'd squeezed into the loaded car back in New York. If only she could feel as optimistic as Decker, she thought.

She remembered her futile arguments with Alec about the temporary move. They had all been in vain. And, even though she had eventually agreed that getting out of the Soho apartment with its countless memories was probably a good move, she still had lingering doubts.

"I think we should have at least gone up there to check the place out first, before making all these arrangements," she had argued with Alec. But she might as well have been protesting to one of her blank canvases, for all the response she got. "I mean, sure, I want to go up there to work. But what if this house is a pile of rubble or something? What if it's not even safe to live in? How could I possibly work there?"

"Well, you're not working here, either, are you, Claire?" His words had struck their intended mark and she had cringed at the truth in them. "Listen, darling, you've got to get out of this rut you're in. And I'm going to see to it personally that you do—if it's the last thing I do."

Watching the tail end of his minivan round the next snowbank, Claire thought about the house they were heading to. She'd had visions of the old mansion, visions of finishing the paintings in solitude away from the noise of the city, away from the people. And now, with New York a good day's drive behind her, she found herself praying that the house would be livable, that she would be able to work there. She dreaded the thought of having to return to New York.

The shadows that had clouded her life for the past eight months lingered back there. Even now, with the sun shimmering off the freshly fallen snow, Claire could still sense those fleeting shadows. She could still envision the memories of Greg—his ski jacket on the clothes tree in the hall, his hiking boots on the shoe rack and his after-shave bottles on the bathroom counter.

With a deep breath, she pushed away the shadows and sought fresh hope in the sunshine around her. As if sensing her inner smile, Decker swung his head around and gave her a canine smirk, followed by a high-pitched whine of excitement as she geared down the Volvo and followed Alec past the "Welcome to Westport" sign.

The buildings of the village huddled along the cold shores of Somerset Bay under the sheltering hills. Along the empty, snowbank-lined streets, storefronts and tourist shops displayed their "Closed" signs behind darkened windows.

Claire rolled down her window and listened to the squeal of snow beneath the car's tires as she pulled to a stop behind Alec's van. He walked toward her, the vapor of his breath hanging in the air.

"I'm just going to see Lubinsky. To get the keys and some directions. You wanna come in?"

"Not really." Claire wrinkled her nose, knowing that Alec had recognized her dislike for the short, corpulent, small-town lawyer the moment they had sat down to discuss the Bramley holdings. "I think I'll just stretch my legs for a bit, let Decker out for a quick run."

"All right, then." He zipped up his coat against the cold. "Just make sure he doesn't kill anyone, okay?"

Claire threw him a wry smile as he crossed the street to the Lubinsky and Ames office. Through the old-fashioned glass doorway she could just make out the squat outline of Henry Lubinsky as he greeted Alec, and only when the lawyer looked toward her car did she turn away. She pretended not to see him as she opened the door for Decker. Watching the retriever trot among the parked cars, she sneaked quick glances into the office and was immediately thankful that Alec had come along with her to Westport.

There had been something about Henry Lubinsky that Claire hadn't liked from the moment she had taken his fleshy hand into her own in greeting. Something about him that she couldn't quite put her finger on. She hoped that he and Alec were now discussing the final details of the estate, and that she would not be bothered by the bumbling, asthmatic lawyer during her stay in Westport.

In time Alec returned with directions and a set of keys. He dropped them into her gloved hand as she leaned against the door of the car.

"There you go, darling," he said. "It's all yours."

She looked down at the keys. Her mind seemed to whirl for a moment as she tried to imagine the house that these belonged to. She'd asked Lubinsky for photographs of the place when he'd seen them in New York, but he'd had nothing to show except receipts, deeds and papers. And now, suddenly, it was all hers.

It didn't seem real.

Estelle Bramley... why had her mother never mentioned the old woman's name? Not that Claire would have remembered at that young age. But even her father hadn't heard of the woman or of the house in Westport.

"Are you ready for this?" Alec's voice broke into her whirling thoughts and Claire looked up at him. She squinted against the brilliance of the sun against the snow.

"What's that?"

"I said, are you ready for this?"

"Sure." Claire shrugged, smiling more to appease his concern than anything else. "Why not? It's just a house, right?"

"Right." Alec looked around him, scanning the shops that lined the quiet street. "Listen, do you want to take a quick look around here and see what there is, or—"

"I can do that another time."

"Lubinsky recommended The Laughing Lobster for dinner and some drinks later. I think we should come back—what do you say?"

"Sounds all right." Claire smiled again. "Why not?" She nodded as her gaze followed Decker. "What else did Lubinsky say?"

"About?"

"About the house. Is everything settled?"

"Most everything. He'll call if anything else comes up. He said that someone's been keeping up the place for you—some guy who's working on the house."

"He told us before that the house was finished." Impatience crept into Claire's voice.

"He said there's just a little more work to be done—mainly stuff like painting. But it's almost finished. I doubt it'll be more than a couple of days max. And besides, this way, the house is being kept up. It's all ready for you to move in. Who knows, maybe the guy's even shoveled the driveway."

THE DRIVE of the Bramley house was indeed cleared of snow, but Claire didn't pay it much heed as she turned her

Volvo in behind Alec's van. Slowing the car to a stop, only vaguely hearing Decker's anxious whine, she stared out the windshield.

The three-story brownstone house loomed above her, rising like some great monolith. The wide terrace that wrapped around the first floor was almost lost under snow drifts. Even the tall Palladian windows, some of which had been securely boarded up, were nearly obliterated by a veil of wind-swept snow that clung to the folds of plastic stapled to the frames.

But what held Claire's eye first was the turret. Jutting up from the second floor to meet the third, the towerlike projection seemed to reach up to the sky. Like a silent sentinel, it overlooked the fields and the sheltering hills above the village of Westport. Claire imagined the view of the cape and the community that the large windows would command. At that instant, she made up her mind as to where her studio would be.

"Alec, this is wonderful."

Alec wondered if it was awe or simply the bitterly cold wind blasting inland from the ocean that caused the breathlessness in Claire's voice. He looked at the boarded-up front door, at the small pile of stones that had fallen away from the building's north wall and at the dilapidated garage just off the drive. "Are you sure, Claire? I did promise you that we could turn back if—"

"No! Alec, this is perfect! I mean, just look at this place. There's nothing around here—just empty fields and the snow. No people, no intrusions, no traffic, no blaring horns or beeping garbage trucks. It's perfect."

Alec scanned the surrounding countryside. Henry Lubinsky had alluded to the fact that the Bramley estate did include land, but he hadn't expected it to be quite as extensive as it appeared now. Tops of fences peeked above the deep snow, and barren fields stretched out to a distant forest. Beyond these, he could just make out the definition of another large house half-hidden by a stand of massive firs. He nodded in its direction. "Well, you've got at least one neighbor."

Claire followed his gaze thoughtfully. "That's half a mile away. And with any luck I won't even have to meet the owners. Come on, let's go in and take a look around." She started toward the steps leading to the back door.

"Looks as if you've already got company," Alec said, pointing to the black Land Rover tucked up beside the house, away from the main drive. "Maybe we should knock."

"Not at my own door." Claire laughed, dangling the keys in one hand. She reached for the door and found it already open. "Come on, Decker. Let's check out the new digs."

The retriever bounded up the steps and through the door ahead of Claire. And Alec found himself grinning at the newfound spring in her step as she walked into the house.

Once inside the house, Alec unzipped his leather coat and removed his gloves. He tossed them next to Claire's on the worn pine kitchen table and surveyed his surroundings.

The kitchen alone seemed to require another two weeks of hard labor to bring it to any level of completion, but when Alec saw the glow of Claire's excitement, he realized that if anyone could make a temporary home out of this century-old relic it was Claire.

Unfazed by the chipped plaster, the stained cracks along the ceiling, the tilted cupboards and the scarred hardwood floors, Claire moved through the kitchen and to what might have once been a sitting room. She wore a

smile that Alec had not seen in quite some time. As he
followed her, he too was beginning to recognize the potential in the old house.

Some work had been done, but just as Claire had
feared, there was still a lot that hadn't. Toolboxes, scraps
of molding and pails of dried plaster in several corners of
the lounge attested to that fact.

"Looks as if Lubinsky was wrong."

"About what?" Claire turned to catch Alec's nod toward the power saw propped up against one wall.

"About the work being done to the house. If you ask
me, I'd say there's at least a couple more months of work
that could go into this place, if the rest of the rooms look
anything like this one."

Claire followed Alec's scrutinizing gaze of the room.
Furniture sat where she guessed it had rested for years,
now enshrouded in sheets. Shelves lined the walls, still
stacked with books. A light dust, stirred by their intru-
sion, shimmered in wide shafts of late-afternoon sunlight
that flooded in through the tall windows.

"Look at all this stuff," Claire murmured, lifting a
corner of one sheet to reveal an ancient yet impeccable
hand-embroidered armchair.

"Lubinsky did say that the entire place was yours.
Lock, stock and barrel. At least this way, you don't have
to worry about trying to fill this big old place."

Claire surveyed the room once more before following
Decker toward the winding staircase. "Well, at least it's
livable. That's all I need. Come on, I'm dying to check out
that turret."

He was right behind her. The occasional creak of the
steps did not come as a surprise to him—it all fit in to the
house's atmosphere of history and mystery.

Rounding the corner of the second-last flight, they were suddenly greeted by the whine of a power tool. Claire paused to look back at Alec. Her smile was gone.

"You'd better call Decker back," Alec suggested when the dog made a beeline toward the open doorway from which the noise was coming. But Claire shook her head and continued on.

It was the man's smile that Claire noticed first when she entered the turret room. His smile...and then the strength of his bare arms as he reached down to pet the golden retriever by his side.

Half expecting Decker to take off the man's hand, Claire could only stand transfixed in the doorway. For what seemed like a full minute she watched him, shirtless, his jeans and leather sneakers covered with a light dusting of plaster and sawdust, as he scratched Decker's chest. All of a sudden, she felt ridiculously overdressed.

Under the weight of her winter jacket, she could feel a trickle of sweat down her spine. When the man finally looked up from the happy dog at his side, she was certain that her face was flushed from more than just the temperature. Caught by the steel gray of his eyes glinting across the length of the room, Claire could only meet his stare speechlessly, craving the power to wrest her eyes from his.

It was Alec's voice that broke the suspended silence. "You must be Michael Dalton."

Only then did the stranger's eyes leave hers. Wiping his hands on his pant legs, he walked toward them and, smiling, extended his hand to Alec.

"Lubinsky told me you might still be doing some work on the place," Alec explained.

"And you must be Alec Thurston." Dalton's voice resonated with warmth. "Henry told me you were coming sometime this weekend. But I really wasn't expecting you until tomorrow.''

"Well, we were anxious to look at the house. I see that you've already made Decker's acquaintance. This is the new owner, Claire Madden.''

Claire took Michael's offered hand, impressed at the firm yet gentle grasp with which he held hers. She couldn't remember a time when she had ever been so overwhelmed by the mere touch of someone's hand on hers, when the eyes of a man had ever pierced her to the very core.

"Claire Madden,'' he repeated, the syllables rolling easily from his lips. "Henry told me you're an artist.''

"Yes, a painter,'' she answered, withdrawing her hand. Forcing her gaze from his and breaking the spell he held her in, Claire looked beyond him, into the turret room. She stepped around him and, almost instantly, felt her initial annoyance return. "Mr. Lubinsky told us that your work here was almost finished, Mr. Dalton.''

"Please, call me Michael.''

He turned to watch her cross the room and gaze out the window. Claire could feel his eyes on her, but would not allow herself to look into those eyes again. She could not let herself feel the disarming pull toward Michael Dalton that she had felt from the moment she'd stepped into the room and seen him stroking Decker.

"Actually, this room is finished. I was just putting the last of the trim up along the fireplace. I'd wanted to redo the bricking as well, but your aunt—''

"I really don't think any of that is necessary, Mr. Dalton. I'm here only for a short time and the house is adequate as it is.''

He nodded, his attention never leaving her. "Fine.''

Out of the corner of her eye, Claire saw him nod and adjust the hammer that hung on the tool belt around his waist.

"I'll just clean up a bit, put my tools away, and I'll be out of your hair."

"Thank you."

"I should tell you, though, I still have a lot of work to do on the rest of the house. I've got someone coming in next week to check on the plumbing, and the furnace is still acting up. Then there's the kitchen and the living room, not to mention most of the rooms on the second floor that Estelle had boarded up."

"What *has* been done, Mr. Dalton?"

"So far? Well, this room. And the downstairs is livable, I suppose. Here on the third floor I've fixed up the master bedroom and a guest room that I thought you might be using. I brought up some of the furniture that Estelle had stored—"

"Then that should be enough for now." Claire turned to him briefly and risked a cold smile. "The rest of the house can be finished if I decide to keep it. I'll be sure to contact you at that time."

"I'm sorry, but I promised Estelle that I would finish the house. In the meantime, I'll be sure to do whatever I can to stay out of your way, Ms. Madden. Now, if you'll excuse me, I'll just collect my things and be leaving." Reaching for his shirt from the back of the desk chair, he picked up the last of his tools and turned from the room. "I'll be seeing you. Mr. Thurston, it was a pleasure meeting you. Good day."

Claire watched the muscles of Michael Dalton's tanned back as he turned out the door, and couldn't help feeling a twinge of shame at her curtness. What had she been thinking?

The room fell into silence. There was only the howling of the wind outside the windows, and a low whine from Decker, who sat staring at the doorway. Then there was the sound of the back door closing and, finally, the Land Rover's motor.

"Well, you sure have a way of making first impressions these days, Claire."

"Alec, please don't start."

"All I'm suggesting is that perhaps you try a more subtle approach."

"I came here to be left alone, Alec. The last thing I need is some hired man around the house, twelve hours a day, running his power tools and hammering at the walls. I came here to get some work done, remember? Besides, he said it's livable. That's all I need for now."

Alec shook his head. "Whatever you say, Claire. I just think you're making a big mistake."

"What? What mistake? You're the one who wanted me to come out here and complete the pieces for the show."

"Yeah. But what happens when your plumbing starts to give you problems, or your pipes freeze? You're not in New York anymore, darling. You can't just call that sleazy superintendent of yours whenever something breaks. At least with Dalton around you've got someone to count on. I think you should reconsider."

Claire was silent for a moment as she took a deep breath. There was some truth in Alec's words. She might need help sometime along the road. On the other hand, she couldn't possibly work on her upcoming show with Michael Dalton hanging around—he was far too disturbing a presence.

She shrugged. "What's to consider? I want to be left alone. I can handle it. Now, come on. Let's get the things in from the van and check out the rest of this place, okay?''

BY SEVEN O'CLOCK, tired and hungry, Alec and Claire had finally hauled the last of her boxes from the van. Michael Dalton had been modest in his reference to the master and guest bedrooms on the third floor. Not only were these rooms finished to the finest of details, they were tastefully furnished and equipped with a closetful of linens and towels. Claire had tried to seem unimpressed with the work that had been put into the rooms, but secretly she wondered what kind of a man Michael Dalton really was, wondered what kind of person hid behind those cold gray eyes that had seemed to pierce her own that afternoon.

She had also wondered how she was going to handle Michael's continued presence in the house. As rude as she had been to him, Claire guessed that she had not gotten rid of the determined carpenter for very long.

Even over dinner with Alec at The Laughing Lobster, Claire found herself thinking vaguely of Michael. She was remembering Decker's immediate fondness for the man, behavior she'd never known of the retriever, when Alec's voice broke into her thoughts.

"Are you with me, Claire?"

"Hmm? I'm sorry, Alec. What were you saying?"

Alec shook his head and gave her a soft smile. "I was asking you about the new studio."

"What about it?" Claire took another sip of her wine and tried to ignore the growing din from the bar.

"The lighting. I was suggesting that you might find the glare of light off the fields too strong through all those windows. You might consider curtaining some of them off."

"Are you kidding, Alec? The light is the greatest thing about that room."

"Well, at least that other house across the fields isn't close enough to be a nuisance."

"Lubinsky didn't tell you anything about that house, did he?"

"No. Why?"

Claire shrugged her shoulders. "No reason. It seems so grand, though, doesn't it? I can't imagine anyone less than the Carrington clan living there, if you know what I mean."

Alec smirked. "Claire Madden, I don't believe it. You? A prime-time TV addict? I never thought it would come to this."

"Drop it, Alec." She laughed. "You know what I mean."

"Well, I'll tell you," Alec responded, leaning farther across the table as if to avoid being overheard, "I'd just like to know why your father knew nothing about Estelle Bramley. All of those years before your mother died, she never once mentioned a rich old aunt up in Maine? Seems a little unlikely to me."

"You're making too much of this." Claire put down her wineglass after swirling it for several seconds. "Haven't I ever told you about my mother's terrible sins? Being pregnant with me was bad enough, but when she eloped with my father, her family disowned her entirely. We had no contact at all with any of them. I didn't even know I had a grandmother when I was a kid."

Claire looked up from her glass. "After the funeral, my father and I just went our own way. There are probably lots of relatives on my mother's side that he knows nothing about. What—you think this is some big secret of his, that he was hoping to cash in on someday?" She caught the mischievous grin on Alec's lips and knew instantly that she had fallen into his little game. There was nothing that Alex Thurston enjoyed more than an intrigue—or creating one.

"Forget it, Alec. You're getting carried away. Just a simple matter of lost family ties. Sometimes I have to wonder about you and your—"

"Hey, Ruthie! A coupla beers down here, huh?" a large, stocky man shouted brusquely from the end of the bar next to the table Claire and Alec shared.

As she and Alec ate in silence for a few moments, Claire listened vaguely to the men speaking over their pints. When the name Bramley came up, she sat up and listened more intently. She looked from the men to Alec, only to see that he too was paying attention.

"... Yeah, that old woman watched everything. Up there on the hill, lookin' over the whole town. Used binoculars, too, I heard." The man in the Cardinals cap swilled back some more beer. "Weird stuff, all that about her murder. Hard to tell what's truth anymore 'round here."

"Well, it's my bet the old woman knew something 'bout the Hobson girl. That's what got 'er killed."

The man wearing the Cardinals cap reached for his pint of beer again. "All I can say is it's no big loss, anyway. Kinda creepy, knowin' that she was always lookin' at everthin' goin' on around here. At least there won't be no more of that."

"Yeah? Well, what about that old house? Used to be able to make a real killin' off that old dame when the plumbing conked out almost every spring. Nothin' like those old pipes that just seem to keep quittin'."

Claire set down her fork, and as if sensing her next move, Alec shot out a hand to catch hers. "Don't, Claire." His eyes warned her to stay put.

"Alec, I just want to ask them a couple of things. Maybe they know something I should know."

"It's just rumors, darling. Relax. You know how these small towns are—people need to gossip. It's their only social life. Besides, you should be keeping a low profile, remember? The last thing you need is a bunch of locals combing your property for the clues to some murder that they've conjured up over Saturday-night beers. Don't get them started."

"But they might have heard something that—"

"Good evening."

Claire stopped short. It was his voice. She hadn't imagined that after one short meeting it would sound so familiar, but even over the din of the bar there was no mistaking it.

She looked up.

Her eyes swept from the faded pair of jeans with its leather belt to the clean white shirt beneath a worn leather bomber-style winter jacket and, finally, to the tanned, smiling face of Michael Dalton. His square jaw was set firmly above the crisp white collar of his shirt, his thick black hair disheveled enough to give him that rugged outdoors look, and his eyes were intent. At that moment, Claire cursed Michael Dalton for looking so good.

"Good evening," she replied tersely.

"Good evening, Mr. Dalton." Alec beamed a smile big enough for both of them.

"Please, just Michael. Formalities are better left behind in the city."

"Michael, then," he repeated, offering him a chair. "Please, join us."

"Thank you." Michael smiled at Claire, and even her cold response didn't faze him as he pulled out the chair and drew up to the table. "Can I buy you two a drink?"

Claire caught the cool gray of his eyes again and a shiver ran through her. "No, thanks. I'm driving."

"Fine. Alec?"

Alec shook his head. "Actually, I'm full up already. I think I've had enough to numb my senses to this Maine cold."

Claire felt Michael's eyes on her as she stared past his shoulder to the men at the bar behind him. She knew Alec was right—there was no sense in creating a scene with a couple of half-drunken men who had nothing better to do on Saturday night than swill beer and watch the final quarter of a hockey game on the twelve-inch black-and-white television above the bar. Then again, there might be something gained by talking to them....

As if on cue, Michael's voice broke through her thoughts.

"If you're interested, that's Jed Henderson on the left. And that's his buddy, Burt Gifford." Dalton smirked when she finally looked at him. "If you need any work done on your car, Jed's your man. And if the plumbing goes, you can give Burt a call any day or night."

"Yeah? Well, I've heard enough about Burt's plumbing."

"What's that?"

"Nothing." She tried to brush him off. "I'm really not interested in the local color, thank you." Claire tried to ignore Alec's glare.

"Well, you're probably right in not getting involved with them. They talk, you know. Local gossip. It's the only thing that keeps them going sometimes. They have to have something to rattle on about in the dead of winter. Are you sure I can't buy you a coffee?''

Claire looked down at the empty wineglass in front of her. She would have loved a cup of coffee, but the last thing she needed was to create a friend in Michael Dalton.

"Actually, no. Thank you, Mr. Dalton. Perhaps some other time. We really must be going." She caught Alec's look of surprise. "I have a lot of unpacking to do. Alec?''

Alec reached for his hat and rose from the table with Claire. "I suppose you're right. And it is getting late. Well—'' he extended his hand to take Michael's ''—it's been a pleasure meeting you, Michael. I'm sorry to say that I'll be leaving this quiet hamlet for the excitement of New York first thing tomorrow, but I hope I'll be seeing you again sometime soon."

Michael glanced at Claire and then back to Alec. "I'm sure you will. I still have a lot of work to do on the house." Then, turning his smile on Claire, he added, "I suppose I'll be seeing you tomorrow?"

"But tomorrow's Sunday." She struggled to break the contact but couldn't draw her eyes from his.

"Yeah." He nodded, and reached for Claire's purse, handing it to her with a challenging grin. "I work Sundays. Don't you?"

Defeated, Claire could only nod her head and take her purse. "Good night then, Mr. Dalton."

"It's Michael, remember?"

"Goodnight, Michael," she repeated, following Alec to the door.

She didn't turn when he wished them a good-night but instead let Alec do it for them. Even while she and Alec sat in her car, waiting for it to warm up, Claire remained silent.

Alec looked across at her from the passenger seat. He watched her breath curl in the light of a parking-lot lamp and wondered if he'd ever seen her this tense before.

"What is it, Claire?"

"What?" She turned an impatient glare in his direction. "I just wanted to get out of there. It was smoky."

"Yeah, right." He looked at her again as she turned away from him.

This wasn't Claire. At least not the Claire he'd known before Greg's death. She was so tense, so defensive. Almost as if she was protecting herself from the rest of the world.

He had hoped that her tension would have eased with New York behind them. But instead, especially with Michael Dalton around, it seemed only to have increased.

"What is it, darling? Is it Dalton?"

"No! Alec, don't be crazy."

"Claire."

She sighed, knowing that she couldn't escape an explanation. "I just want to be left alone. I don't need some handyman around the house while I'm trying to put the rest of this show together. I'm going crazy with the thought of the amount of work I have to get done out here and I just don't need someone like Michael Dalton underfoot. That's all there is to it, Alec. Don't read anything more into this, all right?"

Alec watched her shake her head and put the car in gear. He let her question hang, but he had no doubt that Michael Dalton was on her mind as they pulled out of The Laughing Lobster parking lot and drove back to the old house.

CHAPTER THREE

CLAIRE COULDN'T REMEMBER when she had woken up to such a cold morning. Certainly not since the last time the superintendent of the old warehouse in Soho had forgotten to pay the utility bill. Tucked beneath two duvets, she lay in her cocoon of warmth, daring herself to take the plunge. Boldly she removed an arm from under the covers and reached for Decker.

Her hand found only emptiness.

She thought she could hear Alec downstairs, but with the bedrooms on the third floor, it was difficult to hear anything below. Still, there was the irresistible aroma of brewed coffee. And unless the Bramley house came with room service, Alec was already up and showered.

Claire looked over at the alarm clock and sat up abruptly, forgetting the cold of the bedroom. Nine o'clock. She hadn't slept this late in months.

She reached for her pack of pills and the glass of water. Popping out Sunday's, Claire swallowed it and looked at the plastic dispenser she tossed back onto the nightstand. She didn't know why she had kept taking them after Greg's death. It seemed a futile ritual. She hadn't even looked at another man since Greg, let alone considered sleeping with one. Old habits died hard.

Slipping a white turtleneck and a paint-smeared sweatshirt over her T-shirt, Claire rummaged through her open suitcases for her two thickest pairs of socks and pulled them up over her wool tights. With any luck it might be warmer downstairs.

But the only shred of warmth that greeted Claire as she entered the kitchen was the residual heat from the coffee-maker and the toaster at the end of the counter.

"Ah, there she is. At last. Not exactly up with the lark, but up nonetheless." Alec finished pouring another cup of coffee before greeting her with a kiss on the cheek. "And how did you sleep?"

"Like a log." She shivered as she accepted the warm mug he handed her. "Is it freezing in here or is it just me?"

He pulled out a chair for her at the kitchen table and seated himself across from it. "It's cool. I think the furnace kicked out sometime around two this morning. Drink your coffee. It'll warm you up."

Claire sat down, drawing her knees up against her chest. "This is unbearable."

Alec looked up from the map spread out over the table. "What? The coffee?"

"No, the cold. Did you take a look at the furnace when you got up?"

He shook his head and gave her a half laugh. "Are you kidding? I'm not going down into that basement. I'm not the one who brought work clothes along."

Claire scanned Alec's attire. He'd already pulled on a Ralph Lauren sweater over a black turtleneck and slacks, and Claire could understand his not wanting to venture down into the dank bowels of the old house. The task was better left to someone equipped with sweats and jeans, as she was.

Claire looked around the kitchen and then to the empty dog dish in the corner. "Where's Decker?"

"I put the miserable mutt out."

The sudden skidding of her chair across the floor caused Alec to look up from the road map. "Alec, how could you? He's not used to the country. He doesn't know his way around. He'll get lost out there." Claire recovered the chair from its near fall as she rushed to the door and fought with the handle.

"Relax, Claire. He's not going anywhere. Have you seen all the snow?"

She wasn't listening. Her attention was focused entirely on trying to get the door open. When she finally did, she started to shout out Decker's name, imagining him belly deep in snow somewhere out in the vast expanse of field. And then she saw him. He was huddled up against the wall of the house beside the door, looking up at her with baleful brown eyes as the wind licked at his long silky fur.

"Come on, Decker." She ushered the dog inside and toward his food dish, opening a fresh bag of kibble and filling his bowl.

"See? He's fine, Claire," Alec gibed, only to be answered by a low growl and the clank of the dog's identification tags against the stainless-steel food bowl.

"Yeah, well, he still could have run off."

"Claire, the dog is slavishly devoted to you. He isn't going anywhere, trust me." He picked up the map, carefully folding it so that Manan county was at the front. Checking for the keys to his van, he reached for his coat. "I gotta run, darling."

"What? You're leaving already?" Claire stood up from the retriever's side and faced him. "Alec—"

"Claire, dear, I was supposed to be back in New York last night. I promised to see Ryan Jackson this evening, remember?"

"Yeah, I know—" Claire edged up to him, wrapping her fingers around his forearm and attempting to conjure up her most persuasive voice "—but who's your favorite and most prolific artist?"

Alec pondered her question for a moment before answering. "Favorite—you, by far. But most prolific? I'm afraid right now that would be Ryan."

The comment hit its mark, and Claire would have pulled away from him if he hadn't taken her hands into his at that moment. "I'm sorry for being so hard on you, Claire. But you know I'm right. And my hanging around here isn't going to get you any further ahead. You need to be alone. You need to work." He leaned over and kissed her cheek again. "Besides, Ryan's show is next week. I have to take a look at his last three pieces."

Alec's bag was already sitting by the back door and he moved toward it, pausing by the oversize kitchen window to look out at the white fields and slip into his coat. "It's stopped snowing. With any luck, the main roads will have been plowed."

And then, with the silence of the house seeming to buzz in her ears, Claire felt, very suddenly, much too alone. The house was unfamiliar and Alec wasn't. If she could only convince him to stay another day, even a few hours—long enough for her to believe that the Bramley house was really hers. For her to begin to feel at home behind these massive stone walls...

He turned to look at her when he reached the door, his bag already in hand. "Claire, you'll be all right."

"Yeah, I know. But..." She couldn't think of anything else to say, anything to convince him that she needed him right now.

"But what? I can't stay. You know I would if it were possible. Now, are you going to walk me to the car or

what?" He opened the door, and a blast of cold air forced
its way into the kitchen as he stepped out into the glare of
the morning sun on snow.

"Alec," she called after him, but her breath was
wasted. She stood there for a moment in the middle of the
kitchen with her arms folded across her chest, her hands
tucked into her armpits for warmth. Why was it that she
so desperately wanted Alec to stay, when all she had
wanted before was to be alone? Hemmed in by the silence of the massive house, Claire felt the sudden com-
pulsion to move.

Grabbing her boots, she struggled to get into them,
cursing the double pair of socks she'd put on only moments ago. Decker followed her out the door.

"Alec!" she shouted, jogging across the driveway to
catch up.

He'd reached the minivan and tossed his bag behind the
driver's seat.

"Alec, I don't have any heat, for crying out loud. What
am I supposed to do for heat?"

He turned back to look at her. At the sight of the shivering form draped in a paint-splattered sweatshirt, wool
tights and two pairs of socks slouching over the tops of
sturdy hiking boots, he walked resolutely toward her,
reached out and took her shoulders in his hands as he
smiled. "Claire Madden, you don't have a degree from
NYU for nothing. I'm sure you can figure out how to turn
a furnace on. And if all else fails, you can wait for Michael Dalton to come to your rescue."

He released her shoulders and got into the van. He
didn't need to see Claire's face to know that she'd rolled
her eyes at his last comment. He turned the key in the ignition. "Now look, I'd love to stay, you know that, but I

have to be back on the main highway before we get even more snow."

"Alec—"

"Claire, you'll do just fine. Trust me. I'll call you to-night and see how you're doing, okay?" He waited for her nod. "Now, go inside. You'll catch a cold. It's freezing out here."

"It doesn't matter. It's freezing in there, too." She nodded toward the house.

"You'll be all right, Claire. I know you will." He stared once more at her, looking deep into those black-brown eyes and seeing the old flame of determination there be-gin to take light. She would make it. Not just with this house, he realized, but with her past as well. She would be able to let go, and this was the first step toward that. He was doing the right thing by leaving her here. He believed that more than anything else right now.

Decker's bark warned them of the approaching car long before the engine, muffled by snowbanks, could be heard. The black Land Rover turned in, bounced up the drive and pulled to a stop. Claire watched Michael Dalton step out. He gave them a nod, followed by a cheery "Good morning," then reached down to pet the eager Decker at his side.

Alec shoved a thumb in Michael's direction. "There you go, darling," he said under his breath so as not to be overheard, "right on cue."

Michael looked up and sauntered over to the van, Decker at his heels. Smiling the entire way, Claire no-ticed. How could anyone be this cheerful in such cold conditions? she wondered as she listened to his boots crunching on the crisp snow.

But Michael not only seemed undaunted by the frigid morning, he seemed to be enjoying it. Claire let her eyes

rove as he approached. The wind had brought a healthy
glow to his face. Beneath a brightly knit ear band, his long
hair whipped back in the wind that battered across the
fields. His parka, zipped up to his throat, hugged his
waist, where snug jeans outlined the muscular physique
Claire had already witnessed. All of a sudden, feeling the
cold on her scantily clad legs, she felt extremely under-
dressed.

"You heading out, Alec?"

"Back to New York." Alec nodded and returned Michael's smile. "Too quiet around here. I can actually hear
myself think, for a change. Scares the hell out of me."

Michael laughed and Claire caught herself staring a
him, letting the swell of his laughter warm her. She looked
away only when he turned his eyes on her.

"Well, I'd better get going," Alec said. He reached ou
the window for Claire's hand and pulled her to him, giving her a quick kiss. "You'll be all right, darling. Trus
me," he whispered in her ear.

Claire forced a smile for his sake, wanting to ease hi
mind. "Drive safely, Alec. And say hi to Ryan for me."

"I will. And you take care of yourself, you hear me?'
He waited for her nod before looking over her shoulder
"Michael, I'll see you in a couple of weeks, right?"

"I'll be here," he answered, and Claire was surprise
at the brief shot of comfort she found in hearing his re
sponse.

Alec backed the van around the Land Rover and pause
between gears to look back at them. "Oh, and Michae
you'll keep an eye on her for me now, won't you?"

Michael nodded and waved. Across the widening dis
tance between her and the van, Claire hoped that Ale
could see her pursed lips and the anger in her eyes at th
comment.

She watched the van disappear at the end of the drive, only its roof visible above the embankment of snow as it headed down the road toward the ocean. Even after it had disappeared from sight, Claire stared at the bend in the road.

It was Michael's voice that brought her back to the reality of the cold, windy driveway where she stood shivering.

"You really ought to get inside. It doesn't look as if you're dressed for these temperatures. It's pretty brisk out here."

Claire turned to him, her eyes catching the steel-gray of his gaze as she watched the vapor from his breath spiral around his face and then disappear in the wind.

She took a step back, feeling too close. With her hands still tucked firmly under her arms, she met his stare for a long moment before speaking. "So, what do you know about furnaces?"

IT HAD TAKEN twenty minutes under a shower of near-scalding water to warm Claire's chilled body. She had left Michael banging away at the furnace in the basement after he'd assured her that the temporary malfunction would not affect the current hot-water supply, and by the time she'd turned the shower off, she could hear a power saw whining away downstairs.

He'd promised her, even as they were stepping in from outside, that he would not be in her way. He outlined the work that he wanted to complete in the living room, and even though it sounded like a couple of weeks worth, Claire felt compelled to consent. After all, he was the only person she knew in Westport. And if Estelle Bramley had already made arrangements regarding pay, Claire wasn't

going to find anyone cheaper to come in and fix the furnace, or anything else that went wrong, for that matter.

Still, his presence in the house was mildly unnerving.
Besides the fact that Decker found it more appropriate to
spend his day with Michael in the living room than with
Claire upstairs, there was the constant whir of power tools
and the relentless hammering to contend with.

She had confined herself to the third-story turret for the
remainder of the morning and the better part of the afternoon, in order to set up her studio. A Vivaldi tape
blasting away on her ministereo helped cover Michael's
presence to some degree, and by late afternoon she had
almost forgotten that he was there.

She had just finished laying down the last drop cloth
and had spread out a fresh canvas, ready to staple it to a
stretcher, when the knock on the studio door startled her.
She jumped, almost dropping the stapler. Taking a moment to collect herself, she called, "Come in!"

The door opened slowly at first, as if Michael were
concerned about possible objects in the way, but before it
was even half-open, Decker pushed his way through.

Foreseeing the potential assault that Claire was about
to receive from the happy retriever, Michael snatched the
dog's collar and pulled him back.

"I hope I'm not disturbing you." He stood in the
doorway, scanning the transformation of the turret room.

Claire watched him. Watched his eyes take in the ea-
sels, the empty stretchers and the stacked canvases, the
tables of supplies, bottles of turpentine and tubes of oils,
the jars of brushes, rags and dog-eared sketchbooks.

"Not at all," she answered him.

His eyes came back to hers, holding her gaze for what
Claire felt was a moment too long. She looked away, to
the corner of canvas pinned under her right knee, and

buried three staples into the wood of the stretcher before standing up. Ignoring the pins and needles tingling down her leg, she moved across the studio toward the table where he stood. As she approached him, she could smell the sawdust on him, mingled with the sweet scent of pine and traces of a subtle cologne—a combination she found strangely enticing. She reached for the box of staples on the desk, hoping to appear unaffected by his presence.

"Looks like you've been busy up here."

Claire responded with a nod and watched Michael out of the corner of her eye as he surveyed the room again. The winter sun, setting early across fields, sent shafts of golden orange shimmering in through the expanse of windows lining the turret walls. Even in the warm glow, Michael's features remained strong, almost hard. The shadow of a day's growth of beard gave him an even more rugged appearance, but Claire couldn't shake the feeling that there was much more to Michael Dalton beneath this tough exterior.

There was a gentleness in his voice, in spite of her abruptness with him. And there was something else, something Claire could not quite put her finger on, that suggested the man working on her house was not a carpenter or a contractor by trade.

"Is it warm enough for you up here now?"

"Yes, it's fine. Thank you." In fact, she'd stripped down to her T-shirt and jeans only an hour ago.

He shifted his weight, slipping both hands into his jeans pockets as he leaned against the doorjamb. "It's no problem. The furnace has always been a bit temperamental. You just have to get to know it. I left my phone number on the kitchen table for you, anyway. In case the furnace goes out again. I'm just down the road, so don't hesitate to call if you need a hand."

"Thanks."

"Listen," he said with a smile, "I couldn't interest you in some dinner, could I? Something quieter than The Laughing Lobster, perhaps?"

Claire was surprised at her hesitation. Why should it be so difficult to say no to this man? She *did* want to be alone. That was the whole point of coming to Westport and the lonely house on the bluffs. To get away from New York—not just from the memories but from the noise, the people, the overly concerned friends.

Claire turned her attention to refilling the stapler, hoping that Michael wasn't staring at her. But she knew he was. She could almost feel his eyes searing through her T-shirt against the flesh of her back. "No, thanks. I don't really feel much like dinner. Besides, I have too much work to get through here still."

"Some other time, perhaps."

And even though he hadn't phrased it as a question, Claire found herself nodding.

"All right, then," he said, disappointment lingering in his smile. "I'll be heading off. I have some errands to run anyway. You'll call if there's anything you need?"

Claire nodded again. "Sure. But, really, I think I'll be fine."

"Okay, I'll see you tomorrow then. Probably late morning." And he was gone. He had turned so quickly from the studio that Claire hadn't even had a chance to give dinner a second thought.

Standing in the doorway of the studio, she let her eye follow Michael's figure as he made his way along the hall and down the stairs. His shirt, still damp with sweat, clung to his back, revealing the outlines of well-defined muscles. His hair, too short for a ponytail but still long, had a healthy sheen except where small clouds of sawdust had settled on it.

He never looked back. And in a moment's time she heard the back door swing shut and the Land Rover's motor rumble to life.

She placed a hand on Decker's head when he whimpered softly. With the emptiness of the house closing in on her once again, Claire regretted having turned down Michael's offer for dinner. And tomorrow seemed a long way off.

CHAPTER FOUR

SWEAT TRICKLED DOWN Claire's neck and below the seam of her T-shirt. She'd been working hard pulling canvas over new stretchers, cleaning palettes and brushes and tidying the studio after another all-night session of painting. Her third in one week. Who said the country was a place for relaxing, she thought as she brushed wide strokes of gesso across a new canvas, preparing it for the next wave of colors.

In less than a week she'd completed two pieces and had begun three others. At this rate, Alec would be able to pick and choose from the new pieces for the show. As soon as he saw the paintings, he would say, "I told you so," over and over in reference to her move up to Maine. She imagined the pleasure he would derive from such juvenile finger waggling and smiled. That was Alec.

In spite of her initial reservations about Michael's presence in the house, she had to admit that the drone of tools and the occasional interruptions didn't bother her as much as she had feared. She and Michael had settled into independent routines, neither seeing the other more than a couple of times a day. They shared fleeting glimpses, brief exchanges regarding the house and little more.

By the end of the week, Claire was becoming accustomed to Michael's comings and goings. Sometimes, intent on her painting, she wouldn't even know if Michael was there or not. In fact, often, when she finally took break and went downstairs, she'd be disappointed not to find him. But there would usually be a note, scrawled in the now-familiar handwriting, letting her know what time he'd be by the next day.

This morning, however, Michael was in. Above the throb of her headache, she could hear the intermittent buzz of the sander. She blamed the late nights for her headache, and the heat in the third-floor studio certainly didn't help.

Standing up from her stool, Claire set down the wide brush and pulled her T-shirt sleeves up over her shoulders. She wiped the white gesso from her hands onto one corner of her T-shirt and turned to the nearest turret window. Wrapping her fingers around the window handle, she pulled gently, but the old wooden frame wouldn't budge. Using both hands, she pulled even harder on the handle of the window.

Sweat trailed down her neck and back as she struggled with each of the six windows in turn. With mounting frustration, she moved to the last window and heaved. But it, too, remained locked in its frame. Even as she recognized the futility of the effort, she continued to tug at the window while yelling Michael's name.

It took Michael only a matter of seconds to race up the two flights of stairs and down the corridor to the studio. By the time he was standing in the doorway, Claire felt slightly ridiculous.

"What is it, Claire?" The concern in his voice was evident.

She turned to find herself facing his bare chest. In the mad rush he hadn't had time to pull on his T-shirt, and now he stood before her, his tanned torso glistening with a light sweat.

"I can't get the windows open," she said finally.

His forehead creased, his eyebrows coming together as he stared at her. "You what?"

"I can't get the damned windows open," she repeated, as evenly as possible. "And it's bloody hot up here."

Claire didn't know if his stare betrayed a flicker of attraction or merely disbelief. She opted to believe the latter and, at the same time, attempted to straighten her hair. She must look an absolute mess—tired, sweaty and paint stained. And, more than likely, adorned with a couple of large gesso splatters across her face.

But she met his gaze nonetheless.

Then he smiled. "Here, let me give it a try."

Muscles flexed along his back as he reached past her. Planting his feet firmly on the drop cloth in front of the window, he gripped the handle and lifted it in one sharp pull. The frame rattled and then shuddered upward.

A welcome blast of cold air rushed in, scattering a stack of Claire's most-recent sketches about the room before Michael forced the window back down to a reasonable adjustment.

His eyes turned on Claire. "Just needed a good tug. Is that better?"

"Yes, thanks." But when Claire discovered herself addressing his bare chest rather than his face, she looked away, embarrassed at her obvious attraction.

As if sensing her discomfort, Michael reached for his T-shirt, which hung from the back pocket of his jeans, and pulled it over his head.

"Here, let me help you gather those up," he suggested, starting to pick up some of Claire's escaped sketches.

"No, really. It's all right. I can manage," Claire protested, having already gathered up several sheets, but Michael continued to carefully retrieve the strewn sketches. "Really, Michael, I can handle—"

Claire's plea was cut short. The mere brush of Michael's hand against hers, as they scrambled for the scattered pages, sent an inexplicable shiver coursing through her. Raising her eyes, she met his steady gaze. She held it for several seconds as she squatted in front of him on the studio floor, wondering how it was that she could become so lost in a mere glance, wondering how long it was that she could go on staring at him without feeling the same delicious shiver race through her again.

She didn't have a chance to find out. Their locked gaze was abruptly broken off by a hideous half gong, half buzz from downstairs, followed by Decker's bark as he barreled down the hall.

"What was that?"

"*That* was your doorbell." Michael straightened up with a smile.

Both of them stood still and listened as the back door opened and slammed shut, and a tentative voice called out, "Hello? Ms. Madden? Hello? Anyone home?"

"Who the hell is that?" She stared at Michael, but he merely shrugged.

"Why don't you go down and find out?"

"What—people just waltz right on in here?"

"Claire, this is Westport. Not New York."

"Yeah? Well, that's Decker down there, not Lassie."

At that moment the voice from downstairs called up again, sounding far less bold this time. "Ms. Madden? Your dog..."

Claire looked at Michael and gave him a fleeting grin. "Guess I should go down there, right?"

"I think so."

Handing him the sketches, Claire bounced down the stairs and finally reached the kitchen at the back of the house. She could hear Decker's low growl and couldn't resist an inward smile at having such an alert dog. And one with good taste, too, she thought as she rounded the corner to find the corpulent Henry Lubinsky cowering against the kitchen cupboards.

"Oh, Ms. Madden, thank goodness you're home." His voice quivered almost as much as his double chin when he spoke.

Claire stepped up to Decker and placed one hand on his head to calm him as she offered the other in greeting to the Westport lawyer.

"And what is it I can do for you today, Mr. Lubinsky?"

He edged away from the cupboards and toward the kitchen table, where he set down his briefcase, all the time keeping a wary eye on the big golden retriever at Claire's side.

"Just a few things. I'm looking for some of Estelle's papers. I'm afraid that we didn't get a chance to go through everything before you moved in."

"What kind of papers are you referring to, Mr. Lubinsky?"

"Well, utility bills, really. Expenses, receipts—that sort of thing. Nothing that you should be concerned about, Ms. Madden. Estelle kept all of her important papers with our office—her deed, her will, bank statements, you know? We've supplied you with copies of all those for your lawyer's records. What I'm looking for is any straggling paperwork, if you know what I mean. Stuff I should tidy up. Have you come across anything at all?"

Claire studied the small man for a moment before deciding that he must be harmless. If there were any unpaid bills or expenses, he was welcome to pay them through Estelle's estate.

"I haven't had much of a chance to go through the house yet," she explained as she led him to the small oak desk in the sitting room. She'd given the desk no more than a cursory glance when she'd arrived. "I certainly haven't had a chance to go through any of that." She raised her hand to indicate the mass of papers and notes piled there. "I suppose it'll mean more to you than it will to me."

"If you'd like, Ms. Madden, I can just box all this up and have my secretary sort through it at the office. I'd be glad to inform you of anything crucial that might come up, although I really doubt there's anything much here."

"That'll be fine, Mr. Lubinsky. I'll get you a box."

When Claire returned with an emptied art-supplies box, Henry Lubinsky had already sorted the papers into several manageable piles. He then stuffed the papers, unopened envelopes and all the scraps held together with string and elastic bands into the box.

With him standing on the opposite side of the desk, Claire leafed through several invoices and bills until her hand fell upon a small black notebook. She lifted the cover and saw Estelle Bramley's name elegantly written across the flyleaf.

"What is this?" she asked, about to flip through the rest of the book.

"Nothing you need concern yourself with, Ms. Madden," he said hoarsely, taking the book from her hands and stuffing it into the box along with several large envelopes. "We'll look after everything."

The creak of the second-last stair alerted them to Michael's approach. Henry Lubinsky turned abruptly, almost dropping the last of the papers.

"Oh, Michael." Claire stepped in between the two men. "You know Mr. Lubinsky, don't you?"

Michael's face remained expressionless, his eyes pinning Lubinsky like a dried beetle to a bug collector's board. His voice was as distant and cold as the gray of his eyes. "Yes, I do. How are you today, Henry?"

Lubinsky shifted beside the desk, clutching the box to his bulging midriff. "Fine. Just fine, thank you, Mr. Dalton," he stammered, his flitting eyes never pausing long enough to make direct contact. "Thank you for your time, Ms. Madden. Sorry to have disturbed you."

Claire followed him out through the kitchen, turning once and seeing Michael staring at the empty desk.

"I'll be in touch if anything comes up, Ms. Madden. And do be sure to call me if you have any problems with the house."

"That's why I have Michael, Mr. Lubinsky." Claire smiled, more at the relief of seeing him leave than out of politeness.

"Yes, well…" He paused, then added, "Good day, Ms. Madden."

When Claire returned to the sitting room, Michael was already packing up his tools. She watched him from behind for a moment, remembering the muscles beneath his T-shirt, and the warmth of his smile only moments before as he'd held her sketches in his broad hands.

Clearing her throat, Claire leaned back against the doorjamb and waited for him to turn around.

"So, anything I should know about?"

He slung his hammer into a toolbox before turning to her. "I don't know what it is you're referring to, Claire."

"Henry Lubinsky. And your reception of the man. Wasn't exactly what I would call glowing hospitality."

Michael shrugged and lifted his forearm to wipe at some of the sweat beaded on his brow. "Nothing, really. He's all right. Just don't have any use for a man like that." He'd finished packing now and, with one hand in the pocket of his jeans, he came toward her. Leaning against the opposite doorjamb, he looked down at her face. For the first time, she realized how tall he was.

"And just what kind of man is Henry Lubinsky?"

"You don't really want to know."

"Humor me."

He shrugged. "The man's a leech."

"He's a lawyer, Michael." Claire caught the glimmer of laughter behind his eyes and his lips curled up at the corners.

"Yeah, well, I've known more appealing leeches. I was simply trying to be nice." He lifted a hand to run his fingers back through his hair.

Claire imagined the callused roughness of his hands, feeling mildly embarrassed at the thought.

"To tell the truth," he continued, "I didn't like the way Lubinsky treated your aunt. He used her. Fed off her money. This house would have been in a much-better state of repair if she'd been able to spend even half the money Lubinsky drained out of her on it instead." Michael scanned the unfinished state of the living and sitting rooms.

"So who did pay for the renovations?"

"Oh, Estelle mainly. I helped out where I could. Here and there."

Claire studied his profile, admiring the defined lines and the strong jaw. "I take it you're being paid out of the Bramley estate's holdings then?"

Michael shook his head.

"Then what is all this you're doing?" Images of lumber and labor bills flashed through Claire's mind. He'd spent *weeks* on the house, from what she could see. Her father was wealthy, but aside from the loft studio in Soho, Claire had always fended for herself when it came to finances. Alec was a good agent—managed to get her several shows a year, not to mention numerous sales, and lately profits had been healthy. But there was no way she could even begin to afford the kinds of hours Michael had put into the old house. "I can't possibly—"

"Claire—" Michael held up a hand to stop her "—don't worry about it. I never started the work on this house for the money."

"Yes, but..."

"Estelle was good company. We got along. I enjoyed being here and she seemed to enjoy having me. Besides, I enjoy the work."

"But she must have paid you at least something."

Michael smiled softly, perhaps in remembrance of the old woman Claire had never met but suddenly wished she had. "She'd make me lunch, mostly."

Claire could only stare at Michael, his closeness seeming to draw her to him. How could he have spent so many days, so many weeks and months, working for no return? Who was Michael Dalton, really?

She cleared her throat. "I guess I owe you a few lunches, then."

"How about dinner?" he asked, his lips stretching into an expectant smile.

"Sure." Claire nodded and extended her hand, finding an oddly familiar comfort in the warm strength of his grip. "Dinner—it's a deal."

STEAM BILLOWED OVER the glass partition, shrouding the bathroom in a warm, dense mist. With the shower on full pulse, Michael basked in the heat of the water streaming over his shoulders and back, relaxing for the first time all day.

He'd built this shower for Estelle. All those hours, hand setting and grouting the small ceramic tiles, and it hadn't even been used until Claire's arrival. Estelle had certainly admired it, but had still refused to move to the third floor. It was almost as if she had been preparing it for someone else, as though she had known that one day it would be Claire's. It just wasn't supposed to have happened so soon.

Estelle's death passed through Michael's mind again but, as he had learned to do over the past several weeks, he blocked out his suspicions.

And then there was Lubinsky. The man couldn't be trusted. Who knew what kinds of connections the small-town lawyer was maintaining? Most of all, Michael didn't like him lurking around Estelle's house. Especially around Claire.

Michael turned and let the water flow over his chest. He knew he should get out soon. Claire was waiting for him. She'd suggested that he shower here in order to save a bit of time and, since he'd always been in the habit of keeping a clean set of clothes in the back of the Land Rover, he'd agreed. But the lull of the water joined with his thoughts and he allowed himself one more minute.

Claire's face flitted before his mind's eye: her smile, her laugh, however brief, and her eyes—depths of black brown that seemed to swallow him whole whenever she looked at him. There was sadness there, behind those otherwise serene eyes, sorrow behind the gentle lilt of her laugh. But Claire Madden was not a person who seemed anxious to share her secrets with anyone, and Michael had resigned himself to mere guessing. He'd nursed enough pain of his own to recognize someone else who wanted to be left alone to sort out her emotions.

Still, he couldn't put Claire out of his mind. At first, in reaction to her coolness, he'd been determined to finish the house, gather his tools and never look back. But then, as the week had progressed, he'd seen another side of Claire Madden emerge in their fleeting encounters—a side that had once known happiness, a former self that revealed itself in the occasional smile or in the flash of bright eyes. For the first time in years, Michael found himself attracted to a woman. But he could not ignore the sadness that lingered behind those dark eyes, and until he understood it, he knew she was unreachable.

Turning off the taps, Michael rubbed his face as if to erase the confusion preying on his mind. He would let it go. See what happened. It was an innocent dinner, after all, nothing more. What could possibly occur?

With a towel around his waist, he padded into the master bedroom for his clothes. The queen-size bed was still neatly made and he knew that Claire mustn't have slept last night. He'd seen the lights of the turret from his house long after midnight, and then at daybreak this morning. He'd also seen the exhaustion in her face this afternoon, and made a mental note to get her home early tonight.

Tucking his shirt into his jeans, Michael's eyes skipped over the various belongings Claire had set out in an attempt to create a sense of home for herself in the large bedroom. But it was the photograph on the bedside table that caught and held his eye.

Framed in polished brass, the five-by-eight glossy looked like it had been taken recently. The dark green of tropical vegetation loomed in a blur behind the two figures standing at the bow of a sailboat. Claire wore her curly, dark blond hair in the same blunt cut that she did now. The man beside her—his dark tan contrasted by shining blond hair blown back in the sea breeze—had his arm thrown over Claire's shoulders in the happy instant caught by the camera.

Michael looked back at Claire. Her bright face echoed the man's, their smiles directed perhaps at a comment made by the photographer or perhaps simply a reflection of their belief that the world was theirs and that everything lasted forever.

He turned away, embarrassed at having peered into Claire's personal life in such a manner. He checked his watch. She'd be waiting for him downstairs. He'd already taken longer than he had intended.

Hurrying down the stairs, he could hear Claire putting dishes into the cupboards. As he rounded the corner to the kitchen, he saw her reach up to put a large bowl on an upper shelf.

"Can I give you a hand?"

She returned his smile. "Thanks, but no. I'm just about finished here. Have a seat. I'll only be another minute."

She had changed into a fresh sweater, and for a moment Michael couldn't recall ever having seen her in anything that didn't have paint all over it.

Feeling Decker's cold nose nudging his hand, Michael looked down at the retriever. He took the dog's head between his hands and scratched his ears.

"He really likes you." Claire's voice held a note of mild amazement, causing Michael to look up. She leaned back, her hips against the edge of the countertop, her arms crossed over her chest, and shook her head.

"Well, I guess I've always had a way with animals."

"Yeah, but you don't know Decker. I've never seen him like this with anyone. He'd sooner take a person's hand off than eat the steak they might be offering him."

"That's hard to believe." Michael looked down at the dog and then back up at Claire. "He just lacks a male role model, that's all."

Claire's mouth curved into an unconscious smile that quickly faded when she realized that Michael was staring at her. But even when she turned her attention back to the last few dishes in the drying rack, Michael continued to watch her profile. The strong jaw and cheekbones reflected her strength and determination. But the satiny glow of her skin and the soft fullness of her lips spoke of a gentle femininity that was undeniably seductive.

He remembered the silky feel of her fingers when they had shaken hands. Even then, as a thrill had rippled through his body, he had imagined the warmth of her soft body against his.

But he couldn't allow himself to think this way. Not until he found out more about her.

"So, are we ready then?"

Claire turned from the empty counter as she set her towel to one side and reached for her coat. "Sure." A smile danced in her eyes. "And where is it you're taking me to, Mr. Dalton? Or is it a surprise?"

"Trust me." He helped her with her coat, smelling a hint of musk as she lifted her hair above the collar. "It's just a quiet place I know along the oceanfront. I promise, no surprises tonight."

CHAPTER FIVE

THE HARBORSIDE RESTAURANT was quiet. Certainly quieter than Michael would have considered appropriate for a comfortable dinner between new friends. They shared a softly lit corner facing the ocean. And, as the overhead lights were dimmed and a candle flickered lazily at their table, dinner became a more intimate affair than Michael had intended.

Over grilled sole and a dry white wine, they eventually eased into the relaxed atmosphere of the dining room. Once their plates were cleared and their wineglasses half-empty, Claire began questioning Michael about Estelle and the old house on the bluffs. He told what little he'd learned of her aunt and the history of the house in the two years that he'd been in Westport. But when she asked about Estelle's death, Michael steered the discussion onto other topics.

Further prompting from Claire led him to explanations of his own presence in Westport. He chatted about his former career as a financial analyst and adviser, but gave no precise details as to why he'd abandoned his Wall Street life-style for this quiet spot on the Maine coast. Michael did mention an associate, Dee Sebastian, who acted as his assistant in New York and as his link with those remaining clients who still valued his foresight and experience. By the time coffee arrived, he had skillfully directed the conversation back to the subject of Claire herself.

She spoke openly of her mother's dying when she was only six, and of how her father had brought her up on his own in spite of his rising career as a diplomat. She described how her parents' elopement had alienated them from her mother's family and admitted that she had not even heard the Bramley name until she received the letter from Lubinsky and Ames.

As they sat with their second cups of coffee, Michael smiled at the animation in her voice while she told him about her father's international life-style, her studies at NYU and her experiences in the New York art world. And for a while, as Claire spoke of brighter days, there was a glow about her that seemed to come from deep within, from a place that she herself had not visited for some time.

Even during the drive back from town, Claire kept up her good cheer. She seemed relaxed and open, happy even, and Michael delighted in this change in her.

When they reached the top of the bluffs, he interrupted her gentle laughter and slowed the car.

"Listen, Claire, would you join me for a nightcap?" He looked at her and then at the lights across the fields that marked her house, one concession over.

Claire paused, as if her fate lay in the choice she was about to make. "You live close by?"

"Right here." Michael nodded at the lights that glimmered ahead of them through the ice-laden trees.

Claire leaned forward in her seat and looked up as he pulled into the driveway of the rambling house.

He had to admit, it really did look far more awesome at night than during the daytime. The expansive, pillared entrance was lit up, as were several of the tall windows along the front of the house, while the massive west wing crept back into the blackness of the night like some sleeping monster. He supposed he might have warned her.

Instead, he parked the Land Rover in the cul-de-sac outside and watched Claire's awestricken face as she stepped out of the car and toward the grand main entrance.

"You're kidding me, right? This is your place?"

Michael nodded, following her along the shoveled walkway.

"You didn't tell me you lived here. This is the house I see through the trees, isn't it?"

Michael nodded again, swinging one of the heavy front doors open for her.

"But why didn't you tell me you lived here?"

"You never asked." He smiled and took her coat as she looked around her.

"This is huge. I thought my place was big, but I think I'd be lost in here."

Michael laughed, thinking about how Dee had said the very same thing the first time she'd see the place. She'd actually tried to talk him out of buying the crumbling house, but Michael had recognized the possibilities behind the old, gray stone walls. For two years he'd been chipping away at the relic, bringing it back to its original stateliness.

Claire stepped farther into the entranceway, marveling at the details he had been able to restore in the elegant main hall. In the glow of the hall light, the floors shimmered under a rich coat of finish and the vaulted ceilings reached up into shadows, making the corridor seem even more spacious than it really was.

He hung up their coats and ushered Claire across the foyer, past the base of the curving staircase and through one of the sets of sliding mahogany doors into the living room.

"This main section of the building is pretty much finished," he explained, offering Claire a seat on the leather couch in front of the unlit fire. "I have four bedrooms upstairs, fully furnished. A kitchen, my study, the library, the conservatory, a couple of smaller sitting rooms and this." He waved his hand at the spacious living room. "I'd give you a tour, but you'll have to come over during the day for that. Electrical problems. You know these old Maine homes. I'll get around to rewiring soon enough."

"So why are you working on Estelle's place if you still have so much to finish here?"

Michael shrugged and chose a bottle of wine from a rack in the corner. "No sense in putting more work into this place right now. It's functional. Besides, there's just me rattling around inside these walls. It's enough to keep me comfortable."

He poured the wine and handed Claire a glass before joining her on the couch. It felt comfortable, being close to her, smelling her perfume, watching the sparkle of her eyes.

"You're here alone then?"

He took a sip from his wine. "Only a maid—Greta. She uses the bedroom on the first floor." He shook his head. "You know, it was Dee who talked me into hiring her. I didn't want anyone lurking around the house, cleaning and picking up after me. But I have to admit, she's been great. Unless a vacuum is running or something, I hardly know she's here." He took another sip of wine. "It's really worked out a lot better than I would have imagined."

"But still, all alone in this massive house. I don't know how you keep your sanity."

"It's not that bad." He smiled. "I get my share of visitors. My assistant comes up on a regular basis. A few weeks a year my mother visits from Florida. And, of course, there's my sister and her family." He nodded to one of the pictures on the table behind the couch and Claire turned to catch the happy faces in the family portrait. "They come up from Baltimore every so often— when their careers allow it."

Michael watched Claire sip the bright wine from her glass and, in that moment of silence, realized how strangely comforting it felt to have her so near to him. To sit next to her on his couch, to feel the ease of her company in his own home.

He stared at her a moment longer and watched her rake her fingers through her sleek hair, prop her elbow along the back of the couch. The grace of her movements brought him back to the discussion at hand.

"I suppose you're right, though," he said, looking around the room again. "The house really is too big for my needs. Even this main section is rather extravagant. But then again, I suppose I did have other plans when I bought it." Immediately Michael regretted having created that opening.

"You were married, weren't you?"

Michael studied the wine in his glass, swirling it around in a slow red wave before looking back at Claire. "Once. A few years back."

And then he felt the touch of her hand on his arm.

"What happened?"

He shrugged, wondering why he felt compelled to tell her, wondering why it was that he *wanted* to tell her. "She was sleeping with my partner," he said in a monotone.

Claire squeezed his arm, catching his eyes with hers. "I'm sorry."

"Oh, hey, it's nothing to be sorry about. She's moved on since, new territory every year or so, from what I hear." He tossed back the last of his wine, wondering if the nightcap had been such a good idea. He was feeling too relaxed, too willing to open up. "We got married too soon. I suppose that was one problem. My career was still too important to me. And Marianne, well, she was just too restless to sit around and wait for me to become established."

"Your partner was better established?" The light note of sarcasm in Claire's question caught Michael off guard and he didn't stifle the chuckle that rolled up from his throat.

"Yes, I suppose in a sense he was. He came from old money. It impressed Marianne and she went for it." Michael looked around the living room. It seemed a lifetime ago that he had packed his things and walked out of the upper Manhattan apartment, a lifetime of bitterness to be forgotten. Somehow, he imagined that it would be easier done with Claire around. "Water under the bridge, as they say." He shrugged, not wishing to discuss Marianne anymore. She was in his past, a past that he'd sooner forget than let dampen his evening with Claire by rehashing it. "So, what about you?"

"Me?" Claire looked up from her own glass.

"Yeah. Ever been married?"

"No." She shook her head slowly, taking a deep breath. "Engaged once."

Michael held her eyes with his, trying to see beyond the impervious wall she seemed to have pulled around herself and her past. All he could see in those dark depths was one image—a face, the photograph from her nightstand.

"What happened?" he asked, and almost immediately regretted his boldness.

She drew her hand away from his arm, and Michael felt its loss almost immediately.

"He's dead," she said flatly, looking down at the glass in her trembling hands.

Michael could hear the incredible loss behind those two words. He could hear it in the control she desperately fought to maintain in her voice, and he could see it in her expression. At that moment, more than anything he could remember wanting, Michael longed to hold Claire. To fold her in his arms and comfort her, to feel her warmth and the reality of her body against his, to absorb her sorrow.

Just as he reached out to touch her, Claire lifted her wrist and checked her watch. "Would you look at the time? I can't believe I'm still conscious." She set her wineglass on the coffee table and stood up from the leather couch. "I've got to get home to Decker."

With a sigh of disappointment, Michael followed her to the front hall. The soft glow of the living room cast enough light for him to find her coat. But even as he eased the garment onto her shoulders, watching her slender fingers lift the soft curls of her hair over the collar, Michael knew that he was going to kiss her. He ached for her touch, longed to feel the satiny fullness of her lips on his, to feel her breath against his skin.

When Claire opened the massive oak door to a glittering display of falling snow, Michael reached out and took her hand. She stopped on the threshold and turned to face him, her eyes staring up into his, her gaze expectant as she leaned against the doorjamb. She didn't pull away. Slowly he closed the gap between them, moving toward her warmth.

Her hand burned in his, and with great reluctance he left its comfort and lifted his hand to a straying curl of her hair. With his eyes holding hers, he played with the curl for a moment before allowing his fingers to caress the velvet softness of her cheek.

There was no need to say anything. He'd given her ample opportunity to turn away, to raise her hand in protest, to voice an objection. But she didn't. She only lifted a trembling hand past his open jacket to his chest, and he could feel its warmth searing through his cotton shirt.

He brushed his lips against her cheek, delighting in the tingle that shivered along his skin as he touched her. With one hand cradling her neck and the other lifting her chin, he watched her close her eyes and followed suit. He lowered his lips to hers, feeling her breath mingle with his. When their lips touched, his heart raced and his breath became short.

Her lips tasted sweet from the wine and he traced their silken fullness with his tongue, encouraged by her breathless response. Her hand fluttered farther up his chest until it reached the hollow at the base of his throat, then inched to the back of his neck. She pulled him closer.

His calm was shattered by the hunger of her response, and in moments he parted her willing lips, his tongue touching hers as he drank in her sweet kiss. Even after their kiss ended, Michael basked in its intimacy, his lips still tingling.

With his hands braced against the door behind Claire, he stood close to her for a moment, his face lowered to hers, feeling the tickle of her hair against his cheek as he waited for his pulse to slow. "I'm sorry," he finally whispered in her ear.

"No." Claire sounded hurt. "Please, don't be." Her hand traced a line to his chin and she turned his face so that he was looking at her. "I'm not."

She reached up, her lips pressing against his once again. And, for that brief moment, he savored their sudden familiarity.

He sighed inwardly. He'd crossed a barrier now that he hadn't intended to but felt he could not have possibly avoided. He blamed the wine and his light-headedness. It didn't matter what Claire said, it shouldn't have happened. As much as he had cherished her closeness and the intimacy of their kiss, he couldn't allow that sense of comfort to return. He'd felt a similar sense of comfort once before—during his marriage, before he'd found out about Marianne's affair. A self-defense mechanism clicked in Michael's head as he remembered the old pain. "I'd better get you home."

They drove back to Claire's place in silence. Snow whispered against the roof of the Land Rover as Michael pulled into the drive and turned off the engine. In the stillness of the car, they sat for a moment, watching the snow tumble to the ground in the twin beams of the headlights that reached across the dark fields.

Claire's mind, drugged by exhaustion and the wine, lurched from one image to the next. Reflections of Greg preyed upon her mind—the life they'd shared, the life they'd planned. Even eight months after his death, she could not deny the devotion for him that she still carried deep within her. Even though his memory was the only thing left for her to live with, Claire had clung to it with all her heart. Now, in the quiet of Michael's car, she clung to it more fiercely than she had in a long time.

But in the same breath of understanding, Claire could not deny the longing she'd felt when Michael's lips had claimed hers with a tenderness she'd forgotten was possible. She couldn't deny the pulse of desire she had felt coursing through her body when he'd touched her.

Watching the white flakes melt against the windshield, Claire wondered if, once she'd slept off the wine and her exhaustion, she would regret what had happened between them.

"I'll see you in," Michael half whispered as he stepped out of the car. Claire followed him up the steps and watched him fumble in the dark with the keys.

After Decker had bolted out the door and whined his greetings on his way to the Land Rover's tires, Michael handed Claire her keys. Snow settled gently on his hair and she watched one flake land on his lips for the briefest moment before it disappeared into vapor.

"I have to go away tomorrow," he told her, taking her hand.

Disappointment must have been apparent in her face because Michael lifted a finger to her lips.

"I'm sorry. I would have told you sooner, only…at the time, I didn't see the need."

"How long?"

"It's only a few days. I have to go to New York. More business. I'll be back Friday night." His eyes wandered to her lips, where Claire could still feel the tingle of their kiss. "If not sooner."

She placed a hand on his cheek and forced a smile through her bleary state. "I think I'm going to miss you, Michael."

She had barely spoken these words before he lowered his lips to hers once again, recapturing their hot desire. "I know I'll miss you, Claire," he whispered, pulling away to see her face more fully. "I'll call you when I get back."

She hesitated for a moment, considering the situation. She didn't doubt that he would call. If nothing else, the house required too much work for Michael to turn his back on it now. "You know where to find me," she said, trying to smile again. But the cold had begun to wear off the effects of the wine, and Claire was regaining her former doubts. She was suddenly relieved that Michael was going away—it would give her the breathing space she needed to straighten things out in her head.

"See you then . . . take care, Claire," he breathed as his lips brushed hers again.

He turned from the doorway. Claire watched him walk across the freshly fallen snow to his vehicle, stopping briefly to bid Decker a farewell. Only before getting into the Land Rover did he turn back to look at her again.

Behind the hesitant smile, Claire recognized his uncertainty. She too felt uncertainty clawing at the pit of her stomach as she watched Michael get into the car and back out of the drive. She felt it challenge her swelling desire even as the headlights of the Land Rover followed the tree-lined road and eventually disappeared around the corner a quarter of a mile away.

CHAPTER SIX

It had finally stopped snowing.

For three days Claire had watched the snow pile up on the drive, and with each day she'd felt more and more a prisoner in the old house. But she had decided to wait for a break in the weather before attempting to clear away a path for her car.

Even with a pair of dark sunglasses perched on her nose, Claire found herself squinting against the sun's glare off the snow. She took another breath of crisp air and hurled a shovelful of snow over the growing embankment.

For three days she had watched the snow fall and for three days she'd thought of Michael. There was no sense in denying her attraction to him—at least she'd come to that conclusion. And yet, along with this admission, Claire felt a stab of betrayal. She had tried to move Greg's picture away from her bed table the night before. But the emptiness had been unbearable. She had put it back and retreated to the studio, turning her attention to her paintings instead.

Even as she heaved another shovelful to one side, Claire thought of the four paintings she'd completed. By the time Alec came up to Westport in a week she might have finished a couple more. He would be impressed. Not only was she ahead of schedule, she had managed to leave the darkness of the previous paintings behind her in New

York. In the flood of sunshine that poured into the third-story studio, the new pieces glowed with color. Color inspired by more than the obvious brilliance of her surroundings.

With the completion of the additional paintings and a sudden explosion of energy, Claire had found it necessary to expand her studio space to accommodate the next series of canvases. In the process, she had gone over to Michael's house. Greta, his maid, hadn't seen any problem with her borrowing a few more drop cloths, and Claire had decided to stop by later today to return the unused ones.

The crunch of snow against tires caught Claire's attention. She straightened up and leaned against the shovel to watch a police cruiser edge around the corner and pull into her drive. Even though Decker had been asleep on the front porch, the muffled engine alerted him and he was at Claire's side in a flash. She put a hand on his back to quiet him as two officers stepped out of the car. Claire watched them cross the drive, the bright yellow piping of their pants glaring against the slick, black-blue uniforms.

"Good day, ma'am." The larger man nodded but kept his eye on the dog. His pocked face eased into what Claire would have defined as an official smile. She watched him remove his glove and take the dying cigar from his lips. "Great morning, isn't it?"

"I suppose it is." Claire raised a hand to block the sun as the officer loomed before her.

"Ms. Madden, I presume?"

Claire nodded. "And you are—?"

"Sheriff Raymond Bannon. This is my deputy, Frank Turner."

Claire looked at the younger man by his side while she tried to calm Decker. He was shorter and had a slighter build than the heavy sheriff. But as she watched a muscle flex along the deputy's strong jaw, she had no doubt of the brawn concealed in his wiry frame.

"How can I help you this morning?"

"We just wanted to ask you a few questions," Bannon replied, but Claire already suspected why they were here.

She hadn't forgotten the snippets of conversation she and Alec had overheard at The Laughing Lobster during her first night at Westport. Rumors of Estelle Bramley being murdered? Until now, she'd allowed Alec and Michael to lull her into the belief that the speculations were nothing more than rumors. But with the Westport authorities here in her freshly shoveled driveway, she was beginning to have second thoughts about the boozy chatter of the two locals at the restaurant that night.

"Does this have anything to do with my aunt and her connection to the Hobson girl?" She'd heard the name only once, but it had stayed with her. She watched the sudden stiffness that registered on both men's faces.

"What do you know about the Hobson girl?" Frank Turner lifted a gloved hand to wipe at his nose, and Claire wondered if it was nervousness she saw behind the squint of his vivid green eyes.

She shook her head. "Nothing, really. I just heard the name. Probably nothing more than a rumor."

"Well, you needn't be concerning yourself with rumors, Ms. Madden," Bannon cut in, turning an authoritative glance in Frank's direction. "You know how people in small towns talk."

"Actually, no, I don't, Sheriff. But I do know that there's probably something I should know about my aunt that no one is telling me."

"I can assure you, there's no great conspiracy going on here. Trust me. Your aunt died in her sleep four weeks ago."

"But you think that she was murdered."

Bannon shifted uneasily. They hadn't expected such a bold reception, Claire guessed. Then again, she hadn't thought herself capable of such boldness, either.

"Look, Ms. Madden, there's nothin' for you to be concerned about. Really. We're not trying to hide anything here. Yes, you should know that we *are* investigating your aunt's death. But only as a technicality—you know, with the inheritance and all."

For a moment Claire wondered if he was referring to her.

"Can we come in, Ms Madden?"

"I don't see the purpose of that."

"Just take a look around. Nothing more."

She held his scrutinizing gaze, determined not to have her day interrupted further. "Don't you need a warrant or something for that, Sheriff?"

Bannon studied her for a moment longer. "We're just here to ask you a few questions, Ms. Madden."

"You can ask me here."

"Fine." He looked past her to the house, as if expecting someone to step out the front door at any moment. "Have you seen Michael Dalton this morning?"

Claire hesitated before answering, uncertain as to how Michael fit in to all of this. And then it was obvious. He'd been working on the house. He was the only person who had been in constant contact with Estelle. Why *wouldn't* they be asking for him? They hadn't come to question her at all—it was Michael they were looking for.

"No, not this morning. He's out of town right now, I believe."

"Do you know how long he's gone for?" Bannon asked, pulling the half-smoked cigar from his parka's breast pocket.

"A few days. He said he might be back today."

Bannon looked at the house again and put the cigar in the corner of his mouth, but didn't light it. "So he's been around, then?"

Claire nodded.

"And he's been working on the house?"

"Yes. Why? What else should he be doing here?" She felt her defensiveness rising again.

"Nothing—"

The crackle and hiss of the patrol car's radio alerted Bannon of an incoming call and he excused himself. Opening the door on the driver's side, he reached for the radio and turned his back to the others.

Frank Turner shifted and took a couple of steps closer to Claire, stopping only when Decker's low growl became more defined.

"That's some guard dog you've got yourself." His green eyes swung from her to the dog.

"He's good to have around."

Frank nodded, burying his hands in his pockets. "Especially up here, I'd say. You're pretty isolated."

"I do all right." Claire didn't like the implications of his last comment. She knew very well how alone she was, especially with Michael away in New York. But she didn't need Frank Turner reminding her of her vulnerability.

He reached into an inner pocket and produced a card, flipping it between gloved fingers once before offering it to Claire.

"Just in case you need something."

"I think I'll manage."

"Please, I'd feel better knowing that you had my number. I hate to think of someone all on their own up here on these bluffs. We get some wicked storms off the ocean once in a while. Wouldn't want you to be stranded."

Claire obliged him and took the card.

"You can reach me day or night at that number. It'll ring through from the station if no one's in."

"Thanks." She looked from the card to Frank again, his thin face sporting the memory of a summer tan, his clean-cut, sandy blond hair peeking out from beneath his cap. He smiled awkwardly and Claire couldn't help thinking that, even though they'd barely met, he might be interested in her. "Sweet on her" was the term her father would have so aptly used, and Claire looked away, not wishing to encourage the deputy.

"Frank," Bannon called from the patrol car, "gotta go. Ms. Madden?" He took a few steps closer to ensure that she could hear him. "We'll be in touch if there's anything we need to ask you."

She merely nodded, glad to see the sheriff on his way.

"I'll be seeing you, Ms. Madden." Frank removed his glove and extended a hand, which Claire felt obligated to take. "Nice meeting you. I'm sure we'll be seeing more of you in Westport?"

"I imagine." Claire nodded, giving him a cursory smile.

Only after Frank had gotten into the patrol car with his superior and they had backed out of the drive did Decker stop growling. Claire watched the roof of the car follow the line of snowbanks until it was out of sight.

There was more in their visit than they had let on, Claire sensed. In spite of Bannon's assurances that they weren't trying to hide anything from her, there were still some nagging questions. And if Claire couldn't get the answers from the authorities, then, for her own peace of mind, she'd have to find other channels.

"THE HOBSON GIRL? You mean Annette Hobson?" The librarian peered at Claire.

Claire had gone to Henry Lubinsky's office first, but when his secretary informed her that he was out for the day, she had decided that the local library would be her best bet for digging up information on "the Hobson girl." She'd passed by The Laughing Lobster on her way and had had half a mind to duck in and see if the same two locals were warming their bar stools. But she had reconsidered. Westport was a small community, and she didn't need to draw attention to herself as a meddler.

Claire nodded to the librarian.

"Jenny," the woman called toward the back room, her eyes never leaving Claire, as a mousy girl appeared from around the corner.

"Yes, Ms. Rosemoore?"

"Could you show... Ms. Madden, isn't it?"

"Yes," Claire stammered, amazed at the librarian's knowledge of her name and realizing just how small Westport was.

"Could you show Ms. Madden where the local papers are kept? She's looking for the stories on Annette Hobson."

"Yes, ma'am."

Claire followed the soft-spoken girl to the back of the library. Behind a row of solid wooden tables lit by individual table lamps, the girl paused in front of a massive oak shelving unit and considered the various drawers before pulling one open. "These are the papers for the past five weeks," she explained, bumping her glasses farther up the bridge of her nose with one finger. "They found

Annette...her body, that is...up on the bluffs almost four and a half weeks ago. It's all in here."

Claire stopped. From the snippets of information she'd heard, she had assumed that "the Hobson girl" people murmured about over their beers was dead. But she hadn't thought of it in such cold terms as "body" and she certainly hadn't imagined that the murder had been committed as close to home as the bluffs.

She pulled out the earliest paper. January 28.

"Actually, ma'am, you'll want to start with January 30."

Putting the paper back, she rifled through the others until she found the right date. "Did you know her?"

Claire looked up from the paper in time to see the young girl nod. She couldn't have been older than sixteen or seventeen.

"She was a friend of mine. We went to school together."

"I'm sorry," Claire offered in the hush of the library, thinking that her words were not much of a consolation.

"It's all right. I just hope they get the guy that did it, is all. If you need anything else, I'll be at the front desk."

"Thank you." Claire watched the young woman weave her way between the tables before turning to the paper in her hands.

After the glut of stories the first week after the discovery of Annette Hobson's body, articles were sparse. She spread the week's worth of papers across a table and moved from one to the next, gleaning what she could from the stories.

They were diluted at best—the Westport authorities had no leads and were refraining from making any comments on the investigation. Only basic information had been provided to the local paper.

The seventeen-year-old girl had been reported missing since January 25. Sheriff Bannon and his deputies, along with several community members, had started a thorough search on the morning of the 27th, since the girl's parents hadn't been able to come up with any leads on their daughter's whereabouts through friends.

By the night of the 29th, one of the coldest nights on record, they had found the girl's body. She had been sexually assaulted and killed before being dumped in a snowy field along the bluffs. The paper referred to the Dalton and Bramley houses briefly as geographical markers in relation to the discovery of the body. Claire felt a shiver run down her spine as she read the Bramley name in print.

It was no wonder that the locals from The Laughing Lobster had thought to link Annette Hobson with her aunt. If something had happened up there on the bluffs, or if Annette's killer had just dumped off her body, it was quite likely that Estelle *might* have seen something.

Claire felt perspiration beading her forehead and realized that she had not taken off her coat. Her pulse raced as she considered the possibilities.

If she herself had come to the conclusion that Estelle might have seen something, then certainly Annette Hobson's killer would have reached that same conclusion. It was no wonder that Sheriff Bannon was interested in the Bramley house.

HOPING TO CATCH Henry Lubinsky in his office before she headed out of town, Claire had finished her grocery shopping and parked the Volvo in front of the Lubinsky and Ames offices. Once inside the overheated building, she removed her sunglasses and tried to adjust her eyes to the dark wood-paneled decor.

"Oh, Ms. Madden—Mr. Lubinsky is in now," the secretary chirped, leaning across one side of her desk in order to gain a view of the office across from hers. She nodded to someone there before looking at Claire again. "You can go right in."

Henry Lubinsky looked up from his desk when Claire stepped around the corner. He had just finished taking a quick puff of his asthma medication and he tossed the small inhaler into the top drawer before shutting it. He stood, greeting her with a fleshy smile.

"Good afternoon, Ms. Madden. Please, have a seat."

"No, thank you, Mr. Lubinsky." Claire had decided, before leaving the car that she was going to make this visit as brief as possible. "I can't stay long. I only wanted to ask you some questions."

"Everything at the house all right?"

"Everything's fine, Mr. Lubinsky, thank you. I was just at the library—going through some back editions of the local paper."

Lubinsky nodded his balding head. "Yes?" he prompted, apparently still not certain what it was Claire wanted from him.

"I read about Annette Hobson."

Claire watched the lawyer's face, wondering if she would see the same reaction she had seen in Frank Turner and Sheriff Bannon earlier that day. But he remained calm.

Maybe she was wrong. Maybe it wasn't some kind of a cover-up, after all. Maybe there was a less sinister explanation of the events around Estelle's death.

"How did my aunt die, Mr. Lubinsky?"

"I'm not sure what you're trying to get at, Ms. Madden. Let me assure you that your aunt died peacefully in her sleep. The doctor examined her and signed the death certificate to that effect. I realize that some people in this town would like to believe that there is some connection between your aunt and that poor Hobson girl. You have to understand, Ms. Madden, this is a small community. People get bored. They contrive elaborate fabrications to amuse themselves in the winter months.''

"I don't think that a connection is entirely improbable."

"The authorities haven't made any such connection."

"Not publicly," Claire challenged.

Lubinsky leaned forward against his desk, his eyes nailing Claire where she stood. He stared at her for what seemed like a full minute, and Claire suddenly felt very uncomfortable in the small office.

"Look, Ms. Madden. Believe me, your aunt died in her sleep. I'm sure that if she'd seen something, she would have told someone. Trust me, the connections you're attempting to draw are not real—they're only rumors. It's Frank Turner's case and he'll handle it. He's a good kid. You'll only wind up getting yourself worked up if you go around jumping to irrational conclusions and making wild insinuations."

The phone on Lubinsky's desk let out a shrill buzz and Claire jumped.

"Henry Lubinsky," he answered, still eyeing Claire as she lingered on the opposite side of his desk. "Yes...um—hmm...no, I think Ames was looking into that. Hang on a second." He placed a meaty hand over the mouthpiece of the phone. "Was there anything else, Ms. Madden?"

Claire, who now found herself despising the man more than ever, shook her head, anxious to escape the confines of his office. "No, thank you, Mr. Lubinsky. I'll see myself out," she replied coldly, and turned from the office.

The brisk air outside was a welcome relief from the stuffy office. Claire stepped out onto the sidewalk and took several deep breaths in an attempt to regain her composure.

She would go home, unpack her groceries and start a fresh canvas. That would take her mind off of its rampant hypothesizing.

And then, as she stepped off the curb, Claire stopped short.

Across the street, leaning against the hood of her Volvo, Frank Turner stood watching her. He nodded and lifted a gloved finger in greeting.

"Good afternoon, Ms. Madden," he said as she approached, his lips curling in a smirk.

"Good afternoon, Deputy Turner."

"Please, it's Frank. Can I call you Claire?"

She looked at him and eventually nodded. He seemed harmless enough. And even though she had never been the type to fall for a uniform like some women did, she had to admit that Frank Turner could be considered a handsome catch.

"I saw your car parked here and figured you were inside with Lubinsky."

Claire nodded again.

"Too bad you got stuck with him. He's a bit of an ass. Ames is the brains in that partnership."

"Funny—" Claire smiled, hiding her dislike of Frank's sharp tongue "—I recall Lubinsky referring to you as 'a good kid.'"

Frank's green eyes sparkled in the late-afternoon sun. "Can't see why he'd tell you that. The man hardly knows me." He grinned, giving her a wink. "Can I buy you a coffee, Claire? Just a quick one. Warm you up before the drive home?"

She was about to decline the offer. She had already spent more time than she'd wanted in town, and had no intention of getting to know too many faces in Westport. But she also recognized this as a prime opportunity to pump the deputy for information surrounding her great-aunt's death.

"Sure," she agreed eventually. "A quick one."

The Happy Face Coffee Shop was only two doors down. In a flood of sunlight, Claire sat down with Frank at a corner table and removed her gloves and scarf. In moments they were cradling steaming mugs of coffee and the deputy was prompting Claire with questions about her work and the house. More than ten minutes passed before she was able to steer the conversation away from herself and onto Estelle.

"My hands are tied, Claire," Frank said at last with what seemed an apologetic shrug. "Sorry, department policy. As long as the case is still under investigation, I can't discuss it with anyone."

"But there doesn't even seem to be a case. Lubinsky said that he'd seen the coroner's report, that her death was natural. What is there to investigate?"

"The sheriff's got it in his mind that there might have been foul play. That's all I can say."

Claire studied Frank for a moment. She didn't dare bring up the subject of Annette Hobson after the reaction it had provoked in him earlier on. Both he and Bannon had seemed to throw up defensive walls at the mention of the girl's name, and Claire didn't want to say anything that might cause Frank to end their conversation prematurely.

"Foul play? Who do you think may have killed my aunt, Frank?"

He shrugged again and Claire wondered if she'd seen a faint glimmer in his eyes, as if he knew who might have been responsible and was just playing with her. "I don't know."

"Any wild guesses?"

He scratched at a day's stubble along his chin. "I don't make wild guesses, Claire. Police training teaches you that."

"Well, who found her?" Claire asked, doubting the pertinence of this question but wanting to prompt Frank into admitting something. Anything.

"Think that has bearing on the case?" he asked.

"I don't know. You tell me."

"All right then, if you must know. It was Dalton—Michael Dalton who found her."

Claire stared at him. Of course Michael would have found her. Who else would have? He was the only one who came and went to Estelle's house.

"Since we're on the topic of Michael Dalton..." Frank leaned forward against the table.

"What about him?"

"He's hanging around quite a bit up there, isn't he? Working on the house, I imagine."

Claire had no intention of answering his question. As far as she was concerned, it was none of the deputy's business what Michael was doing at her house.

"What are you getting at, Frank?"

"I'm just wondering how well you really know Dalton."

Claire's pulse quickened, fearing the worst. "What do you mean?"

"Just that. You don't know Dalton very well. Don't suppose he told you why he left New York, did he?"

He'd hated Wall Street. He'd hated the life-style. That's what he'd told her. Was there any reason to doubt it? "Well no, I suppose, not really. He told me he wanted to get away from the city. I just assumed—"

"Don't assume, Claire. Never assume. Gets you into trouble every time."

"Oh, and is this something one learns in police training as well?" she asked sarcastically, but then forced a smile. She was not about to lose the one connection she'd made with the Westport authorities.

"Nope. That I learned from life."

Claire looked out the window to the wintry street. It had started snowing again, she noticed before looking back at Frank. "So what are you trying to tell me?"

"Not trying to tell you anything, Claire. Just saying that I wouldn't trust the guy if I were you. I'm just saying that *I* don't trust him. That's all."

He stood up from the table and rummaged in his pocket before pulling out two one-dollar bills. "Just be careful, Claire. Hate to see a woman like you get mixed up with a guy like Dalton."

"Well, thanks for the warning, Frank. I'll keep it in mind."

He nodded before turning from the table. "You've got my number?"

Claire patted her coat pocket. "Right here."

"I'll see you around, then." He gave her a quick smile before leaving, and Claire watched him lift the collar of his parka and walk off down the street.

Ms. ROSEMOORE WAS just tidying up the front desk when Sheriff Bannon entered the main doors of the library. He caught the head librarian's eye with the wave of his hand before he realized he still held his unlit cigar. He tucked it into his breast pocket as she approached.

"I'm sorry, we're closing, Sheriff."

"That's all right, Ms. Rosemoore. I only wanted to ask you a quick question. That woman who was here earlier—short, slender, blondish hair?"

"You mean Ms. Madden?"

Bannon nodded his head and stared at the woman. Of course she knew. The nosy librarian made it her business to know everyone and everything around Westport. It was damned eerie, he admitted, shifting his weight to lean against the counter.

"Yeah. Can you tell me what she was looking for?"

The librarian seemed to inspect him before answering. "She was asking about Annette Hobson. I had Jenny show her where the papers are."

Bannon leaned even more heavily against the front desk. The last thing he needed was the Madden woman prying into their investigation.

Frank was handling it. That was best. But, knowing Frank and his weakness for good-looking women, anything could happen.

He'd have to keep an eye on the boy.

CHAPTER SEVEN

WHEN CLAIRE TURNED into the drive of Michael's house an hour later, another car was parked next to his Land Rover. She pulled up behind it, grabbed the extra drop cloths from the passenger seat and bounced up the front steps, surprised by her girlish enthusiasm at the thought of seeing Michael again. She hadn't expected him to be home so soon, and wondered who his visitor might be.

Greta answered the door.

"Oh, good afternoon, Ms. Claire," she said excitedly, ushering her out of the cold and into the front hall. "Mr. Dalton is in the study. I believe he tried calling you earlier."

Wiping her boots, Claire headed to the study. The massive mahogany sliding doors were partially closed, and as she reached out to open one, she heard Michael's laughter mingling with a woman's.

Sliding the door further open, Claire peered into the room and saw the woman who was laughing with Michael. She sat perched on the corner of his desk, and her long, slender legs seemed to extend forever. Her tall body, exuding sensuality, was clad in a skintight, short black dress, and her flaming red hair cascaded in loose curls down her back.

All of a sudden, Claire felt extremely out of place. She didn't need to look down at herself to realize the disheveled image she presented. She knew that the jeans she had so hurriedly slipped into had their share of paint smears across the faded denim. And she didn't have to look to guess that the tails of her shirt were probably hanging out from under the sweater she'd pulled on.

Michael saw her first. A smile spread across his face as he held the telephone receiver under his chin.

"Claire. What a lovely surprise. Come in."

The woman stood up from the desk. As she turned toward the doorway, Claire could see that her angular face matched her sleek figure.

"This is my assistant, Dee Sebastian. Dee, I'd like you to meet Claire Madden."

Claire took the hand offered to her, aware of how cold hers must feel in the slender warmth of Dee's.

"So you're Claire," the woman said demurely. "Michael's told me about you."

Claire nodded, doing her best to maintain a smile. "Yeah? Well, you should hear my side of the story sometime."

Dee laughed, apparently feeling more at ease in her surroundings than she did.

"Have a seat, Claire. Greta's just making some tea. I'll only be a minute. They've got me on hold here."

"I'm sorry. I really can't stay, Michael. I was only returning some of your drop cloths. Greta let me borrow a few the other day, but I don't need them all."

"You can just leave them there. I'll put them away later," he offered, pointing at the leather wing chair in the corner. "Are you sure you can't stay?"

Claire nodded and started to back out of the room. "Maybe some other time—I can see you're busy. I'll put these in the shed on my way out."

Before Michael could change her mind, the party on the other end of the line came back on. "Yes, Bill. Yes, I'm still here. The Delaney account... No, Dee filled me in on it. I have the figures right here...." He shuffled through some folders on his desk and then looked at Claire as he mouthed the words, "I'll see you later."

She nodded and turned to the alluring Dee Sebastian. "It was a pleasure meeting you, Dee. Perhaps another time?"

Dee nodded and Claire wished that the woman hadn't given her such a warm smile. It would have been a lot easier to dislike her.

The shock of cold air quelled Claire's nerves. Why had seeing Michael with a stunning woman bothered her so much? She couldn't possibly be jealous when she barely even knew the man.

But as she struggled with the frozen latch of the shed to one side of the drive, she was cursing herself for having foolishly believed that she could have meant something to a man like Michael Dalton. With women like Dee Sebastian around, why would he look any further?

"So THAT WAS YOUR Claire Madden?"

Michael had finished his conference call seconds before Claire's Volvo roared out of the drive, and he knew that there was no sense in running after her now. He leaned back in his chair.

"She's not *my* Claire Madden," he assured Dee with a faint sigh of exasperation.

"Well, she's certainly not your ex-wife, either."

Michael threw her a look he hoped Dee would recognize as a warning. But the glance was unnecessary. She knew him, perhaps better than anyone else did.

"Just kidding, Michael. Lighten up." She took a deep breath and began gathering her papers.

Michael watched her, watched her slender fingers shuffle through the paperwork on the desk and sort the files into her eel-skin briefcase. She did know him. Too well, probably. And, over the past couple of years, he'd tried to understand the protectiveness she displayed on occasion.

"You know," she said, pausing long enough to give him a hard stare, "I'd be inclined to say she's your type, except that I don't really know your type, do I? I mean, there hasn't exactly been anyone steady since that ex-witch of yours."

"Dee." Michael tilted his head, putting a stop to her chiding. She hadn't even met his ex-wife. He'd taken on Dee as an assistant after the divorce and the downfall of his partnership. But still, after all this time, Dee held more of a grudge against his ex-wife than Michael did himself. She had seen the near ruin he'd let his life slip into, and from the outset had carried a resentment toward the woman who had caused his pain. Her loyalty was admirable. She was most likely the closest friend he'd ever had.

And it wasn't as if there had never been an attraction between them. Earlier on in their business relationship, there had been a spark of physical temptation, but it hadn't amounted to anything more than a couple of lingering yet awkward kisses and fleeting thoughts of further possibilities. The fact remained, always, that they were friends. Business friends. And even though their friendship had crossed the line from professional to personal at times, there had never been any passion between them. Attractive though she was, Michael had never felt that he wanted Dee as a lover.

But with Claire it was different. He felt close to her in a way that could not even compare to the friendship he'd shared with Dee over the years. Indeed, he'd felt linked to Claire from the moment he'd first met her.

"Did you hear me, Michael?"

He looked up. "What's that?"

Dee's briefcase was already packed and she had her coat draped over one arm. She smiled with characteristic gentleness and edged up to the corner of the desk. She lay her hand over Michael's. "I said, I'm happy for you. About Claire. She seems interesting, from what little I saw of her. She's certainly pretty. I can understand your attraction. In fact, if you were to ask me—which you aren't, but I'm going to tell you anyway—I think you should let go of all that garbage in your past and go for it."

Michael smiled. "Go for it? This is the bit of wisdom I receive from the great Dee Sebastian, the queen of broken relationships? Go for it?"

"Give me credit for recognizing a good thing when I see it. You know what I mean, Michael. Haven't you spent enough time being afraid of feeling something for someone? Just go with it."

"Dee, I'm not afraid of caring about someone."

"No—" she stepped away from the desk as if to leave "—maybe not. But you've had your emotions turned off for so long now I'm beginning to wonder if you've forgotten how to act on them. You do realize that a woman like Claire Madden doesn't cross your path every day, don't you?"

She waited for Michael's nod before shifting her briefcase to her other hand and heading to the door. "Good. Now, are you going to see me out or do you want me to leave you here daydreaming?"

In the front hall Michael helped Dee with her coat before opening the door for her.

"You take care of yourself, Michael. I'll be seeing you in a few days then?"

He nodded. "I'll be here."

"And when I get back from Chicago, you'll fill me in on your progress, won't you?" she asked with a twinkle in her eye, letting him know that she wasn't referring to the Delaney account.

"I will." He returned her smile. "Now get out of here before you miss your flight."

"Anything you say." She gave him a quick kiss, then tiptoed down the shoveled walk to her rental car.

"Drive carefully," he shouted after her.

She raised a hand of acknowledgment and started the car.

Even as Dee was pulling out of the drive, Michael was thinking about Claire. She had seemed uneasy when she stood in the doorway of the study, confronted by Dee. And Michael hoped that she hadn't come to the wrong conclusion.

CLAIRE WOULD NOT HAVE heard the front door open if Decker hadn't lifted his head to warn her. And she wouldn't have known it was Michael on the stairs if it hadn't been for the dog's wagging tail.

A tape of New Age music played quietly on the stereo in the corner and Claire kept on painting. She looked away from her canvas only when Michael walked in through the doorway of the studio.

He hadn't changed his clothes. Still wearing the black turtleneck and gray tweedy sweater she'd seen him in earlier, he looked too handsome to ignore.

She gave him a smile and a quick "Hi" before turning back to her painting.

"It's getting dark in here. Do you want the lights on?" he asked, lingering by the door.

"No, not yet, thanks."

He walked across the drop cloths and stood beside the canvas she was working on. With one finger under her chin, he tilted her face and kissed her, the softness of his lips clinging to hers. And then he moved behind her, to wrap his arms around her shoulders.

She hoped Michael wouldn't feel the tension gripping her body as he held her. What was it? Why did she feel this apprehension, this sense of betrayal? Was it because Greg used to do the very same thing? Was it because one of her strongest memories of Greg was of him holding her from behind, cradling her for what felt like hours at a time, watching her paint?

At that moment, Claire resented Greg for not being there, for not being with her as he had promised.

She felt Michael's breath against her ear as he let out a long sigh and she closed her eyes, trying to ignore the tingle of desire that shivered up her spine and through the very core of her being. Why did he have to feel so good, so familiar?

"I missed you, Claire," he whispered.

She smelled the trace of his after-shave—a smell that stirred deeper cravings and memories of the other night. Claire gripped the paintbrush firmly in her hand and continued to paint.

And then there was Dee. She couldn't forget Dee Sebastian and the ease the woman seemed to feel with Michael.

As if sensing her thoughts, Michael relaxed his embrace. "She's only my assistant, Claire."

Claire stopped painting, hoping that he wouldn't notice how white her knuckles were from clenching the brush. "What, you think I'm jealous?"

"No, I didn't say that. I just thought...well, you seemed a little uncertain. I wanted to explain."

With one fluid movement, she broke from his embrace and walked over to one of the turret windows. She leaned against its solid wooden frame and stared out into the impending night. "Look, Michael, you don't owe me any explanations. We hardly know each other."

The truth was, she was trembling and didn't want Michael to see it. So many thoughts scattered through her mind, so many doubts. On top of her own misgivings, Claire had not been able to shake Frank's warning from her mind all afternoon. Seeing Dee Sebastian had only acted as a reaffirmation that she had to be cautious—in matters of the heart as well as those surrounding her great-aunt's death.

"Claire, what is it?" Michael's voice seemed to fill the emptiness of the studio as he came up beside her again and placed a hand on her shoulder. He looked out the window, following her gaze to the darkening fields. "What's bothering you?"

Claire was silent for a moment, then took a breath and asked, "She saw it, didn't she?" she nodded toward the snow-laden fields.

"Michael?" Only after a long moment did he look back at her, and Claire knew she'd struck a sensitive area. "Estelle saw something out there. That's why she was killed."

"Maybe—no one knows."

"No, but that's what you believe, isn't it?"

"Who have you been talking to, Claire?"

She looked back to the fields. "Bannon and Frank Turner were here this morning. I think they were looking for you." She picked up a rag and started to clean her brush. "I wanted to find out for myself what had happened, so I went to the library."

"And?"

"And I went to see Lubinsky. Then I ran into Frank again."

"You've been talking to Frank Turner?"

Claire nodded, not certain if it was defensiveness or simply dislike for Frank that was discernible in Michael's voice.

"Actually, he did most of the talking," she confessed.

"And what did Frank have to say about Estelle?"

"Nothing. He said his hands were tied."

In spite of the doubts that had been haunting her all day and still whispered in the back of her mind, Claire reached out and touched Michael's arm. "Tell me what you know, Michael. Please. Did Estelle see anything?"

He took a deep breath, running strong fingers through his hair, and looked at Claire as if deciding whether or not to trust her. "I think she probably did."

Claire watched a muscle flex along his jaw but didn't dare interrupt.

"She wouldn't talk about it. Even when Bannon and Turner came up here, badgering her with questions, she wouldn't talk. It made her nervous, the fact that it had happened practically right outside her door. That's why I stayed with her more often after that—worked on the house whenever I could."

Claire hung on to every word now, anxious to hear concrete information from someone at last.

"She called me the day before Annette Hobson was reported missing. Lied about something gone wrong with the water heater just to get me over. Even then she wouldn't admit anything to me, just said it felt safer with me around. It was obvious she was nervous, so I did what I could—spent as much time at the house as I could afford and checked up on her every so often. But *I* think she saw something out there, because she was frightened even before they found the girl's body. Even before they'd reported her missing.''

Michael paused, staring out the window as the studio behind them fell into darkness.

''But Estelle wouldn't tell you anything?''

He shook his head. ''No. I think she feared so much for her own life that she probably assumed she was helping me out by not getting me involved.''

''She trusted you, didn't she?''

''Of course she trusted me. But I think her fear of whoever was responsible for Annette's death was far greater than any trust she might have had for anyone. She was scared, Claire.''

The tape on the stereo had ended and the studio filled with an ominous silence.

''Five days later she was dead. I can't accept that it was merely a coincidence.''

Claire squeezed his hand, feeling the strength in his response. ''I'm sorry, Michael. I know she meant a great deal to you.''

She watched his profile in the dying glimmer of light over the trees in the distance, and for some reason, she wanted to touch him, almost as if to make certain that he was real.

''Claire, you have to stay out of this.'' His voice and eyes were equally steady as he took her shoulders in his hands and turned her to face him. ''Estelle was concerned for my safety. I'm even more concerned for yours right now."

"Michael, I—"

"You have to promise me that you won't do any more rooting around, that you won't go stirring anything up."

"What are you saying, Michael?" She shook her head in disbelief.

"Don't you see? The community has quieted down now. They believe that an outsider is responsible for the Hobson murder—just some drifter. And that's the way it's best left. As long as you stay out of it and don't provoke people like Frank Turner and Raymond Bannon, you won't get hurt. I don't want anything to happen to you, Claire. Please, promise me that this will be the end of it."

"Michael, I don't understand."

"Claire, just trust me, please. I don't want you to get hurt, too."

The fierceness with which his fingers dug into her shoulders eased gradually when she finally nodded. "All right, Michael. I promise."

She held his eyes as they burned into hers. And then she felt him move closer to her, against her, the heat of his body searing through her oversize shirt. He cradled her cheek in his hand, his thumb tracing the line of her eyebrow. He bent his head down and brushed his lips against hers, tenderly at first and then mounting to a hunger that she, too, felt swelling within her.

She moved against him, almost instinctively, longing to feel the intensity of his touch. When his tongue reached in to explore the silky recesses of her mouth, Claire thought she heard him moan softly.

And then she panicked. Her head reeled—too many thoughts, too many questions, too many memories. With a gasp, she pulled away from Michael, pushing him back with one hand on his chest. She couldn't do this.

"I'm—I'm sorry, Michael. I can't." She looked down so he couldn't see the tears welling up in the corners of her eyes.

"Claire, what is it?" He lifted her chin until she was forced to look up at him and read the intense concern on his face.

"I can't do this, Michael. I'm sorry. Everything's moving too quickly." She pulled away from the circle of his arms. "I came up here to find a quiet little corner, a place to finish my work. I just wanted to be left alone. And all of a sudden I find myself talking about police investigations and murders and cover-ups, and God only knows what's next." She looked up to meet his eyes squarely. "And on top of all that, there's you."

"Claire—"

"Michael, please . . . I mean, I can't even get myself straightened up enough to figure out why I feel the way I do about you."

"It's all right, Claire. Look, I'm sorry. I shouldn't have—"

"No, Michael, it's not you. It's nothing you've done. I just think that maybe I need to take it a little slower."

Michael gave her hand a gentle squeeze before letting it go. "It's okay, Claire."

Crossing the room, he reached for his coat and slipped it over his shoulders. He adjusted the collar and walked back to where she stood in the middle of the studio. For one last time, he took her hands in his.

She recognized the understanding in his expression, and even before his gentle voice had broken the stillness of the studio, she knew what he was about to say.

"It's all right, Claire. I can wait." His lips whispered a kiss along her forehead, and when she opened her eyes again she was embraced by the sincerity of his smile.

"I'll see you tomorrow," he said softly as he turned away.

The silence closed in on her. As if sensing her sorrow, Decker whined and nudged her hand with a wet nose. Claire stroked the dog absently for a moment. Finally, with a resolute sigh, she flipped on the lights and turned back to her painting. With any luck, it would help her get her mind off everything that was happening.

CHAPTER EIGHT

CLAIRE REACHED OVER and pulled open one of the studio windows. Since her battle with them two weeks ago, Michael had come up and loosened the frames for her. Now if only they could get the furnace fixed, Claire thought as she wiped the sweat from her forehead with the sleeve of her shirt.

She was sure Alec would like the painting she'd just completed. In fact, it would probably serve well as an opening piece for the entrance wall of the gallery. She'd ask him tomorrow. He was due to arrive in the morning from Boston, and Claire had been anxious to see him for days. With any luck, she'd be able to talk him into staying longer this time.

She needed a break from the tension.

During the past week, she and Michael had gone about their business as usual. At first she had made a deliberate attempt to avoid him, staying in her studio for hours on end. But it was Michael who had finally seen the futility in such an arrangement and had broken the ice.

They'd gone out to dinner several times, during which he'd made a conscious effort to maintain a comfortable space between them. Claire had to admit that his understanding and restraint were commendable. Many times she felt certain that he was feeling the same pull of desire as she was whenever they accidentally touched, whenever one of them found the other staring. Still, Michael maintained a safe distance.

It was her own inner frustration that was causing her mounting tension. As much as she tried, she hadn't been able to block out her attraction to Michael. She hadn't been able to ignore the fact that she wanted to be around him, to spend time with him. She wanted to touch him, to feel the hunger of his lips on hers again and to be the subject of his frankly appreciative eyes.

Claire focused her attention back onto her work. She tilted the large canvas in an attempt to catch the last of the dark red-orange rays of the setting sun. When the canvas wouldn't stand on its own, she balanced one side of the stretcher against her hip and reached for the small desk that still stood in the turret.

In spite of its solidness, the desk was remarkably light and Claire pulled it easily across the drop cloth. It shuddered along on its four legs until it was close enough for her to lean the canvas against it.

That was when she saw the black journal. It lay on the drop cloth, obviously shaken loose from the back of one of the desk drawers, its cover speckled with dust.

"Are you all right up there?" Michael shouted from the bottom of the stairs.

"Yes, I'm fine," she assured him. "It's okay. Just some minor renovations."

Claire bent to pick up the small book. She opened it slowly, almost as if she were expecting a spider to scramble out from between its covers. Instead, she found pages upon pages of meticulous handwriting.

Abandoning the painting, she crossed the studio and plopped herself into the oversize chair near one of the windows. She turned to the first page, tilting the book to catch the last fiery glimmer of the day's light, and began to read.

In painstaking detail, Estelle Bramley's narrations of life in Westport carried Claire through the journal, leading her from one episode to the next. She read about Estelle's afternoon chats with Andy the mailman, about the occasional tourists who stopped for directions after getting lost on the bluffs. A smile crossed Claire's lips as she read Estelle's definitive comments about the lack of service at the new supermarket, followed by a perceptive criticism of several books she had borrowed from the Westport library. Estelle had devoted several pages to pictorial descriptions of her summer garden and the migrating birds.

Even in the most mundane events, Estelle was able to find something interesting. Nothing escaped her. Life in and around Westport had been chronicled in unforgettable detail.

She even wrote of her visits with Henry Lubinsky and the arrangements she had made to have her will written. When Claire saw her own name penned in the elegant handwriting, she read on. Estelle reminisced about her favorite niece, Julia, and how, since the young woman's estrangement from the family years ago, she had not seen her or heard from her. Only after Julia's funeral, at which Estelle had seen the sweet little girl with Julia's bright blond hair clinging to her father's side, did she realize her family's mistake in disowning her niece. But by then it was too late. Now, with Henry Lubinsky's aid, she resolved to find Claire Madden, Julia's only child, and attempt to make up for the years of silence.

From there, Estelle's writing rambled on to details of her newest friend—Michael Dalton. Claire drew her legs up beneath her as she sank further back into the chair and read on. Perhaps it was being able to see Michael through the eyes of another person, or perhaps it was just a simple matter of Estelle's endearing descriptions of him that caused her to smile to herself.

At first he was merely "the lad who bought the old Farnsworth place." But gradually, as he visited more often, driving her into town, arranging to have her leaves raked and her drive shoveled, fixing a leaking pipe in the basement and rescuing a year's worth of preserves, it was obvious that Michael was playing a much-greater role in Estelle's life than she could have anticipated.

She wrote of their friendship with great devotion. She described her concern for his well-being, particularly at one point during the winter when he had been working too hard and she feared for his health. She also maintained a belief that Michael was lonely and that he needed someone in his life to "bring him around." She had even pondered "fixing him up with the Robertson girl," but she didn't know if the young woman was still in Westport.

To Claire, Estelle's descriptions of Michael were a warm confirmation of who she had come to believe he was. The echoes of Frank's warning faded as she turned the pages of the journal.

"You'll ruin your eyes, reading in the dark like that."

Claire jumped, almost dropping the diary from her lap. "You scared the hell out of me, Michael," she accused, finding little immediate humor in his grin.

But her indignation faded quickly as Estelle's words tumbled through her mind. Michael stood in the doorway of her studio, his faded blue jeans and shirt covered with a light dusting of sawdust and his hair slightly disheveled from working. As she stared at him, Claire wondered just how long she could go on ignoring the feelings that she harbored deep within her.

In the last glimmering shred of light, Michael's features softened and his apologetic smile glowed across the space of the studio. "I'm sorry. I would have knocked, but from the looks of it, I don't think that would have been any easier on your nerves. You were quite absorbed."

Claire lifted the book for Michael to see.

"Ah, you've found one of Estelle's journals." There was a fondness in his voice as he crossed the room to stand behind her. "She really liked to write. That's pretty much all she did every day. I often used to wonder what she might have churned out if she'd had a word processor or even a typewriter."

"It makes interesting reading, nonetheless." Claire stood, needing to place a cushion of distance between herself and Michael. "She had a lot to say about you."

"Oh, yeah? Guess you'll have to fill me in on it sometime."

"Sure. But not before you tell me about this 'Robertson girl,'" Claire challenged with a smile as she slipped the journal into one of the desk drawers.

Michael let out something between a laugh and a grunt. "Come on then, I'll tell you all about it at dinner."

OVER DINNER, Claire found herself laughing for the first time in a long while. She listened with amusement as Michael described, in great detail, Estelle's failed attempts to link him up with one of the local high school teachers. He related several of her great-aunt's staged meetings with Helen Robertson, and then how he had finally been forced to convince Estelle that he really was not interested.

Then, over a glass of white wine, Michael eased the conversation around to the topic of Claire. Initially, she was surprised at her willingness to answer his questions.

But Michael's knowledge of the art world was remarkably comprehensive, and by the time she was on her second glass of wine, Claire felt as though she were talking with a longtime friend and colleague rather than a man she had known only a couple of weeks.

He listened intently as she discussed her schooling, her year and a half studying in Europe and finally the whirlwind of gallery shows that Alec had steered her way during the past two years. As his cool gray eyes held hers, Claire couldn't help but be flattered by his genuine interest in her life.

She remembered the ardent heat of his lips on hers and the eagerness of his embrace. She could still feel the hunger that had swelled within her at his touch, the same desire that rushed through her every time she saw him walk into a room or heard his voice or felt the brush of his arm against hers when he came too near. The desire was as undeniable as it was discomforting.

It was the waiter who mercifully broke the unnerving intimacy of their locked gazes. "Any more drinks here?"

Claire watched Michael as he turned and ordered coffee for them. She studied the relaxed smile lines around his eyes, the proud outline of his nose and jaw when he nodded to the waiter and finally turned back to her.

"So, how long have you known Alec?" he asked, returning to their conversation.

Claire swirled the last of her wine around the bottom of the long-stemmed glass, watching it for a moment before looking back up at Michael. "We met as undergraduates at NYU." She grinned, remembering Alec's misguided first year at university. "He majored in fine arts until he realized he couldn't draw. It didn't take much to convince him to switch to art history after that. We kept in touch during our masters' programs and while I was away

in Europe. He had started to work with artists around
New York. So, by the time I got back, we had already decided that he would represent me." She took another sip
of wine. "We've been together ever since."

"You seem very close, the two of you."

"Alec's a good friend," she confided. "I don't know
what it is exactly. I suppose it's because of the years we've
known each other and the background we share, but he
looks out for me in more ways than just as an agent. He's
more like a brother than anything else. He's always been
there for me."

She watched Michael nod as he sipped the last of his
wine. She looked down at her own glass. Memories
seemed to swirl there in the remnants of wine, haunting
memories that she had still not managed to escape. "He's
seen me through some pretty rough times. Especially
lately."

And then the memories were back, clear and vivid. For
a moment, Claire forgot about Michael. Everything
around her faded—the buzz of people's voices, the drone
of the hockey game on the television set behind the bar,
the smoky haze that filled the pub, the nondescript music
coming from the speakers. The only thing she was aware
of was the throb in her head as she remembered those
endless days. The nightmares, the long sleepless nights.
Alec had stayed with her through it all, comforting her,
holding her as she cried.

Even though she had hardly recognized his presence at
the time, she knew that without his support and understanding, she might never have pulled through Greg's loss.
He had been her only light, her only solace. And she
would never forget how much Alec had given to her.

She felt the warmth of Michael's hand on hers and
looked up, surprised at the tenderness of his touch.

"I'm sorry, Claire. I didn't intend to bring up any painful memories." His voice eased across the short distance between them, dispersing her fading memories.

"Water under the bridge, right?" Claire forced herself to smile. Feeling the strength of his fingers and the warmth of his skin against her hand, she returned his caress.

It felt good to be here now with Michael. To feel the embrace of his hand on hers, to feel comfort in his closeness, and to hear the sincerity of his voice.

"So, tell me about Dee," Claire suggested when the coffee arrived.

"Dee?" Michael used his free hand to stir cream into his coffee. "There isn't much to say. She's a good friend and one hell of an assistant."

"You've known her a while, then?"

He shrugged. "I guess it's been a few years now. Since my divorce and the breakup of my partnership. When I left New York and moved here, I needed someone to act as a contact between me and my clients. And I suppose I also needed someone who was willing to tolerate a quick-tempered and somewhat bitter divorcé."

"Oh, I find that difficult to believe." Claire gave him a quick smile.

He grunted wryly. "You weren't there. Trust me, it wasn't a pretty sight. If it hadn't been for Dee, I'm not sure how I would have pulled myself back together."

"Were you two ever...?" Claire realized that she should have been surprised at the forwardness of the question, but within the intimacy of their conversation it seemed perfectly normal.

"Who, Dee? No." He let out a half laugh. "I suppose there was a time...I don't know, when we may have entertained thoughts. But Dee's the kind of person who needs more than freedom. She needs complete control, one hundred percent of the time. She flits in and out of relationships at a whim. I don't know if she'll ever be ready for a commitment. But, hey, she's happy. Most of the time, as long as she's in control." He set down his mug, and when he looked up again, Claire was surprised at the mischief that seemed to play behind his eyes.

"What about you and Alec?"

Claire laughed, both at the abruptness of Michael's question and at the thought of being involved with someone she adored like a brother. "I don't think so." She shook her head. "I mean, Alec *does* mean a lot to me, but I don't know, I guess we're too much like brother and sister. It doesn't even seem right thinking about it."

Michael reached across and squeezed her hands, sending a shiver through her. "*Do* you know what's right for you, Claire?"

She wanted to say "no" and at the same time whisper "yes." She wanted to tell him how vulnerable she felt against the desire that had been building within her during the past couple of weeks. At the same time, she wanted to explain her hesitancy, explain how it was that she'd become trapped by a memory. How, until she could free herself of it, she could not find comfort in the feelings she had for Michael.

The spell of intimacy shattered in a split second. Their table was jostled, and Michael reluctantly withdrew his hands from hers.

"Michael, dear. How are you?"

Claire followed his gaze up to the teetering woman who leered down at them. One aged hand gripped the edge of the table for support as she looked blearily from Michael to Claire and back again.

"I'm very well, thank you, Mrs. Adams," he said with a nod. "And yourself?"

"Oh, I'm quite fine, thanks," she said, slurring the words. "And who's your friend?"

He cast an apologetic glance at Claire. "Mrs. Adams, this is Claire Madden—Estelle's niece. Claire, this is Ruth Adams."

"Oh, Estelle's niece." Mrs. Adams extended a wobbly hand in introduction. "So you're the one living in Estelle's house now?"

Claire looked from Michael to Mrs. Adams and offered her a hesitant smile. "Yes, for the time being."

"Well, I hope you're staying. You mustn't dream of selling your poor aunt's house. Too much history there."

"Ruth is the head of the Westport Historical Society," Michael explained as he waved to their waiter for the bill.

"You can be sure that we are most interested in anything you come across of Estelle's that might be of some...historical significance. *Have* you come across anything at all, dear?"

Claire caught the slight shake of Michael's head. She cleared her throat, suppressing her smile. "I'm afraid I really haven't had an opportunity to give the house a real go-through yet, Mrs. Adams. But I'll be certain to get in touch with your society if I do come across anything."

Mrs. Adams turned back to Michael. "By the way, Michael, did you hear about my Joey? He's a lieutenant now. With the Bangor police."

"I believe Estelle mentioned something about that to me, Mrs. Adams. Please give Joey my congratulations the next time you speak with him."

"Yes, well, he's certainly a heck of a lot better off in Bangor," she said, slurring her words, "than working here under Bannon. Don't get me wrong, I do miss him. He's my son, after all. But better off in Bangor than having to deal with that no-good, shifty sheriff of ours, huh?''

"I don't know about that, Mrs. Adams. Sheriff—''

"No, Michael, don't you go defending him now. You just can't trust him. Not after the way he treated my boy. Not promoting him and all.''

"Whatever you say, Mrs. Adams.'' Michael cut in before she could ramble on. He stood up from the table and once again gave Claire an apologetic shrug. "Listen, can we give you a lift home? It's very cold out tonight and I'd hate to see you get chilled.''

"Oh, I'm fine, son. Don't you go worrying about me. 'Sides, I wouldn't dream of interrupting your evening with your lady friend here. You go on. Ms. Madden, you'll call me if you come across anything now, won't you?''

"I promise, Mrs. Adams. You'll be the first to know.''

Before Claire could say anything else, Michael had taken her hand and was pulling her toward the door. Only when they had cleared the entrance did he pause to help her with her coat.

"More of the local color?'' she asked with a whispered laugh.

"Right.'' Michael swung his own jacket over his shoulders, and Claire noticed the hint of a smile flicker across his lips. "Just be glad we got out of there when we did.''

She followed him across the snowy parking lot to the vehicle and waited as he held the door open for her. After she had settled into the passenger seat, she reached out for his hand, stopping him before he could close the door.

"Thank you for dinner, Michael.''

"It was nothing,'' he said softly.

She squeezed his hand gently. "And thanks for the conversation."

"*That* was my pleasure." He looked back at her, his face lit softly by the warm glow of a street lamp. Claire could see the same tug she felt within her reflected in his eyes. She wanted to feel his lips caress hers again, feel the strength of his body embrace her.

But it wasn't that easy. The ache from her past still gripped her tightly, sometimes threatening to overwhelm her.

Claire released his hand. Silently, Michael closed her door, walked around the vehicle and got in. He didn't say anything as he pulled out of the parking lot, and Claire relaxed in the silence.

It was after eleven by the time Michael turned the Land Rover into Claire's drive. Exhaustion coupled with a lingering light-headedness from the wine lulled Claire into a dreamy sense of comfort.

It had stopped snowing some hours ago, and a three-quarter moon hung above the distant stand of trees that marked the Dalton property. The crisp air challenged Claire's drowsiness as she stepped out of the car, resenting the level of consciousness it demanded of her.

Neither she nor Michael noticed the tire marks in the freshly fallen snow, nor did they see the footprints leading around the side of the house. And it wasn't until she heard Decker growling that Claire looked up and saw the open door.

She stopped. The dog bounded toward her. Her hand slipped under Decker's collar as the hair on the retriever's withers bristled. She held him firmly. Her heart raced with a rising fear. Familiar fear. Memories thundered through her head. She clutched Decker's collar, using him to support herself.

"What is it, Claire?" Michael came up behind her, putting his hand on her shoulder.

And then she heard her own broken voice, as shaky as the legs that supported her. "Somebody's in the house."

CHAPTER NINE

"MICHAEL, DON'T GO in there." Claire clamped her hand tightly onto his arm.

"Claire."

"No, Michael. Please. Don't go inside."

He stared at the partially open door and then at the tire tracks in the snow. "Claire, it's all right. Whoever was here has gone now. Look at the tire marks."

Her eyes, wide with fear, jerked to the ground and then back up at the house.

Michael couldn't remember if he'd ever seen anyone so frightened, and for a moment, he wondered if she was on the verge of shock. Her eyes widened even further, the vapor from her breath came out in short, ragged gasps, and as he took her shoulders in his hands, he could feel her whole body trembling.

"Claire, listen to me. It's all right. They've gone."

Still she was shaking her head.

"Look, we have to go inside. We have to see if anything's been stolen."

"I don't think you should go in, Michael. Please, let's just go to your place." She pulled Decker back toward the car.

"Claire, wait. You're being unreasonable. Listen to me, it was probably nothing more than a couple of teenagers on a dare. They were up here, driving around, and saw the dark house. They probably thought it was empty. I'll just go in and check around. Then I think we should call Sheriff Bannon.''

"No, I don't want Bannon here."

Michael turned her to face him, lifting her chin so that she looked directly at him. "Claire, trust me. It's okay. Just let me go in and take a look around, all right? Then we'll decide if Bannon should be called."

He could see her lips trembling, and perhaps hoping to give her courage, he bent his head to kiss them. "Okay?" he asked again as he traced her bottom lip with his finger and waited for her nod.

"All right," she said, giving in. "But I'm coming in with you."

The front door had not been forced. The bolt had been turned from the inside, Michael guessed, realizing that whoever had invited themselves in must have gained access to the house through a window. With the front door left swinging open, they certainly hadn't been concerned with concealing their tracks.

Claire followed Michael through the rooms on the main floor. At the back of the house, as Michael had suspected, one of the old, single-pane windows had been broken enough to allow someone to turn the latch.

They went through the empty rooms of the second floor and finally up to the third. Claire's studio seemed as untouched as the rest of the house. Nothing seemed to be out of place. But then, with the air of disarray throughout the house due to the renovations going on, it was difficult to tell.

"Does anything appear to be missing?" Michael asked Claire as he watched her take another quick scan of the bedroom.

"No...I'm not sure." She shook her head. "No, I guess not. It's hard to say."

Even Decker had calmed down by now, seemingly satisfied that whoever had been there earlier had vacated the premises some time ago.

"So what do you think? Shall I call Bannon?"

Claire looked at her watch. "It's late. No, I don't think so. You're probably right. It was probably just a couple of kids," she added, as if trying to convince herself. "Maybe I'll call him tomorrow and just let him know what happened."

"You know, Claire, you can come and stay at my place if you're uncomfortable here."

She studied Michael's face for a few moments, but finally shook her head. "Thanks. But, no. I should stay. If I don't sleep here tonight, I might never come back."

Right then, in the stillness of her bedroom, Michael wanted to hold Claire. More than anything, he wanted to take her in his arms, to ease her fear, to stop her trembling. But he'd vowed to himself that he would wait for her to break down the wall between them. He was not about to press himself on her, to take advantage of her. Especially at a time when she seemed most vulnerable.

"Well, look, I'm just going to board up that back window before I go. I—"

"Michael, don't go." She reached out and took his hand into hers. "Please? I can fix up the spare room across the hall," she pleaded. "I just—I just don't want to be alone tonight."

He nodded slowly. He hadn't wanted to leave her, either, but he'd been afraid to suggest he stay. "Sure, I'll stay with you." He lifted his hand to caress the velvety smoothness of her cheek. "Are you going to be all right, Claire?"

She forced a smile and turned her lips into his palm, kissing it softly. "I'll be fine, Michael. Thanks."

Taking a deep breath, he quelled the wave of desire that swept through him. All of a sudden the air in the bedroom seemed suffocating and Claire's warmth far too close. He stepped back toward the door. "I'd better take a look at that window now. I'll be up in a while."

After sweeping up the shattered glass, Michael stapled two sheets of plastic over the window frame and nailed several boards over the broken window. Satisfied with the makeshift barrier, he closed the door to the room and stuffed a couple of rags under the door to cut down the draft.

At least the furnace hadn't decided to quit on them, he thought as he carried the broken glass into the kitchen. The front door must have been open for some time and the house was just beginning to warm up.

Still, a shot of brandy wouldn't hurt. He rummaged through the cupboards until he found the bottle and a couple of glasses. Claire had just finished making up his bed when Michael reached the doorway of the guest bedroom. She turned with a start and he realized that she was still on edge.

He lifted the bottle and set the two glasses on a dresser to start pouring. "I thought you could use a bit of warming up."

"No, I'm all right, Michael. Really."

"Drink it anyway, Claire," he said, handing her a glass. "It'll help you sleep."

She obliged him, taking the glass and tossing back the dark liquid.

"Feel better?"

Coughing slightly, Claire smiled and nodded. "Sure. I should sleep like a bear now. And how about you? Will you be all right in here?"

"Can't see why not."

"Thanks, Michael," she whispered, setting down the empty glass and taking his hands into hers. "Thanks for being here."

"That's what neighbors are for, right?"

"Right." She gave him a knowing smile and stood on tiptoe to give him a lightly brandied kiss before turning from the room. "Good night, Michael."

"Good night, Claire," he called after her. And even as he nodded off to sleep, he could still feel the gentle trace of her lips on his.

IT WAS TWO-THIRTY when Michael awoke with a start. He'd been sleeping lightly and had already woken up a couple of times to find Decker pacing restlessly from room to room, unsure of whom to spend the night with. But this time it wasn't Decker who'd roused Michael. It was Claire.

Through the open doorway of his room, Michael heard her. He strained against the silence of the house to make out her words.

Then he heard her groan.

Without a moment's thought, Michael left his bed, tightening the drawstring of his sweatpants, and padded barefoot across the hall.

Certainly Decker would have warned him if she'd been in any danger. But the anxiousness in Claire's voice urged him on. She called out the moment Michael stepped into her bedroom; a cry that clutched at his heart and quickened his pulse.

In a flash he was by her side. "Claire?"

A shaft of moonlight raked across the four-poster bed, and in its cool light he could see her face, her forehead contorted in what seemed like pain. She groaned again, this time louder. She writhed and struggled with her dream now and Michael, knowing full well that he shouldn't wake her, realized that he couldn't watch her suffer. He reached for her, touching her arm first and then her shoulder. Still she didn't wake from the visions of her nightmare.

"Claire?" he whispered, bringing his face close enough to hers that he could feel the heat of her breath. He moved his hand to her cheek, his fingers reaching into her hair as he brushed her skin with his thumb. "Claire?"

And then her eyes fluttered open.

She didn't jump. Nor did she jerk away from him. Instead she lay in the silvery moonlight, her chest rising and falling as she drew in quick breaths, collecting herself by degrees, as if this was a dream from which she'd awakened many times.

"I'm sorry I woke you," he whispered as he drew back, giving her room to sit up.

"It looks like I woke you first." She smiled apologetically and shivered as she pulled down the sleeves of her nightshirt.

"Are you cold?"

She nodded, brushing her tousled hair to one side. "A bit."

Michael looked toward the stone fireplace, grateful that he'd had the chimneys cleaned before Claire's arrival. "I'll start a fire."

Claire trembled again as she watched Michael set a small fire in the hearth. Drawing her knees into the circle of her arms, she was determined to shake herself from the images of her dream. She tried to focus on Michael in order to suppress the tears she felt rising within her.

Eventually he came to her side, taking the hand she offered him, and sat down next to her.

"Can you sleep again?" he asked, brushing a straying wisp of hair from her cheek.

Claire shook her head and took another shaky breath. She was afraid to speak for fear that her voice would sound as ragged as she felt. Eventually she cleared her throat. "No, I don't think so. Would you just sit with me awhile?"

And then, for the first time, Claire did not reject the comfort and familiarity she felt with Michael. As he eased himself farther onto the bed, resting his back against the headboard, she welcomed the security of his arms and curled up next to him.

They sat quietly for a long time, listening to the crackle of the fire licking at the logs in the fireplace as Michael stroked Claire's hair. In time, his voice, no more than a whisper, slipped into the mesmerizing stillness.

"Claire . . . do you want to talk about it?"

She fought back the tears and shivered again. "I don't know, Michael."

"Come here." He lifted her easily into the warmth of his arms, drawing her back slowly so that she sank into the curve of his body. Her spine followed the sweep of his stomach and chest as he wrapped his arms around her.

"You're freezing," he said, starting to rub her arms slowly.

Claire rested her head against his chest, feeling his breath on her neck, and sank into the refuge of his embrace. "I don't know," she repeated when she felt his lips brush her temple.

"Who's Greg?"

Covering his hand with her own, Claire stroked it thoughtfully. As much as she wanted to tell Michael, there was something holding her back. Michael was the first person in almost a year whose company she enjoyed. He was someone who hadn't known Greg, someone who didn't feel sorry for her. Someone who didn't question her stability or her loss.

Claire shivered again, but this time it wasn't from the cold.

"If you don't want to talk about it . . ."

"No, Michael . . . no, you should know. It would probably explain a lot of things." But where to start? She took another deep breath and felt the reassurance of Michael's caress.

"Greg Adler." Another breath shuddered through her chest. "We met at NYU. I was in the last year of my master's and Greg was finishing up his doctorate. I don't know, I guess it was what people call love at first sight. Whatever it was, it worked. And when we graduated, all we wanted to do was run away together. But I had other commitments." She lapsed into silence for a few moments, then went on.

"I spent the next year and a half studying overseas, and when I came back . . . he was still waiting for me." Claire smiled inwardly, remembering the welcome she'd received at the airport. Greg standing in line with hundreds of other anxious faces, cradling eighteen red roses—one for each month she'd been away. They'd driven straight back to his apartment and had spent the next four days in bed, vowing they would never be apart again. "We didn't even date. I just moved in. He had a spare bedroom where I set up a small studio and started to paint. He was working as an architect, already established in a good firm and was doing well. He worked on designs for our house in his spare time. We'd even bought the land.

"Anyway, my art was taking off. Alec was finding me more and more shows, more and more sales. I needed more room to paint. Greg's apartment was getting crowded and so we started looking. I guess it was Alec, or maybe one of Greg's friends, who warned us about the neighborhood, but the warehouse studio-apartment was perfect. It was only a block or two out of Soho. And the lighting . . . we couldn't believe the lighting when we first looked at the place. I guess that's what really sold us on it. The light and the space. It wouldn't have mattered if it had been located in the Bronx. We wanted it. We moved in last February, after three months of renovations. Greg put his heart and soul into that place.''

Claire tried to imagine the studio-apartment now— empty and lifeless. It had never been the same without Greg there. There had been no laughter, no love. Even the light had seemed different to her after Greg was gone.

Claire lifted her hands to her face. Hot tears traced irregular paths down her cheeks and neck. She dabbed at them, then covered her face again to suppress the sobs caught in her throat.

Michael whispered in her ear as he stroked her hair. ''What happened, Claire?''

She took a ragged breath. She had to go on. As painful as it was, she could already begin to feel herself letting go for the first time. ''It was June. Saturday morning. Only four months after we'd moved into the warehouse.'' Even now, she could remember the unseasonably cold drizzle that had plagued New York for three days straight. It had been ominously gray and cold. And miserably damp.

The details were still so clear to her, as if it had been only yesterday.

''Greg was taking a shower. I told him I was going to the bakery for bread. We were planning to go back to bed and have breakfast and spend the rest of the day under the covers.''

Claire squeezed Michael's hand and he responded by pulling her closer to him, giving her the strength to go on.

"Decker and I were just getting home. We were stepping off the elevator when we heard the gunshot."

She bit her lip, fighting the tears, fighting the memories. She could still hear the shot—its echoes seemed to pierce through the silence of the bedroom even now.

Blindly, she had raced down the warehouse corridor, but Decker had beaten her through the open door of the studio. He had barked twice and then she'd heard the slam of the studio's back door. "Rawley, one of our neighbors, heard the shot, too. He called the ambulance."

How many images had sped through her mind in that instant? And yet none of them prepared her for what she saw when she ran into the apartment.

Greg had dragged himself up against the bottom two steps of the loft stairs by the time Claire had come in—his face twisted with pain. But what she remembered most was the blood. Rushing to his side, she had taken him into her arms.

"I tried to stop the bleeding." Her voice was no more than a hoarse whisper now. "But it wasn't any good. There was just so much of it. And even as I sat there holding him, even as I watched his life slipping away before me, I—I kept thinking that if I had locked the studio, none of this would have happened. If I'd only bothered to take my keys, the bastards wouldn't have tried to rob us and Greg wouldn't have been there to try and stop them."

Her body heaved with great sobs and Michael pulled her even closer to him, rocking her as she cried in shuddering gasps. It all made sense to him now. The fear in her eyes when she'd seen the open door of the house, the desperation with which she'd begged him not to go inside.

She'd even held Decker back, afraid of what might be waiting for them in the house.

"And ... sometimes ... I still believe that he wouldn't be dead if it weren't for me." She clung to Michael's embrace as if, without it, she would be lost.

"Claire, don't. Don't do this to yourself. You know that's not true."

But she didn't speak after that.

The dying fire sputtered at the glowing remains of the logs in the hearth and Claire's sobs eventually subsided. Michael rocked her in his arms until the fire was nothing more than a cluster of embers.

She wasn't moving at all, but Michael knew that she was still awake. Her head rested against his chest and he felt the heat of her body through the thin shirt she wore, felt her breathing fall into the same rhythm as his. He was amazed at how delicate she seemed, wrapped in his large arms. He'd always seen Claire as a strong woman, but tonight, in the warm glow of the fireplace, she seemed almost fragile. And in the hush of the bedroom that night, he realized that the woman in his arms was the woman he wanted to be with forever.

Eventually Claire stirred and Michael eased her from his embrace, laying her back so that her head rested on her pillow. He brushed her hair with his hand and, when she looked up at him, bent down to kiss her forehead.

"Sleep now, Claire," he whispered.

But when he stood up, Claire still held his hand.

"Stay with me, Michael. Please."

CHAPTER TEN

EXCEPT FOR WEDNESDAYS, when the cleaning woman came in, the Westport Sheriff's Station usually smelled of burned coffee and Raymond Bannon's cigars. By Friday, the place would really be getting stale and by the weekend it was almost unbearable. Frank and Wesley, the two deputies, often commented on the smell, but Bannon never seemed to notice it. He carried the odor of the cheap, plastic-tipped cigars wherever he went.

This Sunday was no different than any other. When Frank Turner stepped through the front doors of the empty sheriff's station, he shook his head in disgust and promptly threw open two windows. He was met with a blast of cold fresh air as he turned to his desk.

It was Wesley's shift this Sunday, but the younger deputy was still not accustomed to the early hours, and Frank suspected he was scrambling to get in before Bannon made one of his surprise visits.

"Cripes, Frank, you'd think we weren't payin' for the heat in this place." *Too late,* thought Frank as Bannon bellowed from the back of the station and thumped into the front room, closing the windows and lowering the blinds.

"Where the hell's Wes? He late again?" The sheriff shook his head as he tossed his gloves on his desk and threw his coat over the back of the chair. "I'm gonna have that kid's pay docked if he keeps this up," he threatened, easing himself into the chair behind the cluttered desk and wiping his nose with the back of his hand. "So what are you doin' here? You had Sunday last weekend."

"Just came to pick up a couple of things," Frank said, shuffling through one of the desk drawers.

Bannon watched him for a moment. He couldn't remember the last time he'd seen either of his deputies in street clothes, but now, seeing Frank in a sweater and freshly pressed jeans, he had to admit that the boy was a smart dresser when not in uniform. Catching a whiff of Frank's cologne, Bannon could only guess what he was up to on a brisk Sunday morning.

"You gonna take some more of those diaries home to read?" Bannon asked, nodding to the box of bound journals that had been sitting on the floor beside Frank's desk for the past few weeks.

Frank cast a disinterested glance at the box and shook his head. "No, there's nothing in those ones. I've been through most of them now. They're too old."

"I keep tellin' you, Frank, I think you're wasting your time with those damned diaries. Even if Estelle Bramley did see something, you don't really think she would have written it down, do you?"

"I can only hope," he replied, taking a swig from a can of Coke that Bannon thought he'd seen on Frank's desk the previous afternoon.

"Did you ever stop to think, Frank, that maybe we didn't even get all of them when we had access to the house? That old woman probably stashed them everywhere."

"Yeah, well, maybe you're right. But someone's gotta go through them, just in case." Frank reached for his keys and turned to the front doors.

"So, where you headed?"

The deputy paused before looking back at him and Bannon wondered if he was even going to answer.

"I'm going up to see Claire Madden."

"Oh," Bannon said with a wink, "so that's what this is all about."

"What's that?"

"The cologne, the shave—"

"I'm just going up there to check on her. That's it."

Bannon turned his attention to the file on his desk. "Well, that's good."

"What's good?"

"That you ain't goin' up there courtin' or anything. 'Cuz from what I've been hearin' around town, that Madden woman is one hot item with your friend Mr. Dalton." Bannon watched Frank's reaction carefully as he spoke.

Since last week, when he'd seen the deputy and Claire Madden walk into The Happy Face, he'd suspected that something was up. Even though Frank had been at the Westport Sheriff's Station for only a couple of years, Bannon knew him well enough to recognize that Claire Madden was too good-looking for Frank to pass up. And a jealous streak was not something completely foreign to the deputy. Bannon had seen that with the Stevenson girl who was now dating Wesley.

"Yeah? Well, maybe that's why I'm going up there. Check on Dalton myself." He held up a hand to stop any protest from the sheriff. "I know what you think, Ray, but I don't trust the guy. He's not telling us everything, and—"

"Easy, Frank," Bannon warned, holding his deputy's hot-tempered stare clear across the station house. "Remember, we already went through all of this. If you think Michael Dalton knows something, fine. But you had better be prepared to prove it before you go flyin' off up there and sayin' something that's gonna jeopardize this case. You understand me? The last thing I need on my hands is a deputy on a one-man crusade against one of Westport's more respected citizens.''

Frank snarled something indiscernible before grunting a farewell and walking out the front doors.

Bannon sat back and looked out the window at the bright morning, watching Frank's car pull away from the snowbank. Sometimes he wondered if the boy was too eager to prove himself, if it was a mistake to have given him the Bramley case. Still, he had to start sometime. And Bannon had to give the boy credit for his persistence.

CLAIRE WOKE UP gradually. She didn't open her eyes, but lay under the warmth of the duvet, delaying her contact with the cold she knew awaited her beyond the bed covers.

She reached behind her, hoping to find Michael, but the other side of the bed was cold. She could still smell traces of him on the pillow and the sheets when she rolled over, and with the familiarity of his scent, she remembered his warmth.

She remembered the firmness of his body pressed against hers as she'd fallen asleep, and she remembered waking several times during the night, always to find his arms encircling her, his breath on her neck and the comforting rhythm of his breathing behind her.

Running a hand through her hair, Claire finally opened her eyes. It was past ten. Groggily she reached for her pack of pills. Perhaps it wasn't a mistake after all to have kept up the ritual, she thought, staring at the circular plastic dispenser in her hand. With memories of Michael's presence in her bed still fresh, she was almost glad that he was no longer there. If he had stayed, if he were still curled up next to her, Claire could not have been certain of her ability to restrain herself.

Tossing the pills back onto the nightstand, she caught sight of the photograph next to the alarm clock. Greg smiled back at her, the same frozen smile that had greeted her for ten long months.

What would he think if, somehow, he could see her now? If he could sense what she was contemplating, what she was feeling?

Claire lifted the duvet, ignoring the cold, and sat up. She took the framed photograph from the nightstand and cradled it in her hands, staring into Greg's features, as if to memorize every line of his face. But she didn't need to memorize it—he was already etched in her memory forever.

Still holding the picture, Claire got up and crossed the room to the closet. She pulled one of her suitcases down from the top shelf and tossed it onto the bed beside her. She would put Greg's photograph away, she decided. It was as simple as that. Tuck it into the side compartment and do exactly what Alec had been begging her to do all these months—let go. Let go of Greg and get on with her life.

But even as she unzipped the pouch, Claire knew that she couldn't do it. She looked down at the picture in her lap, at the face she had woken up to countless mornings, the face she had once touched so lovingly, the face she had looked into as they had made love, as they'd whispered the shared dreams of their future together—the face that had once radiated such life.

No, it wasn't this easy. It wasn't as simple as hiding a photograph in some pocket of a suitcase and pretending that nothing had happened. It was a lot more than just a picture—it was the letting go of everything she had once hoped for. The dreams, the aspirations and the bond of love that had encompassed them—these things could not be tossed aside so casually, left in some forgotten corner like a photograph in a dark suitcase. She and Greg had shared too much, loved too much, for her to simply shuffle his memory aside.

From the photograph, Greg stared back at her, and Claire could almost feel the warmth of his skin as her finger traced the line of his jaw. She lifted her hand from the picture and wiped at the tear on her cheek. She reached over to return the brass frame to its place on the nightstand.

No, she couldn't do it. Not yet.

She turned to the bathroom, hoping that a long hot shower would wash away the clarity of the memories that now haunted her.

Twenty minutes later, dressed in her heaviest sweater, jeans and two pairs of socks, she bounced down the stairs, revitalized by her shower. The aroma of freshly brewed coffee reached her long before she rounded the corner of the kitchen. And when she did, Michael looked up, a warm smile lighting up his face.

He sat at the table, his feet resting on another chair, yesterday's newspaper spread out before him and Decker's chin set comfortably in his lap. The retriever merely wagged his tail a couple of times and raised his ears perhaps an eighth of an inch. He remained glued to Michael, committed to his newly discovered position.

"How are you feeling?" Michael folded the paper and pushed it aside.

"Probably better than you. I can't imagine that you caught too many z's."

He shrugged. "I did all right."

She caught herself staring at him again, riveted by the sparkling gray of his eyes. She took a few steps closer to him, wanting to touch him but remembering Greg's picture. "Thanks for last night, Michael."

"You have nothing to thank me for, Claire. I'm glad I could be there for you."

"Well, thanks just the same," she repeated, hoping her smile reflected her gratitude. "It meant a lot to me." She stepped past Decker, but before she could reach the counter, Michael's hand wrapped itself around hers, stopping her beside him.

"You're more than welcome." He squeezed her hand. "Let me get you some coffee. I heard you taking a shower so I started a new pot."

"No, no, don't get up. I wouldn't dream of disturbing Decker." She looked down at the dog—anything to break the intensity of Michael's stare—and pulled her hand away from his to walk across the kitchen to the counter.

With a steaming mug of coffee in hand, Claire had barely sat down when there was a knock on the door. Startled, Decker bounded into delayed action. Putting on his fiercest bark and racing across the kitchen, his nails slid against the tiles when he reached the front door. "Hey, Decker. Getting a wee bit lax, aren't we?" Claire said with a chuckle. "It must be Alec. He's always like this when Alec's around."

She slid her hand under the retriever's collar and pulled him firmly to her side as she unbolted the door and swung it open.

It wasn't Alec at all.

It was Frank Turner. He gave her a nervous smile, his eyes shifting down to the growling dog at her side. "Good morning, Claire."

"Good morning, Frank." Claire heard Michael's chair scrape against the kitchen floor. "What brings you around on a Sunday morning? Police business or a social call?"

"No uniform," he pointed out, opening his parka to reveal a sweater and jeans.

"Guess it must be social then. Well, would you like to come in?" She held the door open for him as he knocked the snow from his boots and brushed past her into the warm kitchen. "Can I offer you a coffee?"

But when Claire closed the door and turned, Frank's smile was gone. He was staring at Michael. "Uh, no thanks, Claire. I really was just passing through. Hello, Michael."

Michael nodded. "Frank."

The tension between them grew as the seconds passed, and eventually Michael stepped away from the table. "Well, I'd better get started on that trim, Claire. Let me know when you've got a minute to give me your opinion."

Claire nodded and watched Michael's back as he stalked out of the kitchen.

"What's he doing here?" Frank's voice was a harsh whisper as he grasped Claire's arm and turned her to face him.

"And what the hell is that supposed to mean, Frank? He's here to work on the house." Claire pulled her arm from his grip.

"This early? On a Sunday?"

"He works every Sunday. And it's not that early."

The deputy frowned. "So he's still hanging around, then?"

"Frank, really. I told you—he's helping with the house. It's got to be done." She turned to the table and began clearing away coffee mugs. "Listen, Frank. I was going to give you and Bannon a call."

"What about?" He helped himself to a chair.

"We had a break-in last night."

Alarm appeared to shadow Frank's face.

"There's nothing to worry about. I wasn't home and nothing was taken. Michael and I just thought that it wouldn't be a bad idea to let you know what happened."

Frank looked as though he were pondering the possibilities. Finally he looked up at Claire, who stood leaning against the kitchen counter. "Hmm, probably nothing more than a bunch of roughneck teenagers back-roading," he offered.

"In the middle of winter?"

"Hey, they get bored out here. Only two cinemas, the drive-in's closed and Morty shut down his arcade two months ago. They gotta do something."

"Yeah, well, breaking into my house would hardly qualify as something they've got to do."

"What can I say?" Frank tilted his cap back a little farther. "But I'll keep my eyes open—make sure it doesn't happen again."

He glanced in the direction of the living room, to where Michael was working. "And where was Dalton when this break-in occurred?"

Claire threw up her hands in disbelief. "Oh, Frank, for crying out loud. As if Michael would need to break in. He's got a key to both doors! Besides, he was with me last night. What are you getting at?"

"Nothing. Never mind. Forget I said anything." He stood up and walked over to her, taking her arm again. "Just promise me you'll be careful, Claire. I hate to think of you all alone up here in this house."

"I'm not alone, Frank. Michael's here."

"That's exactly what I'm referring to."

Claire held his stare then, trying to find some shred of reality behind his warning. But she couldn't believe that his words had anything to do with the man who had just comforted her through the night.

"I think I can take care of myself, Frank. Honestly. You don't have to worry."

Frank nodded curtly. "I'm still going to check in on you from time to time. Make sure you're all right. If that's okay with you."

"Sure, Frank. Whatever's going to make you feel better."

He let go of her arm and crossed the kitchen to the door. Claire followed him, holding it open as he adjusted his cap once again.

"I'll be in touch, Claire," he said before striding down the path to his car.

She watched as he backed out of the drive. She was too tired to even attempt to figure out Frank Turner this morning.

Leaving the top step, she was about to close the kitchen door when she heard a car horn and turned in time to see Alec's rental car swerve around Frank's vehicle and pull into the drive.

If she hadn't been wearing only socks, Claire would have sprinted across the drive to meet him. Instead, she stood on the top step, smiling as she waited for Alec to collect his overnight bag from the passenger seat.

"Grand Central or what?" Alec nodded to Frank's departing car and then to the Land Rover parked in the drive. "Have you thought about installing traffic lights at the end of your lane?" He paused on the step below Claire, which made their heights about equal, and took her into his arms. "How ya doing, darling?"

"Good, Alec. I'm doing good. God, I've missed you."
She gave him another hug before guiding him into the
warmth of the kitchen. "How was the trip up?" she asked
as she poured him a coffee.

"Well, at least the arrival at Bangor was on time. Lousy
flight, though. And then the rental car—I can hardly
move in that thing, and on top of that, the heater barely
works. I'm freezing."

"Here, wrap your hands around this." Claire handed
him a coffee, It wasn't as if Alec had such terrible luck, at
least not more than any other person. But he did have a
knack of complaining about it in such a way that made
you believe he was the most hapless person around. She
gave his shoulder an affectionate squeeze. "It's good to
have you here, Alec."

She was interrupted by Decker's low growl and the jin-
gle of his tags as he skulked into the kitchen.

"Oh, and how's my favorite puppy?" Alec crooned as
the dog retreated miserably to his food dish. "Happy as
ever, I see. Has he bitten anyone yet?"

Claire only shot him a smile and turned to the counter
to start making toast.

"Good morning, Alec." Michael's bright voice rang
through the kitchen, sending a tingle through Claire's
body.

"Michael," Alec said with a warm handshake. "Hey,
how's it going? I can't believe you're still here. I was almost certain that Claire would have driven you out long
ago."

He caught the roll of her eyes and laughed. "So, between the two of you, painting and renovating, I guess
you have a lot to show me. Do I get a tour or what?"

ALEC HAD BEEN IMPRESSED with Michael's progress on the house. More importantly, he'd been overwhelmed at the development of Claire's paintings. He agreed with her that they were a huge step forward, fresher than anything she'd been working on in the past several months, and had spent half an hour snapping Polaroids of the newest canvases. But instead of being ahead of schedule, according to Alec she had actually taken a step backward as far as her timing was concerned. She was now faced with the task of filling a gallery with the new pieces, rather than relying on the darker works of the past. She agreed with Alec that what she had to do now was complete as many canvases as possible before the deadline for the show in three and a half weeks.

That day, however, Claire relaxed in the comfort of Alec's and Michael's company. They sat at a corner table in The Harborside overlooking Somerset Bay and filled a couple of hours with conversation until Claire and Michael could no longer conceal their exhaustion.

Also tired from the flight and the drive, Alec was more than willing to head back to Claire's house when Michael suggested they leave.

"Will you be over tomorrow?" Alec asked Michael before hopping out of the Land Rover.

"Maybe later in the day. My associate's coming up from New York tomorrow. She's bringing a stack of reports and research that I've got to go through. Have to subsidize this life-style somehow," Michael told him with a wry grin.

"I know what you mean. Well, we'll see you tomorrow then. Have a good night, Michael." Alec turned to Claire, extending his hand. "Keys?"

From her coat pocket Claire pulled out the house keys and handed them to Alec. "Watch Decker doesn't kill you."

He gave her a sarcastic grin, taking the keys and heading up the path to the side of the house.

Michael had taken Claire's hand into his own shortly after pulling on the emergency brake, and he squeezed it now. "You're going to get some sleep tonight, right?"

"Promise," she whispered, smiling back at him. "I'll see you tomorrow?"

He nodded. How could he not see her? How could he possibly stay away for more than a few hours? "You will. Maybe not until later, but I'll give you a call."

Michael closed the short distance between them, sliding his fingers back through her hair, pulling her closer to him. He lifted his hand and caressed her cheek for a moment before their lips touched and she pressed her lips to his, embracing his mouth more than kissing it.

Raising his mouth from hers, Michael gazed into her eyes. He wanted to tell her right then that he loved her. He wanted to tell her how desperately he ached to feel her body next to his, the tingle of her skin against his own. And he wanted to tell her how he'd imagined making love to her and waking up together the next morning. How he'd imagined waking up with her every morning.

Instead, he whispered, "Good night," with promises of seeing her tomorrow. With one last kiss, Claire left the vehicle, thinking how impossibly far away tomorrow seemed.

She half expected to find Alec cowering in a corner of the kitchen, with Decker closing in. But he was cheerfully putting some water on for tea, while Decker merely grunted as he padded back and forth through the kitchen.

"So," Alec said, watching her as she hung up her coat. "Anything you want to tell me, darling?"

She turned to face him, her lips still warm from Michael's kiss. "And what is it you want to hear?"

"Oh, I don't know." He shrugged, throwing his hands up in a mock gesture. "How's the weather been?" He crossed the kitchen and slung an arm over her shoulders. "Come on, Claire, tell me. And don't leave anything out."

"Alec, really, there isn't much to tell."

"Oh yeah? So what were all those stolen glances and lingering looks over the dinner table, then? Just my imagination? Come on, let's hear it."

Claire turned to the counter where her stash of teacups and coffee mugs from the studio had been piling up. Running the hot water, she began washing them.

"Alec, honest to God, we're just good friends."

"Uh-huh, and you're the New Age Rembrandt the world's been waiting for."

"All right, all right." She took a breath and reached for the next cup. Alec's persistence, as always, had won out again. She put the cup on the drying rack and shrugged. "It's nothing right now. We're taking things slow."

"And he spent the night here last night?"

She looked back at Alec in time to see his sly smile. "It's not what you think, Alec."

"Right. That's what my sister's husband told her when she found him with his secretary."

"Alec."

"Okay, okay. But tell me one thing."

"What's that?"

"Do you love him?"

Claire stopped, her hands lingering in the hot water. It was such a simple question. Such a familiar one. Hadn't she been asking herself the very same thing, over and over again, every time Michael walked into the same room, every time she heard his voice, every time their eyes met or they touched?

Slowly she turned to face Alec, drying her hands on a dish towel as she leaned back against the counter. She didn't know why it should be so difficult to say yes, so hard to believe that she could be falling in love with Michael after all.

Perhaps it was seeing Alec again, seeing a part of her former life, remembering the times she had spent with him and Greg. Now, with Alec standing only a few feet away from her, the memories of Greg washed over her as if she had left the Soho apartment only days ago.

"I don't know, Alec," she confided, wishing that she had been able to say "yes" but hearing her voice, small and uncertain in the silence of the kitchen. "I really don't know."

CHAPTER ELEVEN

THE WEATHER HAD NOT BEEN kind. It had snowed lightly all day, and as the oppressive clouds that hovered over Westport and Somerset Bay cloaked the sun, the temperatures had plummeted. Now, as the early evening sky grew even darker, Claire imagined that the mercury was dropping lower still.

Tucked warmly away in her studio, grateful that she and Michael had not bothered to fix the overzealous furnace, Claire let her paintbrush move across the canvas as if of its own accord. Impressions of Michael filtered through her thoughts and mingled with the swirls of colors she saw before her. Memories from her night with Michael followed the dance of her brush against the canvas—the concerned gentleness of his touch, the comfort of his smile, the haven of his embrace.

Fingers of excitement shivered up her back as she remembered his body pressed up against hers, his breath hot against her neck while she slept within the circle of his arms. It didn't matter that she couldn't define what it was she felt for Michael—the important thing was that she did feel something. Closing her eyes, she wished she could be with him now, to feel his lips possess hers again, to feel his body tense beneath her touch.

No, she hadn't lied when she'd answered Alec's question last night. And she wasn't about to fool herself either by thinking that what she felt for Michael was love.

She did care about Michael. Cared about him in a way that she hadn't felt about anyone in a very long time. But not in the same way that she remembered feeling about Greg. It was different. It was incredibly real—perhaps more intensely real than she cared to admit.

After Greg, Claire had never imagined that there would be anyone else. Certainly, after his death, she'd never entertained thoughts of even looking at another man. Dreams of a life that she had hoped for before—a home and a family to share with Greg—had died the day his life slipped away in her arms. Since that black moment, Claire had not dared to dream again. And she would certainly not dare to love.

In the few short weeks she had known Michael, he'd touched a side of her she had thought long since dead. He had awakened her spirit and her passion after nearly a year of utter numbness. And whatever it was that she was feeling for Michael, it was the closest thing to love she had felt in a very long time.

Decker's whine broke Claire's reverie and she looked down at the dog.

"I suppose you want to go out, don't you?"

He nudged her with his wet nose, wagged his tail and watched her as she cleaned her paintbrush on a rag.

"All right. Come on, then." She followed him down to the first floor and opened the door for him.

The weather forecaster had not been exaggerating when he'd warned listeners about the dropping temperatures, she thought. She waited for Decker to bound outside, but when he refused to budge, she closed the door firmly behind them and walked back through the kitchen to the living room.

Michael had worked hard on the room during the past couple of weeks. Claire reached over to the dimmer switch

and soft light flooded the room. The refurbished hardwood floors gleamed with fresh lacquer and the oak
wainscoting was sanded and primed for its own finish.
The walls, a subtle shade of beige, lent a natural warmth
to the room. Claire stopped, leaning against the frame of
the widened doorway, and tried to imagine how the rest of
the old house would look when completed, what it would
look like filled with furniture and personal belongings,
what it would be like as a home for a family.

She stopped herself. She couldn't do this. Michael
seemed the surest thing that had come into her life in as
long as she could remember, but that didn't mean she
could allow herself to put faith in the possibilities.

As much as she believed that Michael felt the same
stirrings she did, there were no guarantees. Life didn't
come with those, she knew all too well.

When Alec had left for town, grumbling about the
weather, Claire had bundled him up in his parka and two
of her scarves. He'd taken her station wagon in search of
hardware for her next paintings and more film for his
Polaroid. That had been over three hours ago. She
checked her watch again and then shook it to be sure it
was working properly. Four-thirty. Surely it didn't take
three hours to pick up several lengths of one-by-one, a roll
of canvas and a couple bottles of turpentine?

There's nothing to worry about, she told herself. Not
yet anyway. More than likely Alec had run into someone
in town, possibly even Michael, and would pull into the
drive any minute now.

Convincing herself that this must be the case, Claire left
the kitchen and headed for the stairs.

She jumped when the phone rang, then reached for the
receiver. "Hello?"

"Hello? Is this Claire Madden?" The voice on the other line had a harsh tone that made it hard for Claire to identify its gender. In the background she could hear voices and buzzers.

"Yes, speaking."

"I'm calling from Westport General. It's about Alec Thurston."

Claire's heart stopped and the room began to spin as the hollow voice over the phone went on, "I'm afraid there's been an automobile accident."

ONE OF THE SMALLER hospitals in Manan County, Westport General nestled quietly at the foot of a backdrop of snow-covered firs, looking more like a large ski chalet than a hospital. Michael had done his best to calm Claire from the moment she'd phoned him. But for the duration of the drive into town, Claire had remained fearfully silent, her eyes glassy as she stared out through the windshield.

Even now, as Michael parked the Land Rover in the hospital lot, Claire was twisting one of the ties of her coat around her fingers. She didn't even notice the hand he offered her in support as they walked across the cold parking lot and into the warmth of the hospital.

Unlike big-city hospitals, Westport General's waiting room was not overrun with the sick and injured. Less than half a dozen people sat in the waiting area. None of them looked even half as anxious as Claire, Michael thought as he joined her at the front desk. He rubbed her shoulders, feeling the iron knot of tension there, while they waited for the receptionist to finish her call.

"Hello, I'm Claire Madden. Someone called me about Alec Thurston?"

"Ah, Mr. Thurston. Yeah, he's in room 307. Elevator's right behind you." She pointed with a pencil.

"I'm sure he's all right, Claire," Michael whispered, as they rode up on the elevator.

"We don't know that," she answered abruptly, stepping off the elevator to the sound of buzzers and voices ringing over the paging system.

They found Alec's room, and as Claire swung open the door, Michael could see the wave of relief that washed over her.

Alec was sitting up in bed, a magazine in his lap and a glass of juice in one hand. He set the glass down when he saw Claire and smiled.

"Alec," she breathed with a sigh of relief. "Are you all right? What happened?"

"I'm fine, darling. Really." He laughed as he welcomed her hug, giving Michael a nod. "Just had a run-in with a snowbank after a mild disagreement with the brakes of your car. By the look on your face, though, I'd say you'd already pegged me as a goner."

"Not quite." Claire's hesitant smile replaced her previous panic as she sat on the edge of the bed. "How are you feeling?"

"Nothing more than a headache." He lifted his hair to give her a full view of the gauze bandage taped to his forehead. "And a real shiner to show the gang back home."

"So, are they going to keep you overnight?" Michael asked.

"Overnight?" Alec laughed. "They love me here. They want to keep me permanently."

"Well, at least you haven't lost your sense of humor." Claire raised a hand to her shoulder and placed it over Michael's. "They are keeping you, then?"

"Just one night," Alec assured her. "I've already called New York to let Janine know I'm going to be a day late."

"You'll be all right to drive by then?"

"I'll be fine, Claire. Trust me." He took her hand and squeezed it reassuringly. "It's not that serious."

THEY DIDN'T LEAVE the hospital until well after visiting hours, and by the time Michael got Claire home, he could see exhaustion coupled with relief etched across her face. They hadn't spoken much during the drive, but Michael knew Claire well enough by now to realize that there was something else besides Alec's accident on her mind.

She immediately busied herself about the kitchen, picking up dirty cups, a paintbrush and rag she must have carried downstairs and some thumbnail sketches she'd been going over with Alec before he'd gone into town. She had pulled the ends of her shirt out from the top of her jeans, and as she paced the length of the kitchen, Michael could just make out the curves of her delicate form beneath.

Once the stray items were put away, Claire ran a hand through her hair impatiently and looked about the room, as if searching for anything else that might require her attention.

"What is it, Claire?" Michael asked.

She shrugged. "Nothing, I'm fine. Just thinking."

"Anything you want to share?"

"I don't know exactly—just thinking about the car."

"Your car?"

She nodded her head. "It doesn't make any sense. What happened to Alec—it shouldn't have occurred."

"Those kinds of things *do* happen, Claire, on occasion."

"Yeah, but not to cars that have had new brakes installed only three months ago. There's no way—"

"Claire, it happens." Michael took her shoulders in his hands. "You can't let yourself feel responsible. If it hadn't happened to Alec, it might have happened to you. And you might not have been so lucky."

"That's just my point."

It didn't take a genius to recognize the suspicion that clouded Claire's eyes. "I'm sorry, Claire. What is it you're getting at?"

"First the break-in, then the car."

"Claire, don't. You're letting your imagination get the better of you."

She paused for a moment, her muscles relaxing slightly beneath his massaging hands. "I don't know, Michael. Doesn't it make you suspicious? I mean, maybe it wasn't just some kids the other night. Maybe someone was actually looking for something. And maybe they did something to my brakes. We used your car yesterday. The Volvo's been sitting there until Alec used it this afternoon."

"I don't think the two incidents are related at all, Claire. I really don't. I think you're tired and maybe stressed. It's been a long forty-eight hours."

Claire nodded, and he could tell that she was trying her best to relax.

"If it makes you feel better, we can go down to the mechanic's tomorrow and see if he can tell us anything. In any case, there's nothing you can do about it tonight, right?"

Claire nodded again, and the corners of her lips curled into a faint smile. "I suppose you're right. It has been a long couple of days." Turning around and reaching on tiptoe, she brushed a gentle kiss across his lips. "Thanks."

The urge to take her into his arms then, to pull her body against his and lose himself in her sweet warmth, was overwhelming. Instead, he lifted a hand to her cheek and touched it tenderly, delighting in the softness of her skin.

She shivered against his touch and Michael took a deep breath before pulling away from her. "I'd better light the fireplace in your room before I go. Just in case the furnace decides to quit again. The temperature's going to drop even lower tonight."

"Thanks, Michael. I'll be up to give you a hand in a minute. I just want to put a few more things away."

With Decker at his heels, Michael climbed the stairs to the third floor. She would be all right, he thought as he flipped on the bedside lamp in Claire's room. It was just too much in too short a period of time, that was all. He could understand.

After all, hadn't he been on edge himself lately? What with Dee's latest rundown of a series of unforeseen complications with several of their clients, and then Bannon and Turner's badgering about Estelle and her affairs, he'd hardly had a chance to unwind in the past few weeks.

On top of all that, there was Claire and the new emotions he felt stirring within him. It was a constant battle to keep his distance, when all he wanted was to bury himself in her radiant sweetness. He wanted to tell her what he was feeling, what surged through his mind when he looked at her, when she touched him, when he heard her laugh. But instead, he had to remain silent.

She needed space. She needed time. He didn't have to be told twice.

In the meantime, all he could do was wait.

Wait and hope.

Standing by Claire's bed with all of her things around him, Michael could almost feel her radiance.

She hadn't made the bed yet—the bed they'd shared. The sheets were rumpled, the covers still pulled back. And from the mass of bedclothes, so faint it was barely discernible, Michael could smell her musk.

He breathed deeply and was about to turn from the bedside when the photograph on the night table caught his eye. The man in the picture was Greg, he now realized. The man whose memory Claire clung to so desperately, the man whose ghost seemed to haunt her spirit even now.

Michael turned from the bed and crossed the room to the fireplace. Perhaps time would widen the gap between Claire and this ghost. But he couldn't be certain of that.

Of one thing Michael could be certain. He would wait for Claire. He would wait for the day that she could let go of her past. He could only hope that it wasn't too far off.

CLAIRE LOCKED UP downstairs and came up to the bedroom, silently crossing the room. She guessed that Michael hadn't heard her.

In the hush of the room, with only the whisper of snow against the window and the hiss of the fire, he squatted before the hearth. He poked at the flickering kindling as it started to blaze, and the logs began to crackle. Claire leaned against one of the bedposts and watched him. In the glow of the fire, his profile held the contained strength she had come to know in him. Whether it was relief after the shock of Alec's accident, or something deeper, something that had lain dormant within her for too long now, Claire knew she wanted Michael tonight. More than anything she had wanted in a very long time, Claire longed to feel his body next to hers.

He stared into the flames. She didn't think he had heard her cross the room and come up behind him. But he didn't start, either, when she reached out and placed a hand on his shoulder. She moved her finger against the line of his jaw, stroking it slowly, marveling at its sharp angle.

Michael didn't say anything. He only looked up at her, and Claire allowed herself to become lost in the familiar gray depths of his eyes. As if sensing her desire, he stood silently, turning to her, and lifted his hands to her face. Long fingers buried themselves in her hair and drew her mouth up to his.

Like a light whisper, his lips brushed hers with a quiet intimacy that reminded Claire of their first kiss. Gently, almost tentatively, she tasted his lips, breathed in his breath, shivered against the brush of his hair on her skin. She felt his tongue reach and caress hers, pull back to trace the line of her lips and then probe again.

"Are you cold?" he asked her after a while, his mouth never really leaving hers.

"Warming up," she answered softly, feeling the curve of his smile beneath her lips.

She lifted a hand to the back of his neck and entwined his long hair through her fingers as his tongue probed deeper, drowning her in its velvety caresses. Claire could already sense his hunger, as intense as her own. His breathing quickened, and his pulse was strong against the hand she rested on his chest.

Eventually, his lips left hers. With exquisite tenderness, he kissed her cheek, her temple, her ear. He breathed delicate kisses along her neck until she ached with longing. And then his voice, no more than a breathy murmur against her ear, sent tremors of longing raking through her.

"I think I love you, Claire," he confided, and the room seemed to whirl around her.

She reached up, taking his face in her hands so that she could look into his eyes. At that moment, Claire feared she might cry. "Make love with me, Michael."

For a long moment he stared down at her, as if allowing her the opportunity to change her mind. But, as Claire watched the fire's glow flicker across his face, she knew what she wanted. Knew what she needed.

He drew her to him then, his lips claiming hers with a hunger that had been confined for too long. A hunger that raged within Claire, as well. A hunger that could no longer be denied.

And only when they became short of breath did Michael pull back, allowing them time to savor the pleasure.

Claire shivered as Michael's fingers traced a line from behind her ear, across her neck and finally to the top of her shirt.

Deft fingers unfastened the top button, then the next and the next, working their way down until the white lace of her bra and the luminous warmth of her skin were revealed.

Then it was her turn. As the buttons of his shirt came undone, Claire marveled at the ripple of tanned muscles underneath. She ran her fingers across his chest, following the perfect contours of his bulk and then the lines of his back. She'd seen his chest before, but now, anticipating the searing touch of his skin against her own, she trembled.

He lowered his mouth to her shoulder then, the heat of his lips unbearable in their tenderness, and Claire felt another shudder drive through her as his kisses trailed sweetly downward.

Cupping one breast in his hand, Michael pulled the lace back with his thumb. Claire gasped as his lips found the taut nipple and enveloped it with the heat of his mouth, tasting it, sucking it.

Her own hands fluttered to his open shirt, sliding downward along his skin until she was blocked by the barrier of his belt. Wrapping her fingers around it, she pulled him closer to her. His lips moved back to hers and he answered her hunger with equal longing as their tongues darted with a consuming thirst.

He unzipped her jeans, seeking the rising heat of her desire, and Claire heard her own quiet moan of pleasure. When he pulled her to him, her breath caught as she felt the immediacy of his arousal. This was what she had imagined over and over—his skin burning against hers, his mouth devouring hers, their bodies melding into one urgent and equally shared passion.

This was where she wanted to be.

Sweeping her easily into his arms, Michael lowered Claire to the thick rug in front of the fire. Beyond the hunger of their kisses, Claire saw the flicker of flames in the hearth and felt the brief coolness of the rug beneath her. But these weren't enough to pull her from the circle of their cresting desires.

Hands and fingers explored, brushing aside clothing, stroking and fondling fiery flesh. Time ceased to have any meaning as they rocked between hungry passion and slow, exploratory caresses.

When Claire reached out and fumbled with the buckle of his belt, twice losing it in her eagerness, Michael moved above her. And finally, hearing his groan as if it had come from her own throat, she slipped her hand beneath the heavy denim. She embraced the straining hardness there, caressing it with trembling fingers, marveling at its readiness.

Their kisses mounted, ravenous and fervent. Claire heard Michael moan again as she grasped his jeans and pulled them free of his waist, running her fingers back along his thighs.

He massaged her breasts, his fingers tracing ever-widening circles along her skin, igniting shocks of desire within her. Claire felt his lips leave hers and trail a hot arch to her breasts, along her ribs and down past the hollow of her stomach.

With one willing movement she lifted her hips, allowing him to slip off her jeans. His kisses continued, hot lips burning along her inner thighs and then working their way hungrily upward again—tasting her, savoring her velvety skin, and then pausing long enough to relish the firmness of her nipples.

When his lips sought hers again, Claire felt him move against her, felt his hardness press against the soft flesh of her deepest longing. She heard her own small cry of ecstasy as he slowly, deliciously, moved inside of her.

She encircled him with her legs. She trailed her hands down the slick length of his back to his buttocks, pulling him down onto her, drawing him deeper within her. She moved with him now, muscles straining in the rhythm of their lovemaking. She felt the hot dampness of their bodies rocking together as her fingers dug into the flesh of his back and shoulders, felt the tautness of muscles in his legs and hips with each powerful thrust.

Throwing back her head, Claire arched against Michael, raising her hips to him as the heat of his lips burned along her neck. And when he took her mouth with his once again, he drove to the inner core of her desire and brought her to a brink she'd long forgotten.

A shudder tore through Claire as she reached her highest peak and cried out Michael's name. She heard her own name escape his lips while he took her one plateau higher and then joined her. Together, their passions culminating as one, they melted into the crucible of their fused ecstasy.

CHAPTER TWELVE

THE FIRE BEGAN TO DIE sometime around four that morning, and by eight the ashen remains of the logs looked cold and lifeless. Claire stared at the hearth, remembering the fire's radiant glow flickering across their bodies as she and Michael had lain in each others arms. The blankets and pillows in front of the fireplace still marked their nest.

In the early hours of the morning, he had carried her to the bed, where they had made love again. It was during this magical time, as they explored each other's bodies, seeking out each other's arousal, that Claire had been overcome by a strange sense of belonging that echoed in her heart now as she stared down at Michael.

Gone was the sense of betrayal she had felt when they had first kissed. Gone was the hesitation that had hung over her like a dark cloud every time she had dared to think of being with him. And yet, in spite of the familiarity she now felt as she lay next to Michael's nakedness, Claire could not be entirely certain of her own feelings anymore.

Last night she had been unable to restrain her longing for Michael. But now, with the light of the morning sun already slipping through the blinds and creeping across the bedroom floor, Claire wondered how much of this new familiarity lay purely in her physical attraction to him and how much of it was real.

Sleeping with Michael had been easier than contemplating the possibility of loving him. But even though Claire wasn't certain if what she had done was right, there was a sense of rightness in lying beside him now.

His breathing was slow and deep as, in the hush of the bedroom, Claire watched him sleep. She propped herself up against the headboard with two pillows, turning so that her eyes could take in the beauty of the man beside her, and watched the steady rise and fall of his chest.

How long had it been since she had felt this fulfilled? So absolute and whole, with this curious satisfaction that nothing beyond the four-poster bed seemed to matter anymore? There was Michael and the space they shared. And, for the time being, nothing beyond this mattered.

She reached out to touch him, as if to be sure he was indeed real, that what had passed between them had truly occurred. She traced the muscles along his chest, the strength of his shoulder and finally the line of his jaw. And, as her fingers fanned back his hair, she pressed a kiss to his forehead.

He stirred, his eyes opening slowly, and smiled.

"Good morning," he whispered.

Claire smiled in turn, placing a kiss on his lips as she felt his strong arms wrap around her waist. In one graceful movement he pulled her on top of him, and she felt a shiver of excitement when their skin touched, as if it were the first time again. Propped up on her elbows, she pressed her breasts against his firm chest as the rest of her body melted into his.

"How did you sleep?" he asked, his voice still husky with drowsiness.

"It depends. Which two hours were you referring to?" She smiled intimately, tracing his lips with her fingertip.

"Oh, that bad, huh?"

She shook her head. "I didn't say that." She stretched forward to give him another gentle kiss. "How do you feel?"

A slow, easy smile of satisfaction crept across his lips then and his eyes lit up with a gleam of fulfillment. "I haven't felt better in years."

Claire continued to trail her fingers through Michael's hair. "So you don't think that last night was a mistake, then?"

"A mistake!" Michael almost sat up, but remained pinned down by the comfortable weight of Claire's body. "A mistake? Are you kidding me?" He feathered his own fingers through her hair now, bringing his hand back to cup her face in his palm. "Claire, last night was the first thing that's felt *right* in years. Being with you, loving you—it's the rightest thing I remember doing in a long time. No, I don't think last night was a mistake. Not at all. Why? Is that how you see it?"

A momentary panic flickered through his eyes as he stared up at her. And then, just as quickly, it faded as Claire shook her head.

"No, I don't think so. I just wasn't sure how you felt."

"Well, maybe I'd better show you again." He smiled and rolled her over so that he straddled her.

Claire could feel his awakened desire, hard and familiar against her thigh, and she smiled up at him, hoping that her momentary hesitation was not apparent to him. She slid her hands under the warm covers and trailed her fingers down the length of his muscular shoulders, fanning across his ribs and then down along his thighs after lingering for a while to savor the hot swell of his arousal.

"I'll show you how I feel," he whispered, just before his lips claimed hers and they spun into the familiar realm of their passion.

"YOU'RE SURE YOU DON'T want me to come along?" Michael stood beside Alec's rental car as Claire turned over the engine.

The late-morning sun had at last found its way clear of yesterday's oppressive sky and now it glared off the top layer of crusty snow. Claire looked up at Michael through her sunglasses and considered the plan of attack she had discussed with him over coffee only awhile ago.

She'd promised Alec that she would pick him up from the hospital at noon, but before she did that, she was determined to speak with Raymond Bannon about the accident and the break-in. If he could offer her any reasonable explanations for the doubts that plagued her, then she would go about her painting as if nothing had happened. "Claire?"

She shook her head. "No, Michael. There's no sense in your coming. You don't like Bannon any more than I do. No reason for both of us to ruin our mornings, is there?"

"I suppose not." He gave in with a shrug. "But listen, Claire, like I said before, don't be too disappointed if you don't get the kind of reception or answers you want. Especially from Bannon. With his retirement only four months away, the last thing he wants is more work. He didn't toss Estelle's case over to Turner for nothing, you know."

"We've been through this, Michael," she said, smiling at his concern. "I'm only going to see if he's looked at the car. That's it. I can handle it."

"All right then," he conceded, and bent down to kiss her through the open window of the car.

Decker, seeing an opening for a display of affection, stepped quickly from the passenger seat, over Claire's lap, and gave Michael a lick across the face.

"Great," he muttered, pushing the dog back and wiping his face with the back of his glove. "I'll miss you, too, Decker."

"Besides," Claire continued, "you should get back to your place. Dee's got to be wondering what's happened to you."

He nodded reluctantly, not anxious to return to the pile of dry reports and computer printouts he had to digest and analyze. "Unfortunately, you're right." He kissed Claire again. "Promise me that you won't mention Estelle or the Hobson girl?"

"I promise." Claire smiled in an attempt to reassure him. He had been right to dissuade her from drawing any connections between the murders, the break-in and Alec's accident. In the light of day, it did all look different. And she understood Michael's concern that the Westport authorities not think she was meddling in their case again.

"Good. And you'll call me when you get home?"

"The very minute," she promised, slipping the car into reverse. "In fact, the very second."

Twenty minutes later, Claire climbed the steps to the Westport Sheriff's Station. When she walked through the front doors, she was overcome by the lingering odor of cigars and considered herself lucky to have caught Raymond Bannon in.

Instead of the sheriff, Claire found one of his deputies behind the front counter. With a shake of his head, he informed Claire that Bannon had already gone out. He waved his hand toward the main street and explained that if she really wanted to see him, she could probably find him at Sarah's Donut Shop down the street.

She did find him there. With a blueberry fritter in one hand and the morning paper in the other, Bannon sat hunched over an oversize mug of coffee at a table near the back.

As the door closed behind her, Claire wiped her boots and crossed the small shop. Even here she could smell Bannon's cigars. A wobbly fan turned lazily overhead, doing little to disperse the heavy smoke.

"Coffee, ma'am?" someone asked her from the counter.

"No, thanks."

Bannon must have recognized her voice—he looked up as she neared his table.

"Good morning, Ms. Madden. Can I buy you a coffee?"

"No, thank you, Sheriff." She pulled a chair up to his table and wasn't surprised at its wobble. "Your deputy told me that I would find you here."

"Well, you found me." He grinned, folding his newspaper and spreading his arms wide. A piece of glazed icing hung on the edge of his lip. "So what can I do for you? Frank tells me that you've been having some trouble with teenagers up at your aunt's house."

"Well, that hasn't been established yet." Claire looked straight at Bannon. "We're only assuming that it was some teenagers on a dare."

"Nothin' damaged?"

Claire shook her head and Bannon waved his hand as if to dismiss her concern. "They were just bored. You know kids these days."

"Actually, no I don't, Sheriff."

"Trust me, Ms. Madden. You've got nothin' to worry about. Frank told me he was going to keep an eye on your place. Between him and that dog of yours, I shouldn't think it'll happen again. The kids probably saw all the lights out and figured no one was living there anymore."

He took another bite of his fritter and washed it down with a mouthful of black coffee. "Is that all you came to see me about?"

"No, not exactly. I heard you pulled my friend Alec Thurston out of an accident yesterday afternoon."

"Um-hmm." Bannon continued to relish his fritter, giving her no more than a quick side glance.

"He told me you saw it happen."

Bannon nodded again and let out a laugh that sounded more like a grunt. "Not much of a driver, that one. Surprised he didn't get himself killed."

"I was hoping that you might look into it for me."

The sheriff stared across the table at Claire. "Already did," he responded, wiping a paper napkin across his wide mouth.

"You already did?"

"Um-hmm. Had a coffee with Fred Trendell this morning. He's the mechanic who runs the shop down the street."

"What did Mr. Trendell have to say?" Claire asked.

"Fred told me it was definitely the brake lines."

"And what about them?" Claire prompted.

"Said that they were wearing thin and probably slipped some fluid."

"Look, Sheriff, I know my car. I had complete brake work done on it less than three months ago. And besides, that car has two brake lines. I find it a little coincidental that they would both wear out at the same time. Don't you?"

Bannon lifted his hands. "Hey, I'm not the mechanic. All I did was ask Fred what he thought happened to the car and he says the brake lines were wearing. He certainly didn't see anything suspicious in that and definitely nothing he felt warranted a report." He started to unfold his newspaper again, and Claire realized that she'd just been dismissed. "But hey, why don't you go ask him yourself? He's just at the end of the street. Gets back from lunch around twelve-thirty."

Claire stood up from the table, her chair scraping against the old linoleum flooring. "Thank you, Sheriff. I think I will. Sorry to have bothered you."

Crossing the street to the rental car, Claire kicked angrily at a chunk of ice that had fallen from some fender. She watched it roll toward the line of cars parked along the snowbank, and when it came to rest by the wheel of a minitruck, she looked up and suddenly froze.

It could have been the red ski jacket or the blond hair that curled down to brush the collar, or maybe even the way the jacket met the faded jeans that hugged his waist, but when Claire stopped halfway across the quiet street, her heart seemed to stop. Blood coursed through her head, pulsed with a nauseating flash of heat as she stared at him.

"Greg?"

It was his walk, his stance, the way he moved, the way the wind whipped at his hair. And even though reason told her that it was impossible, that it couldn't be Greg standing across the street with his back to her, for one hopeful and sickening moment Claire stared at him and saw Greg. His name echoed through her mind. She wanted to call out to him, to run to him, to throw her arms around him and feel his embrace again. But when she heard her own voice, shaky and desperate, whisper his name, Claire suddenly felt foolish.

She watched as a woman in a turquoise parka trotted to his side and planted a kiss on his cheek. When he turned at last, getting into the minitruck, Claire's heart sank with disappointment as she saw that his features were nothing at all like Greg's.

Raking her fingers through her hair, Claire let out a long breath and walked to the rental car. Her heart was still pounding when she closed the door behind her and pulled the seat belt across her chest. Ten months after Greg's death, and she was still seeing him. Fighting back the tears she felt building, she tried to think of Michael and of the night they had shared.

But even as she started the car and pulled away from the curb, it was Greg's face she saw in her mind.

FRED TRENDELL TOLD HER exactly what Bannon had, only in mechanics' lingo.

After leaving the garage, Claire had headed to the hospital. Now, as she rode the elevator up to the third floor of Westport General, she hoped that Alec wouldn't complain about her being late.

She walked along the corridor of the east wing to his room.

The only difference between Fred's assessment of the car and Bannon's was that Bannon's version had been easier to understand, Claire thought now in reflection on the lengthy conversation she'd had with the mechanic. Fred had rambled on about the details of the Volvo's braking system in such detail that Claire had begun to wonder if there was anything other than brakes in the man's life. Finally, she gave him the go-ahead to fix the car, and Fred promised that she could pick it up the following day.

Alec was already dressed and sitting at the edge of his made bed when Claire walked into his private room. He closed the issue of *GQ* he'd been flipping through and tossed it to one side.

"Hi, darling." He beamed her a smile as she crossed the room.

Claire blew a stray wisp of hair from her face before giving him a quick kiss on the cheek. She lifted the hair from his forehead to inspect the gauze bandage. "So, how's the patient?"

"Better than you, by the looks of things." He nodded to the chair behind her. "Take a load off and tell me about it."

Claire stared at him for a moment and then let out a long sigh. She sank into the chair, eased her head back and closed her eyes.

"That bad, huh?" Alec asked, stepping behind her to rub her shoulders.

"It's just been a crazy few days," she admitted, trying to relax under his massage.

"You mean the break-in and stuff?"

Claire nodded, running a hand through her short hair. "The break-in, the car. And then there's this thing about the Hobson girl and Estelle's death. As much as I've tried to stop thinking about it, I just can't seem to let it go."

"Well, darling, you'd better start trying real hard. You've got a helluva lot of work ahead of you for this show. You can't play Nancy Drew and finish your paintings at the same time."

"I'm not playing Nancy Drew, Alec," she said in an attempt to convince him and herself, even though the same thought had crossed her own mind just this morning. "Really. I'm just bothered a little by everything that's going on."

"What *went* on, Claire. Past tense, remember? All of that stuff has nothing to do with you."

She thought for a moment, recognizing the truth in his statement. As much as she doubted the word of Westport's sheriff, she could not waste her time searching for clues that weren't there. She could not exhaust her energy worrying about something that *had* happened in the past and was no business of hers. "No, you're right," she said at last. "If Estelle had any secrets, they died the day she did."

She let out a half laugh, half moan of exasperation. "Oh, man." She rubbed her face with both hands as if to wipe away the past couple of days. "I went to see Bannon today. Practically demanded that he look into the possibility that someone tampered with my car. Do you believe it?"

"And what did he have to say?"

"It's not *what* he said so much as the way he said it, Alec. I swear the man thinks I'm just another neurotic from New York."

"Good." He slapped her shoulder playfully. "That means he'll leave you alone. Did you talk to the mechanic?"

She nodded, remembering how foolish she'd felt after that visit. "Just a bad brake job. I couldn't make out half of what he said, but when he asked me if my mechanic had read the manual, I knew I'd be making a fool of myself if I pursued the issue."

Alec moved around the chair and stood in front of Claire. He reached down to take her hands in his and held them as he looked down at her. "And what about Michael?"

Claire looked away. "He thinks it was an accident, too."

"That's not what I was referring to, Claire."

She didn't look up at him now, didn't dare. She knew if she met his stare she would not be able to hold back the tears of confusion she had been choking back.

"I can tell there's more than this accident on your mind, darling. I know you too well. What is it?" He waited for her response, but she only shook her head. "It's Michael, isn't it?"

She looked up to him at last and felt herself about to cry.

"Claire?"

She let out a long breath, hoping he couldn't hear the shakiness of it. "I don't know, Alec. It's more Greg than it is Michael."

"Let me guess," he said, lifting her chin so that she was forced to look at him. "You're beginning to feel more than just a passing attraction to Michael and you can't shut off the guilt, am I right? You can't stop thinking of Greg in spite of Michael."

"Pretty much," she admitted, feeling a certain comfort in Alec's perception of her feelings. "You know, I actually thought I saw Greg in town today?" She forced a smile through the blur of unshed tears. "It was just this guy wearing a red ski jacket like Greg's. You know, the one we got in Aspen last year? He had the same hair, same build, everything. And...even though I know Greg's gone, even though it's been almost ten months, for that split second I honestly thought it was him."

She felt Alec's hands tighten around hers as he pulled her up from the sagging cushions of the chair into the familiarity of his embrace.

"It's all right, Claire," he whispered. "You still miss him. That's perfectly understandable. Especially now, with Michael in your life. But you have to put Greg behind you now. I know it takes time. I know it can't be easy. But I'm also sure that Greg would want you to, Claire—especially with someone like Michael. I've seen the way he looks at you, Claire. He's crazy about you."

He stroked her hair as she nestled her face against his shoulder and held him tighter, unable to stop the tears now. Alec was right. One way or another, she had to get on with her life, no matter how difficult or frightening that might be.

"It takes time, darling," Alec repeated. "And I know it's difficult, but you have to try. For yourself...and for Michael."

CHAPTER THIRTEEN

ALEC LEFT WESTPORT in time to miss the storm. When he backed out of the drive, waving goodbye to Michael and Claire, the sun had been shining and the skies looked promising. By nightfall, it had started snowing again. And the next morning Michael and Claire started shoveling.

They couldn't keep up with it, though. For three days the snow continued its assault along the coast, three days of snow and bitter winds that drove even the most courageous of souls behind closed doors.

Michael and Claire had ventured into town only once for groceries and supplies. Dinner at The Laughing Lobster had confirmed Michael's theory that there was little else to do during an extended storm such as this, and they had warmed themselves with hot cocoa and coffee until the bartender called for last rounds.

Dee had gone back to New York on Thursday, hoping to beat the worst of the storm. With her gone, Michael had little reason to leave Claire alone. He'd completed the work on the living room and lounge and had started to move his equipment up to the second floor.

Now, as Claire perched on the stool in front of one of her paintings, she was almost grateful that Michael had to return to his house to make several phone calls and go over some of his own work. She was beginning to doubt whether she would ever complete all the pieces she'd promised Alec.

Michael's presence in the house was a constant and irresistible distraction. Even though she felt the pressure of the work she had to complete, Claire could not bring herself to say no to his advances. But when she was able to put in a few hours in the studio, she surged on ahead relentlessly. She'd stretched half a dozen new canvases based on the thumbnail sketches Alec and she had gone over. She'd even had to open the extra box of supplies he'd brought from New York.

Claire leaned back on her stool and cocked her head. The color just didn't seem right. She had become so accustomed to the flood of light in the studio during the daytime that now, with darkness closing in around the turret and the overhead light glaring down on the wet paint, she had to second-guess how natural lighting would eventually play on the canvas. She'd have to wait until the morning to make any kind of final decision on the amount of blue she'd been using. It seemed a little murky.

She took a deep breath and jumped down from the stool. Crossing her arms over her chest, she paced across the studio and turned to look at the painting again. No, it was working. They were all working. For the first time in months, her pieces were coming together. And with an ease that amazed even her.

The abstract forms seemed to pulsate with a life of their own. They undulated within the boundaries of the canvases' edges. Their subtle tones shimmered with a new sensuality, with a serenity that seemed almost palpable, yet remained mysteriously elusive. These paintings were utterly different from those of the past eight months. Claire could see the power emanating from them. It was as if she had breathed life into these new pieces. The kind of life Michael had breathed into her.

She began to clean her brush.

Gently rubbing the bristles in a turpentine-soaked rag, she walked over to the turret windows. The snow had piled up against the screens along the north windows, allowing her no view of the road or the driveway. But then, even in the daytime, there was nothing to see but blowing sheets of snow.

Claire continued to work the brush with the rag and leaned up against the solid frame of one of the east windows. Looking past her own reflection, she could just make out the lights of Michael's house glimmering across the fields.

They had spent a lot of time together, she and Michael—almost every moment since Alec and Dee had left. She had spent hours watching and helping him work, only to have him follow her upstairs later to sit with her as she painted. And for all her good intentions of getting some work done, they usually ended up in the bedroom, in the shower or in front of the fireplace.

And with each passing day, Claire realized that Michael Dalton was addictive. For a person who cherished time on her own, she had certainly become accustomed to his constant presence.

Even now she missed him.

He'd left only a couple of hours ago, but she had already begun to feel his absence. She wondered if he would be able to make it back to her house tonight. Then again, the county had been pretty conscientious about keeping the roads cleared. During the past three days she'd heard the snowplow cruise by almost every three hours.

She turned away from the window, thankful that it wasn't she who had to drive the short distance between the two houses. The mere sight of the snow chilled her now, and she reached for her sweatshirt.

And that was when she remembered Decker. A wave of hot panic jolted through her. How long had he been outside?

She couldn't remember when she'd last let him out, but it had been quite awhile ago, well before dark. She'd returned to the studio and made certain to leave the stereo off in order to hear his habitual bark.

But he hadn't barked. And she hadn't let him in.

Echoes of the weather warnings she had heard over the radio for three days now raced through Claire's mind as she clambered down to the first floor.

Hoping against hope that she would find Decker pressed up against the screen, Claire threw open the door. But the only greeting she received was a blast of frigid air and pelting snow.

The light mounted on the side of the house did little to penetrate the darkness. Claire strained to see, ignoring the snow that blew in through the door to the kitchen.

"Decker!" she screamed above the howling winds, realizing that her voice carried no more than a few hundred yards.

"Decker!" she called again, then strained to hear the jangling of his tags, a bark, anything.

"Decker!"

She stood in the doorway, calling for almost a minute, the wind whipping at her hair, the cold biting her skin, until finally she closed the door and scrambled for her coat and boots.

This couldn't be happening, an inner voice screamed. He never strayed very far for very long. She pictured Decker huddled behind some snowdrift out in the fields, his sense of direction lost by the icy winds and howling snow.

Throwing a scarf around her neck, Claire was about to open the door when the phone rang. Praying that the caller had news about Decker, she went to pick up the receiver.

Michael's voice came across the lines. "Hi, sweetheart. I'm just taking a short break in between calls, but I wanted to hear your—"

"Michael," Claire gasped, realizing only now how breathless she had become in her panic.

"Claire, what is it?"

"Decker, he's gone." She raked a hand through her hair and looked out at the darkness beyond the kitchen windows. "I let him out and he's still not back yet. I've tried calling him. He's nowhere around."

"Calm down a second, Claire. What time did you let him out?"

"I don't know. It was still light out. I guess an hour, hour and a half. Listen, I have to go. I'm just on my way out to look for him."

"Claire, no, wait," Michael almost shouted at her. "You don't know your way around out there. And besides, with the storm—"

"Michael, I have to find him."

She heard him take a deep breath. "All right, but listen to me, Claire. You're not going out there alone. It's too dangerous at night with a storm like this. You wait for me."

She didn't answer him, only bit her lower lip and listened to the wind rattle the windows of the old house.

"Claire? Do you hear me?"

"All right, Michael. But hurry."

"Just sit tight. I'll be there in a few minutes. Don't go out on your own, Claire. Promise you'll wait for me."

There was silence as Claire clutched the phone to her ear. Eventually she hung up and took a breath to regain her composure. Ten minutes was not going to make a big difference. Besides, she thought, looking down at the clothes she'd scrambled into, she was hardly dressed for venturing out into a storm.

Racing upstairs, she pulled on another pair of socks and slipped on a turtleneck beneath her sweatshirt. By the time she saw the headlights of Michael's Land Rover, she was thoroughly bundled up.

Closing the door firmly behind her, Claire ran out to meet him. In her gloved hands she carried the small plastic flashlight she'd found in one of the kitchen cupboards, and she flipped the switch on it, shaking it until a dim yellow light flickered from the bulb.

Michael gave her a quick kiss as she came up beside him, his lips moist from the snow that had melted there.

"Okay, we'll do this right," he assured her, squeezing her hand before reaching into the Rover. From behind the driver's seat he pulled out two pairs of snowshoes, tossing them down on the ground in front of Claire.

"Ever use these things before?" he shouted above the wind.

Claire shook her head, her hair already matting with snow as Michael bent down to start strapping them to her hiking boots. In the light of his torch, Claire could see his hands already turning red as his fingers worked the buckles. Only when he'd fastened on his own pair, did he stand up.

"Okay, now just walk. Keep your legs apart a little. And whatever you do, don't step on your own feet." His quick smile eased Claire's tension momentarily.

He reached down to take her flashlight. Tossing it into the car, he handed her a large torch like his own and put on his gloves.

"Okay. You ready?"

Claire nodded and was about to attempt her first steps in the oversize snowshoes.

"Wait." His hand on her arm stopped her. "Here," he said, removing his ear warmer and pulling it down over her head. Lifting her chin with one gloved hand, he kissed her again. "Now follow me. And keep me in sight. I don't want to lose you."

It took several minutes, but eventually Claire fell into the rhythm of Michael's step and the snowshoes began to feel less awkward. They had crossed the first field in a matter of minutes and now followed the line of trees that marked the edge of the forest. Through squinted eyes and the blur of melting snow, Claire watched Michael's back as she followed him. The outline of his broad shoulders was clear enough through the heavy curtain of snow. And only when she stopped every few minutes, bringing her hands to her mouth to shout Decker's name across the empty fields, did she begin to lose sight of Michael's fading shape.

Fighting the punishing winds and the knife-sharp snow that thrashed across the fields was a constant battle. The light of the flashlights struck the thick sheets of blowing snow, hardly breaking through the pitch black of the night.

After forty minutes, Claire was losing hope. Stopping, calling and then jogging to catch up with Michael again, she was beginning to doubt that she would even hear Decker's bark over the force of the wind.

Suddenly, Michael stopped moving, causing her to bump into him and tread on his snowshoes. He lifted his hands to his ears, trying to warm them, his flashlight sending its beam skyward. "It's no use, Claire," he shouted to her.

She was shaking her head, her cheeks long since numbed from the stabbing cold. "Don't say that, Michael!"

"We'll never find him this way. It's too dark. Besides, if he was around, he would have heard us. He would have come to us by now."

"I'm not listening to this, Michael," she screamed at him. "You can go back if you want, but I'm not leaving here without him!"

"Claire! He's probably holed up somewhere safe, out of the wind. Come on, we've been out here for almost an hour. He would have heard us by now."

"I'm not going anywhere until I find him!" Claire almost tripped over her snowshoes as she turned defiantly and pushed on. How could Michael even entertain thoughts of leaving Decker out here, she thought angrily as another gust of wind almost forced her off her feet. Visions of the animal struggling against the storm urged her on and her legs plowed through the drifts of snow until she felt sweat dampen her back.

And then Michael was beside her, grabbing her arm, pulling her to a stop. "Claire!"

She felt tears searing her frozen skin, burning their way down to her chin.

Michael must have seen them. He took one gloved hand from his ears and reached out to wipe her face. He stared at her a long moment, his dark hair matted white, his face red. "All right," he shouted. "We'll keep looking. But we'll head to the woods. Maybe he's farther in and can't hear us."

For another fifteen minutes they struggled through the underbrush. Claire found the traveling more difficult now—fallen branches caught in the mesh of her snow-shoes and large rocks hid just below the drifts of snow. But she struggled on, playing her flashlight on the ground in front of her, until she heard Michael's voice yelling back to her, "There he is."

Claire's heart skipped a beat and she sprinted to Michael. By the time she reached him, he had aimed the beam of his flashlight ahead of them. He stood motionless. And before Claire could even call out, he lifted a hand to her mouth.

"Don't call him," he said. "Look." He pointed his flashlight to the ground encircling the snow-matted retriever. It was stained a dark red.

Claire's heart stopped. "It's a trap. If you call him, he could get too excited and hurt himself more."

But it was too late. Decker had seen them. With his ears down and his tail wagging madly, he was already trying to pull toward them.

How could he hurt himself any more? Claire wondered, taking in the horror of the blood-stained snow.

"Just walk slowly with me and be firm with him. We don't want him jumping around."

Her attention focused fully on Decker, Claire tripped several times as they closed in on the dog. In spite of her firm commands for him to sit and stay, the retriever's excitement mounted as they neared. And only when they were finally on top of him did Michael break his silence.

With the two flashlights proppped on the snow and trained on the bloody scene, Michael squatted down beside the dog and tried to hold him down. "All right, Claire," he called between Decker's elated licks, "just hold him as still as you can. Hang onto his leg and don't let him pull it out until I say it's okay.''

Wrapping her arms around Decker's neck, Claire straddled the retriever and fought to keep him still. Once she'd grabbed hold of his front leg, he settled down enough for Michael to begin work on the trap.

The teeth of the trap had buried themselves into the flesh of the dog's leg, and as far as Claire could tell he was still bleeding heavily. She watched Michael. He worked quickly, pulling the chain to give himself another inch of slack, brushing the snow from the trap's springs and then bracing himself.

Gripping the springs, Michael gritted his teeth and squeezed. Claire watched as the toothed jaws slowly opened, and she fought with Decker's instinct to yank his leg free.

"Okay," Michael yelled.

Claire saw his arms shaking with strain as she finally pulled the dog's leg clear. She shouted to him the second the animal was free.

Decker quivered with excitement and cold as Claire struggled to wrap his paw with her scarf. Forcing him to lie down in the snow, she took up a flashlight and shone it at Michael.

She had never seen Michael angry before and she hadn't really expected the violence with which he yanked at the trap now. He threw his weight against the chain, cursing under his breath, until she heard something snap and the trap broke from its anchor, almost sending Michael flying back into the snow.

Holding the trap in one hand, Michael picked up his flashlight and searched the area until his boot kicked up what he had been looking for.

"Bait," he shouted to Claire, who was only a few feet away and could see the semifrozen piece of meat half-buried in snow. "It's fresh."

She turned to Decker. Squatting in her snowshoes, oblivious of the wind and snow, she loosened the scarf and shone the flashlight onto the bloodied paw.

"How's it look?" Michael asked as he knelt beside her and scratched Decker's head.

"I don't know. It's hard to tell."

"We'd better get him to the vet's anyway. Could be some broken bones. Here," he said, handing Claire the trap, "we'll let Bannon have a look at that."

Wrapping the paw again, Michael lifted the retriever into his arms with a grunt and staggered after Claire toward the house.

They spread out a blanket in the back of the Land Rover and Michael eased Decker onto it, commanding him to lie down. Stopping at the house only long enough for Claire to grab her purse, they drove into town.

DR. BRETT MONROE, the local veterinarian in Westport, did not hold clinic hours on Saturdays, especially at nine o'clock at night. But Michael had assured Claire that a knock on her back door was known to elicit a concerned response no matter what the hour.

"Are you sure someone will be in, Michael? Maybe we should take him to Bangor, or..."

She stopped talking as she heard footsteps approaching the door, followed by the glare of the back-porch light. Michael shifted his weight and Decker struggled uselessly in his arms.

"This isn't going to be easy, Michael," Claire warned, remembering the last time she'd had to take Decker to the vet without Greg. But then the feeling between the dog and the vet had been mutual, which had only made matters worse.

Dr. Monroe, on the other hand, did not seem intimidated by the low growls issuing from Decker's throat. She ushered them through the door and turned on the lights of the clinic that occupied the bottom half of the two-story house, waving her hand when Michael apologized for their unannounced visit.

"Just set him down there, Michael," she said, indicating the stainless-steel examining table. And then, looking Decker in the eye as another low growl rattled up from his throat, she smiled. "Oh, you'll be all right, boy."

Decker shifted his brown eyes distrustfully from Michael to Claire and then back to the vet.

"So, tell me. What mess has this one been getting into?"

Michael maintained a firm grip on Decker's head and watched the vet unwrap the scarf from around his leg. "Had a run-in with a fox trap up on the bluffs."

"A trap?" Brett continued her examination, oblivious of Decker's complaints as she swabbed and cleaned the cuts. "Surely, no one's trapping around here?"

"That's what I thought," Michael said.

"You're going to talk to Sheriff Bannon, I hope."

"That's our next stop."

Brett spent the next five minutes silently inspecting the damage and finally stood back from the table. "Well, our friend here is pretty lucky, I'd say. It was a fox trap, you said?"

Claire and Michael nodded.

"It could have been a lot worse. No broken bones, fortunately. No severed tendons. Everything else seems fine, other than these lacerations. There's some bruising, of course—that's what's causing the swelling—and maybe even a touch of frostbite. But look, there's really nothing to worry about. I can put in a few stitches, help the healing a bit and wrap him up. I think we'll give him a sedative for tonight, at least, and here are a couple of painkillers for you to give him tomorrow. He'll be smarting some tomorrow, and it's better if you keep him quiet."

She moved to the other table and started to get her supplies ready. "You'll want to keep him wrapped up for a while. He's gotten quite a chill out there," she said, filling a syringe with serum.

"At least he doesn't have a temperature. The bait couldn't have been poisoned. They do that sometimes, you know." She returned to the table and gave Decker his first injection. "Yes, I'd say you're one lucky pooch."

BRETT MONROE HAD SEEN them on their way by nine-thirty, with extra blankets to wrap around the drugged Decker.

Claire sneaked quick glances at him as they drove through town, his head jerking whenever the Land Rover hit a bump along the snow-packed streets. The wind had died down and now the snow, thick as ever, drifted aimlessly downward.

Several windows were lit up when Michael pulled up to the Westport Sheriff's Station ten minutes later. He pulled the emergency brake and looked over at Claire.

"I'll only be a minute. You're sure you don't want to come in?"

Claire shook her head. "I've had enough of Bannon, thanks. You go ahead."

"All right, then. I'll be right back." He reached over and kissed her, and at last Claire felt her lips beginning to thaw.

With the vehicle idling and the heater blasting, Claire reached out and warmed her fingers in front of a heater vent as she watched Michael jog up the steps of the station, the trap dangling from his hand. He opened the door, and as the light cascaded out across the steps, Claire could see traces of blood on the jagged teeth.

She shivered and looked back at Decker, who was dead to the world. She smiled to herself, out of relief more than anything, and reached back to pet the sleeping dog.

In less than two minutes Michael returned to the car. He wasn't carrying the trap, Claire noticed. And he wasn't smiling, either.

"What did he have to say?" she asked, once he'd sat down behind the wheel again.

He took a deep breath. "Bannon said he'd look into it."

"You don't believe him?"

Michael stared out the windshield of the Rover and shook his head. "I don't know, Claire. Seems all Bannon's thinking about these days is his retirement. He's not interested in anything that's going to force him to get off his butt."

"Did he at least have an explanation?"

Michael shook his head again and turned to look at her. "He says he doesn't know of anyone who's trapping on the bluffs anymore. He figures it was just an old one that had been left behind."

Claire was shaking her head. Even in the dim light of the street lamp she could see doubt etched in his expression. "But the bait was—"

"I know, Claire. I know. Let's talk about this later. Right now, we'd better just think about getting Decker home."

CHAPTER FOURTEEN

"WHERE DO YOU WANT HIM?" Michael carried Decker into the kitchen. Blankets trailed behind him and the dog's head hung limply over his arm.

"I suppose the studio would be best. Can you handle him?"

Michael nodded and started up the stairs.

They had driven in relative silence back to her house, neither one of them anxious to begin voicing their suspicions. Claire had decided this was best left for discussion over a hot cup of tea, or at the very least in the warmth of the house.

The lights in the studio were still on, Claire's paintings still out and drying. Michael eased the retriever onto one of the drop cloths in the corner and arranged the blankets over him.

"I imagine he'll be out all night," Michael said, leaving the dog's side and rummaging through one of the closets until he produced a small space heater.

Claire settled down on the drop cloth beside Decker and stroked his head. Only now was she beginning to warm up. Despite the heat that had blasted through the Land Rover's vents during the drive home, a chill still gripped her. She shivered.

"I think you should take a hot shower, sweetheart. You need to warm up," Michael suggested as he eased himself down to the floor and wrapped an arm around her. He turned her face and kissed her, his lips hot against hers. "Hey, are you all right?"

Claire shook her head and looked at Decker again. How could she be all right? Her dog had just gotten snared in a trap that might possibly have been set with him in mind, and Michael was asking her if she was all right? So much for the peace and quiet she had sought at Westport.

"No, Michael, I'm not. I want to know what's going on around here."

"Claire—"

"Is it just me? Am I being paranoid or something?"

Michael took her hand into his and stroked it reassuringly. "No, I don't think you're being paranoid, Claire."

"So what do you think is happening?"

He shrugged and stared at Decker. "I don't know. Either someone doesn't want Decker around, or they think they're still going to catch themselves a fox around here."

"Michael, the trap was only a couple hundred yards from the house. I don't claim to be an expert hunter or anything, but wouldn't you say that that's a little too close for fox trapping?"

"Look, sweetheart." Michael took her hands into his, shifting his position so he could face her. "I can't give you any explanations. I'm sorry. I wish I could, but I don't know what went on out there. I don't know why someone would do this."

"Someone wanted Decker out of the way." Claire heard her voice waver in the hush of the studio. She hoped it didn't sound as anxious as she was beginning to feel. "Either that or they were trying to frighten me out of this house."

"What would anyone have to gain by doing that?"

"I don't know, Michael. I don't know." But Claire was thinking about Estelle and Annette Hobson. There had to be something about the house, something someone wanted. And until proven otherwise, she was going to act upon those suspicions. No matter what Michael believed.

"Whatever *is* going on around here, Claire, there's nothing we can do about it right at the moment. Bannon's got the trap, and first thing tomorrow morning he's going to look into it. Either that or get Frank to take care of it."

"And how are we to know that it wasn't Bannon who set the trap in the first place?"

The crease on Michael's forehead deepened. "Why on earth would you think that?"

Claire shrugged her shoulders. "I don't know, Michael. I don't know what to think anymore. I'm living off hunches now."

Michael was silent for a moment, his fingers stroking Claire's hand as he followed her gaze to the drugged dog.

"Look, sweetheart, why don't you take a hot shower and get a bit more painting done? It'll take your mind off this."

"You're leaving?"

He stood up, pulling her along with him. "Not for long. I promise." He checked his watch. "I have to make a couple of calls still. Shouldn't take me more than an hour. You could come along with me, if you like."

She shook her head. "No, I don't want to leave Decker alone."

"It'll be all right, Claire," he whispered to her as his lips brushed her cheek and then her ear. "I don't know what's going on yet, but I won't let anything happen to you. I promise."

She pulled back and returned his gentle smile of concern. "I'll be all right," she assured him and kissed him again. "Just lock up on your way out."

FIFTEEN MINUTES under scalding water had finally taken the chill out of Claire's bones. She had pulled on a thick pair of socks, wrapped herself up in a heavy terry robe and now paced the bedroom, toweling her hair.

As she wandered into the studio to check on Decker again, Claire wondered how much of her fear was unreasonable. She really had no basis for questioning Raymond Bannon's integrity. In fact, when she thought about it, she couldn't isolate a single incident that might have caused the mistrust she intuitively felt toward the sheriff.

With all that had happened, she couldn't allow herself to trust anyone but Michael. It wasn't just the break-in. And it wasn't just Decker.

Whether or not Estelle's death had been natural, the fact remained that *someone* had assaulted and killed a seventeen-year-old girl and had left her body out in the snow-covered fields. That reality could not be ignored. She wanted to believe Michael when he'd explained that the sheriff had no suspects, that everyone believed the murder had been committed by an outsider. But now, reinforced by Decker's injury, the link Claire had imagined between Estelle's house and Annette Hobson's murder was only getting stronger.

She could not allow herself to be lulled into the false sense of security that the stone walls around her seemed to represent. And she could not rely on the security Michael's presence offered her if he wasn't even there. She'd have to take care of herself.

Walking back to the bedroom, Claire opened the drawer of her nightstand and pushed aside a back issue of

Cosmo, revealing the leather holster underneath. Wrapping her fingers around the smooth case, she took it from the drawer and snapped open the flap.

The cool metal of the .22 semiautomatic felt like ice against her skin. Turning the compact piece over in her hands, Claire let the magazine drop from the grip and stared at the loaded cartridge.

Alec had forced her to buy the gun shortly after Greg's death. He'd gone with her to the shooting range for practice and had seen to it that she kept it loaded and in her nightstand at all times.

When she'd arrived in Westport, Claire had smiled fondly when she unpacked her suitcase and found the gun. In his unfailing concern for her safety, Alec had undoubtedly packed the Beretta when her back had been turned. Although she was certain she'd committed at least one federal offense by taking it across the state line, it was here now and she was not about to ignore the security it represented in her mind.

Carrying the gun with her into the studio, she set it down on one of her worktables and looked at Decker. He twitched in some deep canine dream, but when she squatted down beside him to caress his head, he settled into a quiet rest. She ran her hand down along the sleeping animal's strong body, her fingers slipping through his silky fur.

Settling back into the armchair, Claire propped her legs up on another chair and picked up her sketchbook. Occasionally she glanced over at the gun resting inconspicuously among the tubes of paint and jars of turpentine. Her hand worked the pencil briskly across the pad as she mapped out some possibilities for the next painting. Only a trace of wind swirled the snow that whispered against the windows, and Claire soon lost herself to the sketch-book in her lap.

She wouldn't have heard the small scraping noise downstairs if Decker hadn't growled out in his sleep.

But when she looked at the retriever, he lay still—lost in some tranquilized dream. The steady rise and fall of the dog's rib cage attested to his deep slumber, and suddenly Claire felt extremely alone.

And then she heard it.

It was a quiet thud—nothing more than a shuffle, really—but she stood up just the same. The sketchbook on her lap crashed to the floor, and when she stooped to pick it up her hands were shaking.

She crossed the studio in a silent bound, and with her senses straining, stepped out into the dark corridor. She took hold of the railing, her palms already slick with sweat.

It had to be Michael. Almost an hour had passed since he'd gone. Surely it was him returning for the night.

But Claire couldn't ignore the quivering of her nerves. All her senses were on edge, crying out to her, demanding action. She had to be certain.

"Michael?" Her voice trembled.

No response.

"Michael?" she called again, this time loud enough that he should have heard.

Still there was silence.

For what seemed like a full minute, Claire hovered at the edge of the railing, peering down the dark stairs, listening for something, anything. And then she heard it again.

This time it was footsteps—soft at first, and then growing louder with a determination that made her shudder.

She called out one more time and then, with a stab of realization that ran through her like a cold knife, Claire knew that it was not Michael downstairs. Even as she turned to the studio again, she could hear the footsteps echoing through the empty living room, heading toward the bottom of the staircase.

In a flash, Claire had closed the door and latched it. Her pulse quickening, she rammed one of the studio chairs underneath the knob and gave the legs a good kick to wedge it securely. Sweat beaded on her forehead and along her back. Her robe felt damp. It clung to her body as she raced back to the worktable.

Wiping her hands on the sides of her robe, she picked up the gun. The Beretta trembled in her hand and the walnut grip threatened to slip in her sweaty grasp.

Claire scrambled to the other end of the studio table and picked up the phone, almost dropping it in her panic. Trembling fingers jabbed at the keys, dialing Michael's number.

But it wasn't Michael on the other end of the line when the phone was finally picked up. Claire tried to say something, but could only manage a gasp.

"Ms. Claire? Is that you? What's the matter?" Greta asked, hearing the distress in Claire's voice.

"Greta!" she whispered harshly. "Greta, where's Michael?"

"Oh, Ms. Claire, I'm afraid he's left already. I assumed he was going over to see you."

"When did he leave?"

"About ten minutes ago. He should—"

Claire's heart stopped as the line went dead.

There's no need to panic, she thought, trying to convince herself as her mind frantically searched for possible explanations. A telephone pole might have come down, a line might have snapped. Then again, the storm had passed some time ago.

He'd left about ten minutes ago. Surely Michael should be here by now.

And then she heard another sound, from down on the second floor. A door closed, and then another. The footsteps began again—slowly, steadily, up the hardwood stairs.

Claire brought her other hand to the grip of the gun and stood across the studio. She faced the door squarely, listening to the hollow sound of the footsteps drawing nearer. They were on the third floor now, coming down the corridor. Only once they'd reached the studio door did they stop.

Claire didn't move.

With her eyes fixed on the door, the gun shaking in her hands, she tried to control her breathing. But when the handle of the studio door turned, Claire drew the gun up farther. Determination steadied the weapon now.

"I have a gun," she called out, amazed at the unexpected control in her voice.

The house fell into utter silence. Claire waited. Her eyes never left the door. The handle stopped moving. A minute ticked by like an hour, until finally Claire heard the quiet tread of footsteps retreating down the stairs.

She didn't move from her stance facing the door. She didn't dare unlock the studio for fear that the withdrawing footsteps had only been her imagination.

And now, with the sounds echoing in her mind, Claire's grasp on the semiautomatic began to loosen again. She lowered the weapon and felt her nerve begin to leave her.

When she heard the front door open, she readied herself to raise the gun again until, with a wave of relief, she heard Michael's voice from downstairs.

"Claire?"

In a minute, the handle of the studio door rattled again.

"Claire? Are you all right? Claire?"

Still holding the semiautomatic in one hand, she ran to the door. She kicked the chair clear and unlatched the door. She was shaking by the time she fell into Michael's arms.

"AND YOU'RE ABSOLUTELY certain that it wasn't just the wind or something?"

"Michael!" Claire pulled away from him. She had already slipped the safety on the gun, and now slammed it down on the wooden tabletop. "I know what I heard! For Christ's sake, I'm not making this up. Listen." She picked up the phone and held it to his ear. "Am I making that up? It's dead!"

"Okay, okay, Claire. I just want to be sure before we go rushing for Bannon."

"Michael, I'm sure, all right? Someone was in this house, wandering around. I don't know if they were looking for something or if they were after me, but I do know that they were certainly interested in getting in here."

"And then they went back downstairs?"

Claire nodded. She'd already been through it all with him once. "Yes, then they went downstairs. And no, I didn't hear the back door close. But how else would they have gotten out if you didn't see anyone?"

"All right, listen, Claire. Why don't we just go downstairs and check the phone line? And then I really think we need to call Bannon."

Once downstairs, Claire turned on all the lights and set a kettle on for tea. He watched her as she took out the teapot and two mugs. Her robe was drawn tightly around her waist, concealing her slender form, and when she turned around, he could see exhaustion and fright etched in her face. For the first time, a feeling of panic gripped Michael as well.

The thought of Claire's safety being threatened—her life even—twisted something deep within him. Something dark and desperate.

Since that night when he'd held her close and shared her sorrow, he recognized the feelings that stirred within him. And then, when they had made love the first time in front of the fire, he knew that he needed Claire—not just wanted her, but truly needed her. She brought something to him, something he hadn't really known he'd missed, something he was no longer certain he could do without.

And looking at her standing in the middle of the kitchen in her robe, remembering the shock of seeing the gun she'd held so casually in her hand, Michael knew that he could not bear to lose her.

"Do you want some tea?" Claire's voice broke through his thoughts.

"Yes, please," he answered, turning to the box above the kitchen telephone. It was here that the main phone line came into the house, and it took only one glance for Michael to see that it had been disconnected.

"Has it been cut?" Claire came up behind him and placed a hand on his back.

Michael shook his head. "Only unplugged. See?" He heard the satisfying snap of the jack as he clicked it back in. "I'm going to call Bannon now."

While the sheriff's line was ringing, Michael promised himself that he would convince Claire to move to his house. The security was better there. And he could keep an eye on her.

"Westport Sheriff's Station," the voice on the other end of the line answered.

"Hello, Wesley? This is Michael Dalton."

"Oh, good evening, Mr. Dalton."

"Is Sheriff Bannon around?"

"Uh, no. Sorry. I think he's gone home. I can ring 'im there if you want."

"I'm afraid you'll have to, Wesley. I'm calling from the Bramley house. There's been another intruder."

CHAPTER FIFTEEN

TWENTY-FIVE MINUTES LATER Claire and Michael saw the headlights of Bannon's patrol car as it swung in alongside the house.

The hand on the kitchen-stove clock had crawled past eleven, and Claire had seen no sense in getting dressed at this hour. She sat at the kitchen table, wrapped in her thick robe, with her knees tucked under her chin, waiting. Now, as the car's engine stopped, she joined Michael at the door.

Bannon heaved his large frame from the cruiser, pushed the door closed and sauntered across the drive. As he kicked the snow from his boots at the top step, Claire could see the vapor of his breath swirl up and encircle his round face for a split second before the warmth of the kitchen swallowed it up.

"'Evening, Sheriff." Michael nodded and closed the door behind Bannon. When he turned, Claire was surprised at the lines of exhaustion etched in his face.

She drew her robe tighter around her and shivered from the blast of cold air that had slipped through the door. She, too, was feeling the strain of exhaustion and hoped she didn't look as worn out as she felt.

"Mr. Dalton, Ms. Madden," Bannon said, giving them each a cursory smile as he unzipped his uniform parka and wiped his boots on the doormat.

"Would you like some tea, Sheriff?" Claire asked in an attempt to be genial.

"Thanks, but no. Getting too late for me." He blew on his hands and rubbed them together, his rough skin rasping loudly in the silence of the kitchen. "So, Wesley rang. Said you had another break-in?"

Michael looked at Claire before nodding his head.

"I radioed Frank. He should be here shortly."

No sooner had he spoken than the second patrol car pulled up outside. Bannon shook himself free of his parka and sat down.

When Frank entered the kitchen, knocking the snow from his boots and nodding an icy greeting to Michael, Claire remembered the tension she had seen between them before and wondered what it was that had created such a visible antagonism between the two men.

"So what do we have, then?" Frank asked.

Bannon shook his head. "I don't know. What do we have here, Ms. Madden?"

"Someone broke into the house again. Tonight, around ten-thirty."

"You were home?"

"Yes, I was up in the studio working."

"The studio?" Bannon asked, his brows arching together.

"The turret," Michael clarified.

"You were home alone?" Bannon asked.

Claire nodded.

"What about your dog?"

Claire looked from Michael to Bannon and shook her head. "My dog? You know about my dog, Sheriff. You've got the evidence sitting on your desk back at the station."

"Ahh, right." He shifted his weight. "So, you were alone up on the third floor, and heard someone come into the house?" He waited for her nod. "And you didn't think that maybe it was Mr. Dalton here?"

"I called out—twice. No one answered."

"Might have just been the wind or something. You know how these old houses are. Full of strange noises."

"There was someone walking around, Sheriff. I heard them going through the rooms." His cynical smirk showed her that he wasn't taking her very seriously. "I know what I heard."

"And you didn't think to phone someone?"

Claire tried to curb the frustration in her voice. "I did, Sheriff. I spoke with Michael's maid for less than thirty seconds before the line went dead."

"It was disconnected," Michael explained. "Someone had pulled the jack where the line comes into the house. We plugged it back in."

Frank shifted his position by the front door, his cool green eyes pinning Michael with an icy stare. "Then I think it's damned obvious that whoever disconnected the jack must have known the house pretty well. Had to know where the main line fed into the box."

Claire couldn't see Bannon's face as he glanced at Frank. Whatever it held, it served to silence the deputy.

"All right then, Ms. Madden, perhaps we should start by getting a rundown of what was stolen."

"Stolen?" Claire shook her head. "Nothing was stolen."

"I'm sorry," Bannon said, clearing his throat. "Did you say nothing was stolen?"

Claire nodded and looked at Michael, hoping for support, but he seemed as lost for words as she was. Why should this be so terribly difficult? Someone broke into

her house, tried to get into her studio, tried to scare her—
or worse—and no one was doing anything about it.
Weren't there laws against someone just walking into your
house in the middle of the night?

"Look, lady," Bannon said finally, "I don't know how
they handle this kinda thing in New York, but I'm afraid
there's nothing we can do for you here. If nothing was
stolen and there was no threat to your life, and—" he
opened the door and checked the frame "—no sign of
forced entry, then there isn't much we can do.

"I'd advise you to get bigger locks. And use 'em. That
is, if you're still convinced that you have an intruder
problem here. But, quite frankly, I'd be more inclined to
think you were just hearing the creaks and groans of this
old place. You'll get used to it in time...if you stay."

Claire was clenching her teeth, her hands balled into
fists. "I know what I heard, Sheriff." She felt Michael's
hand on her shoulder.

"If it'll make you feel any better," Bannon said, pausing to take his cigar from his breast pocket and starting to
chew on the end, "we'll look around. Frank, why don't
you go check out the back door. See if you can find anything."

Frank moved through the house, his footsteps hollow
against the hardwood floors.

"Did you see a car or anything come up the road before any of this supposedly happened?"

Claire shook her head. "The windows of the turret are
covered with snow right now. I can't see much of anything through them."

"And did you see anyone leave, Mr. Dalton, when you
arrived?"

"No."

"Did you have the doors chained?"

Claire shook her head again. "Michael was returning within the hour. He locked up on his way out, but we didn't chain the doors, no."

Still chewing on the end of his cigar, Bannon reached back and pulled a wallet from his pants' pocket. He opened it and fumbled through its contents until he drew out a green credit card. Wordlessly, he turned, opened the door, swiveled the lock and shut the door behind him.

Claire heard several muffled scraping sounds, and after a moment, Raymond Bannon stepped in through the unlocked door.

"No problem. Little bit of practice and anyone can get through the old locks you have on these doors. That's what the chains are for. Did you have the lights on?"

"No. Only upstairs." She turned as Frank came back into the kitchen, and felt Michael's grip on her shoulder tighten.

"Nothing, Sheriff. Everything looks fine. Tight as a drum."

Bannon took the cigar from the corner of his mouth, turning it in his fingers thoughtfully. "Well, Ms. Madden, all I can say is, if you're still determined to believe that there really was someone in this house tonight, you're probably lookin' at another case of some kids lurking about. Lights off, door unchained. They probably figured no one was home."

"I called out Michael's name. Twice. You're telling me that they were deaf, too?"

She was about to relate how the intruder had been able to hear her say she had a gun, but thought better of making the admission. She didn't need Bannon slapping her with a charge for possession of an out-of-state weapon and lose the single self-defense tool she possessed.

"Look, Ms. Madden, I wish I could help you. But there's nothing for us to do here. As I said before, without anything being stolen or broken...well, there's nothing to investigate."

"Trespassing?" Claire offered.

"Can't prove it. Besides, it looks more like you left the door unlocked. Maybe even invited the guy in yourself. I'm saying this only in terms of writing up a report, you understand."

Claire took a deep breath and pulled away from Michael's grip to take a step toward Bannon. "So, let me see if I'm getting any of this straight. What you're telling me, Sheriff, is that if you had to come up here with a body bag, like you did for my aunt, only *then* you would have something to investigate? Is that—"

"Claire," Michael cut in softly.

She twisted her arm from his grasp. "No, Michael. I want to know what it's going to take before someone starts believing me around here." She could feel her face flush with anger.

"Now, just relax, Claire," he whispered. "I'll take care of this, okay?"

Claire hitched the knot of her robe tighter and crossed her arms over her chest, as she watched Michael approach the sheriff. When Bannon spoke again it was in a loud whisper, as if he thought she might not hear them.

"All right, Dalton. I don't know what's going on here, but you should know better than to drag me and one of my deputies out here in the middle of the damned night without good reason. I am not about to waste my time reassuring your lady friend here that no one is trying to kill her. I would have expected that you, of all people, would have had more sense. You know how these old houses make all kinds of noises."

"Sheriff, trust me, I realize the hour. But I believe Claire when she says she heard someone tonight. Now, I don't care what you and your deputy are willing to believe. I don't even care if you don't do anything about this incident. But what I do care about, as a tax-paying resident of Westport, is the safety of the members of this community. And since Ms. Madden is now a resident of Westport and her taxes are paying *your* wages, I think you might be just a *little* more concerned with her safety."

Claire watched Michael's profile. She saw the squint of his eyes as he stared Raymond Bannon down and she saw the muscle along his jaw flex sharply.

And then she saw a fiercer anger flare up in Frank's eyes, a hostility that had been seething somewhere deep inside the deputy from the moment he'd set foot in the Bramley house. "Just where do you get off lecturing us on protection, Dalton?" he spat out.

"Take it easy, Frank," Bannon said.

But the deputy didn't listen. He took a step closer to Michael. "And where the hell were you tonight, huh? No, don't bother. Probably don't have an alibi again. Just like with Annette Hobson. And Ms. Bramley. What were you doing over here anyway, Dalton? Trying to add a third name to the list?"

"Easy, Frank," Bannon warned him again.

"I just want you to know, Dalton, I'm keeping my eye on you. You're not clear, you know. We may not have anything on you yet, but one wrong move and I'll have you on both counts, as well as harassment—"

"Frank! That's enough." Sheriff Bannon's face was flushed with anger now, but Claire didn't notice.

She was staring at Michael, staring at the only man she had thought she could trust.

Frank's words echoed through her mind.

Even after Bannon had apologized for the scene and mumbled something about giving them a call, Frank's accusations clouded her thoughts as she measured the significance of his allegations.

When the door closed behind them, she stared at Michael. He stood against the door with his back to her and only after a long moment did he turn to face her.

RAYMOND BANNON PULLED up the zipper of his parka when he reached his patrol car. With one gloved hand he brushed the freshly fallen snow off the windshield and with the other he grabbed Frank's arm.

"Don't you ever do that to me again, you hear?"

Frank stopped, his coat open, his lips tightly pursed. "Ray—"

"I don't want to hear it, Frank. You messed up in there. Don't ever threaten someone openly like that again, you hear me? Not while you're under my supervision. I don't care if he's a suspect or not."

"But, Ray—"

"No. You just keep that hot-tempered mouth of yours shut for one minute and listen to me for a change. Now look, I'm only four months from retirement here and I'm not going to have you mess things up for me, Turner. You've been whining about taking over my position ever since you came to Westport and I've been more than obliging. I've done everything I can to show you the ropes. I gave you this Bramley case because I thought you should learn how to handle your own investigation. I was trying to give you a break. But if you don't start cooling it, I'm going to have to reassign the case to Wesley. And I know you wouldn't want that." Bannon paused, then added in a more conciliatory tone, "You have to relax about this, all right? We don't have anything on Dalton and we won't *get* anything if you keep on harassing him like that."

"I just don't trust the man, Ray."

"Yeah? Well, you're going to have to get over that one pretty damned fast if you want to get anywhere with this." He opened the door of his cruiser, its interior light spilling out onto the snow-covered ground. "Now, let's get the hell out of here. I'm freezing."

"YOU TOLD ME the sheriff's office had no suspects." Claire fought to control the shakiness in her voice. She kept her eyes on Michael.

He took a step toward her. "Claire—"

"You said they thought it was some drifter, an outsider. You never told me *you* were their only suspect."

He came toward her, one hand extended. His eyes seemed to plead for her to understand. "Claire, please, let me explain." He took her hand in his, but she pulled away as quickly as if his fingers were burning metal.

"No, Michael. Please. Don't touch me." She backed away from him until her hips were pressed against the kitchen cupboards. She clutched the collar of her robe and pulled it tighter around her neck.

How could she have been so gullible? How could she have entrusted her life, and Decker's, to a man she had known for only a few short weeks? And hadn't Frank done his share in trying to warn her? "Hate to see a woman like you get messed up with a guy like Dalton." Weren't those Frank's very words?

And hadn't he also mentioned something about why Michael was really in Westport? Something about "the real reason" he'd left New York?

"Claire, let me explain."

"Why *did* you leave New York, Michael?" Claire's voice was cold and hard as it cut across the distance between them, and she realized that if she didn't sustain her anger, she would shatter from the pain.

"What?" Michael's face was a composite of confusion and hurt.

But not the incredible hurt that she was feeling, Claire thought as she held his cold gray eyes, watching them plead with her. No, he was not feeling the pain she was now. Not the humiliation, not the sense of betrayal.

"Why did you *really* leave New York, Michael?" she repeated.

Michael stared at her from the middle of the kitchen, his hands hanging by his side. His entire body seemed about to collapse, until finally he reached over and pulled out a chair for himself.

"Claire, I don't see how my reasons for coming to Westport have any bearing on—"

"Look, Michael. I just want to know. I want to know the truth. I obviously haven't been told the entire truth about everything else that's going on."

"It's nothing, sweetheart. Really."

"Frank didn't seem to think so."

"Frank Turner. Is that what this is all about? Frank Turner? Can't you see the guy has it in for me? He'll say anything to get you to believe the worst about me so that he can move in on you himself. God, Claire, trust me."

"I did trust you, Michael. Perhaps too quickly. Now I'm not sure I trust anyone." Such a simple statement. No disguised messages, no hidden meanings. And yet it had taken every fiber of Claire's courage to say it.

"All right, Claire. You want to know why I left New York? You want to know what Frank Turner seems to think is such a big scandal?" He took a deep breath. "I went into partnership with the wrong person—that's what the scandal was all about. We were both ambitious to get ahead. But he took a shortcut and was charged with insider trading. I was acquitted on paper, but it was difficult not to be tarred by the same brush. I lost a lot of business. Some of my best clients wouldn't return my phone calls—that sort of thing. Seemed like it was time to get out. My partner was being sent to one of those country-club prisons and decided to spend one last night with my wife. By then, even I knew it was time to cut my losses. There certainly wasn't any reason for staying."

Claire remained silent.

"But this has absolutely nothing to do with what is going on here tonight. I wasn't trying to keep my past a secret from you, Claire. There just hasn't been any reason to tell you until now."

"So what about tonight, Michael? What about the things Frank said?"

"Do you really believe any of what he said?"

"I didn't see Bannon denying his allegations."

Claire felt the hard edge of the counter cutting into her back. She wanted to sit down, but didn't dare go near Michael. She needed her distance now.

"All right." Michael took a deep breath and seemed to gather his strength before going on. "I knew Annette Hobson. I tutored her a year ago, over a six-month period. Her mother asked me. Annette was having problems in school, she also didn't have a father and Nora Hobson thought I might be a good influence on her daughter. I did what I could for the girl, but eventually I got too busy with my work and then this house.

"Annette still came to visit me sometimes. She visited me the afternoon she was killed. It was after school. I wanted to drive her home, but she insisted on walking. It was a couple of hours before dark and still pretty warm for January. So I let her go. How could I have possibly imagined that she would have gone anywhere but home?

"Obviously, when Bannon and Turner found out that I was the last person to see her alive, other than her killer, they started questioning me. I had stayed in that night working. I had absolutely no alibi. But, fortunately, those bumbling idiots haven't found anything that might be construed as evidence against me or I would have been hauled in long ago."

"So why are they still after you, if they haven't found anything?"

"Claire, they've got to pin this on someone. Bannon's only a few months away from retirement and Frank's up for his job. Bannon doesn't want something like this hanging over his head when he leaves, and Frank isn't a likely candidate for the position if he can't bring in the person responsible for Annette's murder."

Too many thoughts raced through Claire's head. Too many jumbled emotions. She felt herself beginning to weaken under the strain of the day's events—the desperate search for Decker, the scare of the break-in and now discovering the sheriff's suspicion of the man she thought she knew and trusted. The man she thought she loved. And yet she found herself struggling with the urge to go to him. To fall into his arms. To plunge into the sanctuary of his embrace.

"Listen to me, Claire," he whispered. "I'm going to be straight with you, and I can only pray that you will hear the truth in what I'm going to tell you. Because, of all the things I want you to know, I want you to understand that I never, ever, intended to hurt you. Claire, I…" He let out a long sigh and buried his face in his hands for a moment before going on. "It's not supposed to happen this way.

I'm not supposed to be telling you this in the same breath
with which I'm defending myself to you, but, Claire, I
love you. And you have to believe me that I truly never
meant to hurt you. You have to know this. Yes, I guess I
did lie to you in a sense. When you first arrived in Westport, I told you that I wanted to finish the house because
of Estelle. That was only a partial truth. There were other
reasons as well for working on the house.

"I needed access to Estelle's things. I needed to prove
my innocence, just in case Bannon or Turner did concoct
something that might falsely implicate me. And I wanted
to find the person who had killed Estelle. She didn't de-
serve to die the way she did.

"I know she had to have seen something, Claire. She
was too nervous whenever I brought up the subject,
whenever Annette's name even came up. I continued to
work on the house, in spite of your initial protests so that
I could look for the proof I needed.

"I can only hope that it's in her journals, Claire.
You've read through bits of one of them yourself. You
know she wrote everything in them. That's all she did all
day—stare out the windows of the turret and write. I
continued to work on the house in the hope that I might
find the last journal that Estelle wrote in before she died."

But Claire was only half listening now. In her mind she
played back the past week. She had bared her soul to Michael. She had shared her pain, let go of her past for him,
allowed herself to believe in his love for her. They had
made passionate love together. Had all of this been a ploy
as well? Had Michael feigned a desire for her, whispered
sweet promises to her, made love with her, for the sole
purpose of searching for Estelle's journals? Had she been
so blind, so naive, that she hadn't even seen through his
facade?

Claire felt the stinging heat of a tear on her cheek. She wiped it away quickly, hoping that Michael hadn't seen. "And I suppose you thought that by sleeping with me you'd be absolutely assured of getting the journals."

"Claire, no!" Michael stood up suddenly, his chair almost crashing to the kitchen floor. "Please, you can't think that for a minute." And then he was closing the gap between them, his arms reaching for her.

But Claire was ready for him. Before he could slip his arms around her, before she could foolishly fall for his false comfort again, she put a hand against his chest and stopped him. The heat of his skin through the soft cotton of his shirt, the familiar ripple of muscle, sent a jolt of hollow pain through her now.

She drew away from him.

"I think you should leave, Michael," she said quietly, her voice calm and distant.

"Claire, please," he pleaded. "Let's talk about this."

"We've talked enough, Michael. I think you should go."

"Claire—"

And then it was Claire who was pleading, her voice beginning to tremble as she fought back the tears that had been choked off for too long now. "Please, Michael—don't make this any harder."

She wasn't certain how long it was that he stood there, no more than three feet away, holding her stare—his eyes boring into hers, glistening with unshed tears. But she knew that if he'd stayed a second longer she could not have maintained her composure.

After a minute that seemed more like an hour, he nodded and turned. Silently, he reached for his coat and opened the door. He looked back once as he paused in the doorway, but Claire did not meet his gaze. Instead, she stared down at the pattern of the kitchen tiles.

Only when she heard the door close behind him and the roar of the Land Rover's engine fade into the distance did she move.

She sank to the floor, her back braced against the cupboards, her face buried in her hands, and cried.

CHAPTER SIXTEEN

CLAIRE TOSSED her paintbrush into the jar on the table next to her. Drops of turpentine splashed out onto her jeans and she grabbed a rag to wipe them, swearing to herself as she did. Nothing was working, she thought angrily as she rubbed the rag against the faded denim.

She stared at the canvas in front of her. She had been trying too hard. For more than two days she had tried to rescue the painting from the murkiness that had enveloped it, but she had only succeeded in further smothering the light of the original idea.

She tilted her head to one side, as if this would allow her a fresher perspective, but the same muddied darkness stared back at her. She let out a long sigh of defeat and picked up the brush again to begin cleaning it. She had hoped to avoid starting the next blank canvas as long as possible, but she knew now that there was no point in delaying it.

A rumble from her stomach reminded her that, other than the endless flow of black coffee, she hadn't eaten in some time. It had been a long four days. Days of painting that had stretched through the darkest hours of night into the early rays of morning. Hours of work that she welcomed as an escape from everything around her. She hadn't wanted thoughts of Michael or Estelle or even Westport to crowd her mind. She hadn't wanted to think about the investigation or Estelle's diaries, because these would only remind her of Michael—remind her of how naive she had been. But even the long hours of painting had done little to banish Michael from her thoughts.

For four days she had neither left the house nor answered the phone. And for the first two days it had rung every couple of hours. Yesterday it rang only three times and today it had remained strangely silent.

But even without the phone ringing, Claire was still haunted by Michael. Everywhere she turned she was reminded of his presence. There were the personal belongings that he had left in the house—his razor, a toothbrush, his after-shave in the bathroom and some clothes in the bedroom. Even though she realized the futility of her actions, Claire had taken Michael's things from the bathroom counter and hidden them under the sink. But the memories persisted.

And she blamed them for the darkness that had returned to her paintings.

Lowering herself from the stool, Claire crossed the studio and looked out the window. The weather had been brilliant for several days now, but she hadn't really paid it much attention. Sunlight glared off sparkling snow, and she squinted now as she scanned the side of the house for Decker.

He was there, at the edge of the driveway. He limped a few steps and stopped, stared out across the fields, perhaps remembering the nightmare of the storm, and sat down. He wasn't wandering far these days, Claire thought, feeling a mild chill pass through her. She stepped back from the cold window and rubbed her arms.

The furnace had been acting up again, but only once had she dared to venture down into that dark hole of a basement to check on it. She had knocked the furnace a couple of times with the palm of her hand, fiddled with some switches and spoken a silent prayer to the oversize metal god. And now, even though the beast hadn't quit entirely, the temperature in the house fluctuated at the furnace's whim.

Claire set down her paintbrush. She was about to turn away from the table when her eye caught the gleam of the gun nestled among tubes of paint and her sketchbooks. In spite of her preoccupation with Michael, she had not forgotten the scare of the other night and kept the semi-automatic with her in the studio.

She shivered again and finally turned from the table to walk down the corridor in search of a sweater.

Her bedroom confirmed the fact that she had done little else but paint for the past four days. The few clothes that she had changed out of lay where they had fallen, the sheets and covers on the four-poster bed twisted in a tangled mass—the same sheets she had shared with Michael only a few days ago. She had still been able to smell traces of him the few times she had gone to bed and had been oddly reluctant to change the bedding.

Giving herself a mental shake, Claire pulled a sweater from the mound of clothes covering the pine chest at the foot of the bed. It wasn't until she pulled the garment over her head that she realized it was one of Michael's. She savored the faded hint of his after-shave on the ribbed collar and wrapped herself in the intimate warmth of its comfort.

She did miss Michael. She couldn't deny that. She missed everything about him, but at the same time couldn't ignore the doubts that preyed on her mind.

Claire jumped when the phone by the bedside rang.

She did not answer it. Instead, she headed back to the studio and picked up her sketchbook. And as the empty

ringing echoed through the silence of the house, she lifted
her pencil and started drawing.

MICHAEL LISTENED to the hollow rings, imagining Claire
sitting in her studio ignoring them, until he finally replaced the receiver in its cradle. He leaned back in the
leather chair behind the sprawling oak desk in his study
and stared at the phone.

He had tried to reach her for four days now, with no
success. He had seen the lights of her studio across the
fields, burning well into the night. Even last night, when
he had finally been able to go to sleep, he had taken one
last glance over the expanse of moonlit snow and seen the
lights, imagining her moving about, working on her
paintings. That had been two o'clock this morning.

And when he'd woken up at six, well before daylight,
the studio lights were still on. It looked as though she'd
gotten into the habit of leaving several lights on throughout the house since the latest break-in, and he had taken
comfort in her apparent caution.

Bannon had called two days ago, asking him why no
one had been answering the phone at the Bramley house,
and Michael had told him something about Claire being
extremely busy these days. So the sheriff had asked him
to inform Ms. Madden that the trap could not be traced.
He had been unable to turn up anything on possible trapping along the bluffs and suggested that Michael tell her
to keep a tighter rein on her dog from now on.

But Michael knew that after what Decker had been
through, it would be a long time before the retriever regained an appetite for wandering afar.

He also had the assurance that, with Decker in the
house and with the gun he had seen Claire wield the other
night, she would be well protected. Yet he could not quell

the urge to go over to her house, to be sure she was all right.

Then again, he knew that she was fine. Hadn't he driven past several times during the last three days and seen movement around the house? Hadn't he slowed down enough to see that Decker had been out and the garbage taken to the end of the drive? Still he could not get over the longing to see Claire again.

Over and over, her words tore through his mind. Over and over, he replayed their final scene. He remembered the tears in her eyes, the pain that had clouded her face when she suggested he had been using her to get to the journals.

What hurt him the most, though, was not being able to touch her, not being able to hold her in his arms and explain to her how he hadn't been thinking about the journals since the night they had first gone to dinner. He wanted her to know that there had been only one thing on his mind from the first time they had made love. He wanted to tell her how he had fallen so completely in love with her that, from that moment, he had forgotten all else.

But the opportunity hadn't been there, and for four days he rehearsed in his mind how he would tell her all these things and more. How he would tell her that he wanted to be with her, that he needed to be with her. That not being able to see her hurt more than anything had ever hurt before.

He stood up from his chair and paced the length of the room. He couldn't keep this up—the silence, the separation. He stopped at the window and held back the blind to stare out at the house across the fields. No, he couldn't lose the only thing that seemed right in his life. He had to see her.

"Why don't you just go over there, Michael?"

He started. The blind snapped back into place as he turned to the door of the study. He had no idea how long Dee had been standing there watching him, but now she crossed the room. She flipped a lock of red hair back over her shoulder and gave him her warmest smile.

"All you have to do is go over there and explain everything to her."

"I'm afraid it's not that easy, Dee." He let out a long breath. "I screwed up. I really hurt her and I wouldn't be surprised if she doesn't want to talk to me again." He buried his hands in his pockets. "At least not for some time."

He looked over the files on his desk, at the pile of computer disks, spiral-bound presentations, reports and financial statements. There was still a small circle of companies and individual clients who had remained loyal to Michael despite all the trouble. He owed them his best advice. He sat down and opened the next manila folder. They had far too much work to do before Dee caught the evening flight out of Bangor.

Dee's presence in the house for the past day and a half had helped a little to take Michael's mind off of Claire. If it hadn't been for Dee, he surely would have gone over to see her by now.

"You have to at least try, Michael. You know that you're only widening the distance between the two of you the longer you stay away. Maybe you're right, maybe she is hurt, but you can still go over there. You've got to make a move before it's too late and the damage is irreparable." She edged close to his desk, took up her usual position on the corner. "Don't worry about this stuff." She waved her hand over the files covering his desk. "I can easily work on these on my own for the next hour."

Michael hesitated and then stood up, placing a quick kiss on Dee's cheek. "All right, I'm going. I'll be back soon."

When he drove up to Claire's house a few minutes later, he had come to the decision that even if she refused to see him, he could at least spend some time clearing up his tools and gathering the bits of trim he'd left in the hallway when he'd last been working. If nothing else, being in the same house with Claire would be a change from the hollow emptiness that consumed him when he was away from her.

Shoving the Land Rover's door shut, Michael looked up at the house. There didn't appear to be any movement and he guessed that Claire hadn't heard him arrive. And then, from around the side of the house, came the tinkling of Decker's tags. Michael squatted down to meet the excited retriever as the dog attempted a lurching trot. A canine grin spread across the animal's lips and Michael could not stifle a smile himself.

After petting the dog for a few minutes, Michael knocked on the side door. After the third try, he used his keys and stepped into the kitchen. Decker, favoring his front leg, trotted ahead of him toward the stairs, pausing only once to make sure Michael was following.

"Claire?"

She didn't answer. Michael heard the music from her stereo as he reached the bottom of the stairs. He called again and started to climb to the second landing.

She must have heard him then, because when Michael reached the second landing and looked up, she was there—leaning against the railing of the top floor, the light from the studio windows flooding into the hallway behind her. Even with the harsh backlighting of the studio, Michael could see the exhaustion etched in her face.

His heart stopped, as he stared up at her. He swallowed hard. "I—I knocked. I guess you didn't hear me."

Claire only shook her head.

"I just wanted to clear up the rest of the trim down here," he lied. Why couldn't he tell her the truth? Why couldn't he tell her that he had come to see her, that he wanted to hold her, to feel her lips on his, to know that it would take more than a misunderstanding to separate them? "I shouldn't be more than an hour and then...I'll be out of your way."

"Fine." Her voice still held the same cool distance it had the other night. But Michael couldn't help thinking that a part of her wanted to say more as she stood by the railing above him.

God, he missed her. The sun from the studio played on the golden highlights of her hair, and her eyes, large and dark, devoured him as he stared up at her. He felt his body cry out for her as he remembered the tingle of her skin against his, the heat of her lips and the soft brush of her fingers, the whisper of her voice and the sound of her quiet moans when they had made love. More than anything, Michael wanted to bound up the stairs to the third floor, take her into his arms and tell her how he had never meant to hurt her, how he loved her and couldn't live without her.

But instead he just stood there, staring up at her. Only when she was about to push away from the railing did he dare to speak. "Claire?"

She paused, lifting a hand to brush back the hair that had fallen across her cheek. She looked pale and drawn.

"Are you all right?"

She nodded slowly, taking a breath before answering. "Yes, Michael. I'm fine." And then she turned from the railing.

Michael watched her back as she retreated into the studio and eventually closed the door behind her. He listened to her move around in the studio until the sound of her stereo drowned out everything else.

In his heart, he wasn't sure he could ever break through Claire's pain again.

CLAIRE DID NOT HEAR Michael leave later that afternoon. But now, as she took a break from her painting, she saw that the Land Rover was no longer in the drive. She leaned against the window frame and stared out at the empty driveway.

She had turned up her stereo earlier for several reasons. She hadn't wanted to hear Michael downstairs, she hadn't wanted to know how near he was to her and she hadn't wanted to be tempted to go down and see him. But most of all, Claire had not wanted Michael to hear her crying.

After she had left him standing on the landing and had closed the studio door behind her, she had collapsed in the large chair by the window. It had taken everything she had to maintain her outward composure, and the moment she turned her back on him she had felt anguish wash over her again.

Looking across the fields in the direction of Michael's house, Claire watched the sun set behind several low rows of clouds. It would be dark soon and she guessed that perhaps tonight she would be able to sleep.

She turned to study the canvas she had started earlier and hoped that she could maintain the freshness she had finally been able to create there. It was a good thing Alec wasn't in Westport now, she thought. Or better yet, that she wasn't in New York. Seeing the familiar darkness invade her paintings again was more than enough pressure for the moment. The last thing she needed was Alec hovering over her, reminding her of the impending deadline. All of a sudden two weeks seemed like no time at all.

It wasn't until Decker nudged his way into the studio that Claire finally looked away from her canvas. Smiling, she watched the retriever hobble across the drop cloths to the chair by the window. She knew what he was up to even before he managed to drag himself onto the chair's ample cushion. And she wasn't about to scold him until she saw the paint he smeared across the faded fabric.

"Oh, Decker," she complained, lifting his paws to clean them with a rag. "You gotta watch where you're treading around here. I thought you would have figured that out by now, you crazy mutt."

After struggling to lift the dog from the chair, Claire tried to rub the paint off the worn cushion. The cushion sagged beneath the pressure she applied, but the paint only spread deeper into the cloth. Realizing that it was going to take more than a cursory wipe, Claire pulled the cushion out, intending to turn it.

What she saw then made her stop. Wedged solidly along the back of the chair, behind the seat, was the black cover of one of Estelle's journals.

With one hand still scratching Decker's head, Claire pulled the book from its resting spot with a firm yank. She turned it over in her hands, noting that although it was bent out of shape, it looked newer than the first one she had found.

Tucking the journal under her arm, Claire finished straightening the old chair and fell back into its contours. Darkness had already begun to slip over the white expanse of the fields, and through it Claire saw the lights from Michael's house. She wondered if this might be the journal Michael had been searching for.

In the warm light of the floor lamp beside her, with Decker's chin resting on her knee, Claire opened the volume.

Estelle's elegant handwriting carried Claire from one page to the next. But as much as she craved the time to cherish every vivid and picturesque detail, she was driven by Michael's words.

He believed not only that Estelle might have seen something, but that she might have actually written about it in one of her journals. Fueled by the hope that this was the one, Claire forged ahead. Without any dated headings to guide her, she skipped over entire sections until she had almost completed it.

It was in the last ten pages that the handwriting became more scrawled, more jagged, and Claire had to struggle to make out the words.

It was definitely January. She'd passed over the section in which Estelle described her quiet Christmas with Michael and she'd picked up on the hints of the New Year.

And then, in a breathless glance, Claire saw it at last. Annette Hobson's name.

She brought the book closer to the light, straining to decipher the shaky handwriting that scrawled across the last few pages of the journal.

"... and I must remind myself to ask Michael about some new locks for the doors. I know he will think I am crazy for wanting them, but I shall tell him that it is on account of the Hobson girl going missing. I hope he will believe me, because I cannot tell him the truth. When he told me yesterday that the poor girl's mother had reported her missing, I wanted to tell him then. I wanted to tell him what I had seen. But I cannot. It is too wicked.

I can still see her from here. From this window, I can still make out the outline of the snow that covers her. She is resting now, but they will not know where to find her. And I must not tell anyone.

He would know it was me, then. He would know that I had seen him.

I am so frightened. I hope that Michael will be able to come over again today. Perhaps I will call him later.''

Claire scanned slowly ahead, her fingers trembling as she traced the words, the writing becoming more and more illegible.

"Sheriff Bannon and his deputy have been up to the house asking questions. They asked me if I've seen anything of the missing girl. I think they believe that Michael may be responsible. Oh, please God, help the boy. And please forgive me for not speaking of what I know. Forgive my cowardice.''

The blare of the telephone startled Claire and she dropped the journal. With a quick gasp, she picked up the book, her heart pounding, and, without thinking, reached for the phone.

"Hello?'' her voice cracked.

"Claire? Is that you?''

"Alec,'' she breathed.

"Are you all right, darling?''

"Yes, Alec. Yes, I'm fine.''

"Are you sure? You don't sound very fine.''

"No, no. I'm okay, really. The phone startled me, that's all."

"Well, what's going on out there? I've been trying to get hold of you for days now. I've been worried sick."

Claire sighed. "I'm sorry, Alec. I wasn't answering the phone. I suppose I should have called. But you know how I get when I'm working," she lied.

"I'll take that as an indication that the paintings are going well?"

"They're . . . coming along."

"Claire, I know what that hesitation means. What's the matter?"

"Nothing, Alec. Absolutely nothing. Now would you just trust me? They're coming along fine. Besides, I still have two weeks left." She could almost see Alec rolling his eyes at her final comment. She knew how much he hated last-minute additions to her shows, but she also knew that he had faith in her—especially when she was under pressure.

"Don't start scaring me, Claire. I mean it. I don't need these surprises. You remember what happened at your last show."

"The last show was fine, Alec. And this one's going to be as well. Now, one more time, trust me."

Alec mumbled something about never trusting an artist, especially an artist in love, but Claire wasn't really listening. Her eyes hadn't left the black journal on the chair by the window.

"So how's Michael these days?"

The mention of his name drew her back to the conversation and Claire looked around the darkened studio, feeling the silence and emptiness again. "He's fine, Alec. Michael's fine. Listen, I've gotta run."

"What, some heavy date? See, Madden, didn't I tell you you'd like the natives?"

"Yeah, right, Alec. No, nothing of the sort. I happen to be in the middle of something right now."

"Well, as long as it's another painting—"

"I'm working on it as we speak. I'll talk to you later."

"All right then. Take care, Claire. And my love to Decker, you hear?"

"Right, Alec. Good night." No sooner had Claire hung up the phone than she was back in the chair under the lamp. She opened the journal and flipped through the pages again until she had reached the last one.

"But I cannot tell Michael. If I were to tell him, it would mean certain jeopardy for him. I will not put his life in danger as well. It is my secret. And I alone must carry the burden.

I can only pray, for the sake of the poor girl's mother, that tomorrow I may feel differently. Perhaps the Lord will give me the courage to speak then. Perhaps even through my journals will I be able to tell of what I know. But, for now, I shall remain silent. I must learn to live with my secret so that I, alone, may die with it."

A quiet desperation gripped Claire as she turned the crisp leaf, hoping that it wasn't, but knowing full well that it was the last page of the journal.

She stared again at the final entry. Despite Estelle's melodramatic writing, Claire felt a chill from her words.

She closed the small book in her lap and looked up. Through her own reflection in the studio window she looked toward Michael's place. And as the silence of the studio rang in her ears, she watched the lights across the fields flicker behind the swaying stand of firs.

CHAPTER SEVENTEEN

DECKER'S WHINE pulled Claire from her thoughts. The journal lay closed in her lap, her hand resting on its cover. Other than the soft glow from the floor lamp behind her, the studio had fallen into darkness.

She looked away from the window, uncertain of how long she had been sitting there, watching the lights across the fields, thinking about Michael. However long she had sat in the big armchair, it had been long enough. Long enough for her to replay the time she'd spent with Michael and long enough for her to realize that, if she had to trust anyone now, it would be him.

He needed the journal she held in her hands. It was the closest thing to proof they had of Michael's innocence. But then, it wasn't really his innocence that Claire had been questioning for four days.

Still, she would have to put her doubts aside for the time being. She could not second-guess his reasons for sleeping with her right now. Regardless of what had gone on between them during the past couple of weeks, he had a right to the journal that lay in her lap.

The thought of searching for a subsequent journal hadn't escaped Claire's consideration. She had cast a probing eye around the darkened studio, wondering where Estelle might have hidden one, but that was as far as she had carried the thought.

Despite Decker's calmness, her own nerves were on edge. Perhaps it was from being in the house for four days straight or perhaps it was the ominous note on which the journal had ended, but Claire was overcome with the urge to leave. Briefly, she considered calling Michael, but when she was forced to cross the dark studio to turn on the light switch, a chill ran through her and she knew that she had to get out.

Fifteen minutes later, when she pulled into Michael's driveway, Claire was still feeling a twinge of nervousness, but now it was coupled with the apprehension of seeing him again.

Decker at her side, she approached the front door. With one mittened hand, she clutched the warped journal tucked under her arm and with the other held Decker's collar. She rang the bell. Within a few moments sharp footsteps approached and the door was opened.

"Good evening, Ms. Claire," Greta said, ushering her in. "What a cold night for you to be out. Is everything all right?"

"Everything's fine, Greta." Claire smiled in an attempt to reassure the woman. As the maid took her coat, she realized she was still wearing Michael's sweater.

Greta wordlessly ushered her toward the study. She could hear a woman's laughter above Michael's own, and recognized the other voice immediately. As she walked through the study doors, she already envisioned Dee perched on the corner of Michael's desk.

Just as she had pictured, Dee was seated on the edge of the oak desk, her long legs stretching to the floor, her red hair shimmering.

Decker pulled at his collar by Claire's side, his tail wagging, but she held him back.

"I'm sorry," Claire said quietly as she stood framed in the doorway. "I didn't mean to interrupt. I'll come back—"

"No, Claire. It's all right." Michael stood up and stepped around the desk toward her. When he placed his hand on her arm to guide her back into the hall, Claire tried to ignore the desire that shivered through her.

"Please, Claire, stay." He put his hands over her shoulders, turning her to face him. His touch alone conjured up too many memories, and Claire gripped the journal under her arm more fiercely.

Looking up into his face, she remembered the sound of his laughter from only a moment ago. How could she have been so foolish to think that just because she was lonely and thinking of him, he was also thinking of her? How could she have thought he would have missed her as much as she had missed him—missed his sawing and hammering, his company at the house, his voice, his laughter and most of all his touch.

"I should go. I'm interrupting."

"No, Claire, please. Please stay." His voice was no more than a whisper in the quiet hallway. "I want to see you. We're just finishing up."

Through the open doorway to the study, Claire saw Dee push away from the corner of the desk and begin gathering files and documents into her briefcase.

"Can you wait for one minute? Please?"

Slowly, she nodded her head. "All right. I'll wait."

"Thank you, Claire." Michael's face broke into a smile and he nodded toward the living room. "Make yourself comfortable. I promise I'll only be a minute."

A low fire flickered in the massive stone hearth, and as Claire eased herself down onto the leather couch, she felt the warmth of the dancing flames.

She would stay only long enough to give him the journal. He could keep it and then she would be on her way—back to the solitude of her house and the studio. Back to the waiting canvases. And when the two weeks were over, when the paintings were completed and her show about to open, she could pack up the Bramley house, go back to New York, to the Soho apartment that now seemed a world away, and pick up her life where it had left off. She could forget that she had ever known the sleepy little town of Westport. And then she would try to forget that she had ever known Michael Dalton.

Somehow, it sounded a lot easier in theory than she imagined it would be in practice.

Claire stroked Decker's head as he rested his chin in her lap, his brown eyes expectant. The flames in the fireplace faltered briefly, perhaps from a draft in the old house, then regathered their strength and curled around the glowing logs with renewed intensity.

Perhaps she'd even visit her father for a couple of weeks once the show was finished. More than likely, though, he would surprise her by showing up at the opening—he always had in the past. Maybe she would return with him to Paris or Geneva or wherever he was going to be for the next month and take a holiday herself. Maybe then she would be able to leave her memories of Michael behind her, along with the old stone house on the bluffs.

When Michael walked in behind her, Claire started. She stood up from the couch, clutching the journal to her chest, and watched him slide the double mahogany doors shut.

"I didn't mean to interrupt your meeting." Claire spoke softly in the hush of the living room.

The doors met with a quiet thud and Michael turned to face her. "Dee was on her way out anyway. She's catching the nine forty-five back to New York tonight."

Claire watched him cross the room. He wore a light gray turtleneck underneath a dark gray sweater that hugged his hips. His faded jeans were snug enough to remind Claire of the toned physique that rippled beneath the worn denim. And she found herself cursing him for looking so good.

Still, she couldn't forget his laughter, his smile, when she had interrupted him with Dee only moments ago. He hadn't been missing her. Couldn't have been. At least, not from what she had seen.

"Thanks for waiting, Claire." He was standing in front of her now.

"That's all right," she said, clearing her throat. When he didn't make a move to sit down, she looked at the journal clutched in her hand. "Here," she offered, holding it up to him, "I found this. One of Estelle's journals. I—I think you'll want it."

She didn't look up when she felt his hand brush across her cheek. She didn't dare. She knew what his eyes could do to her.

"I missed you, Claire," he said, lifting her chin with strong fingers so that she was forced to look at him.

Her breath quickened as he stared at her, and afraid of what might happen if she held his gaze, Claire pressed the small black book up to Michael's chest. "The journal, Michael?"

His eyes never leaving hers, he took the journal from her grasp and tossed it onto a side table. "I don't care about the journal, Claire," he said, taking hold of her shoulders again with his big hands. "It's you I want."

She didn't pull away when he lowered his mouth to hers. She didn't shrink back when the heat of his lips covered hers, when she tasted the sweetness of his kiss. Instead, she swayed under his spell, her longing pulsing through her with an intensity that frightened her.

When Michael pulled away and stared into her eyes, she recognized the restraint he was exercising. "I've missed you, Claire." He shook his head. His thumb followed the line of her jaw. "These past four days—it's been hell without you. I've missed you so much. I can't sleep at night."

Claire had already seen the exhaustion in the dark lines around his eyes and in the deep furrows across his forehead. She lifted a hand to where his rested on her shoulder and gave it a light squeeze.

"I lie awake every night, trying to think of the words that might convince you of the truth. I keep going over in my head how I might have done things differently. How I should have told you everything before you had the chance to hear it from someone else.... I haven't thought about Estelle's journals in weeks. Not since I met you. You've got to believe me, Claire. There was only one reason I ever had for sleeping with you." He traced her lips with his thumb and Claire longed for the solace of his embrace.

Why was it so easy to believe him? Why was it that every fiber of her being cried out for him? Cried out with renewed faith in his words?

Whatever it was, Claire couldn't deny it. She believed him now.

With all of her heart, she believed Michael when he told her he loved her. Now it was her turn. She wanted to tell him how much she had missed him, how empty her world had been for the past four days and how she had wanted

to run down the stairs this afternoon and fall into his arms
when he'd looked up at her from the second-floor landing.

But she couldn't. His lips eagerly claimed hers again,
and this time Claire responded with a hunger equaled only
by Michael's. With her lips still throbbing from their kiss,
she felt his breath against her cheek and then against her
ear.

"God, I've missed you, Claire," he whispered again.
His lips drifted from one electrifying point to the next,
igniting surges of yearning deeper than any she had
imagined possible. His fingers brushed lightly over her
skin, following the arch of her neck, until they were buried in her silky hair.

Abandoning herself to the rapture of his touch, Claire
drew closer to him. She longed to feel his body burning
against hers, ached for the caress of his embrace. She
hadn't been wrong about Michael. She hadn't been blind
and naive. And now the doubts that had clouded her life
for the past four days were driven away as Michael's love
shone through like a long-awaited ray of sunshine after a
dark storm.

"Say something, Claire," he pleaded, pulling back
from her.

As she stared up into his eyes, the glow of the fire lending a warm radiance to his features, Claire swallowed
hard. When she finally spoke, her voice threatened to
break.

"You want me to say something?" She waited for his
nod. "I think I love you, Michael."

She had not uttered those words to anyone in so long
that she had thought herself incapable of voicing them
again. Yet she had said them. And she knew, with the

certainty of day and night, that she meant them with all of her heart.

"Oh, God, I love you, Claire." His voice was more a moan than a whisper as he lowered her to the supple leather of the couch, his lips claiming hers with the same passion that surged through her own body now.

Her hands found their way beneath his sweater and traveled along the contours of his back, the play of muscles there sending an agonizing thirst quivering through her. She wanted Michael more now than she ever had.

She lifted her sweater over her head, taking her shirt along with it. As he eased her back, Claire felt the smooth coolness of the leather pressing against her hot skin. She ran her hands up along Michael's jeans-clad thighs, and when she started to work the buckle of his belt, his desire for her already straining against the heavy denim, he pulled away.

"Not here," he whispered. "I want you to share my bed tonight, Claire."

His words sent another wave of longing shuddering through her, and Claire struggled to calm her impatience as he led her through the dark house.

Through the tall cathedral windows, silvery moonlight lit their way up the wide curving staircase to the second floor. Michael held Claire's hand as she followed him down the corridor and, finally, into the master bedroom.

Delicate fingers of light reached through the two sets of French doors that overlooked the ocean in the distance and reached across the floor to the enormous carved-oak bed in the center of the room. Michael didn't turn on the lights. Instead, he led Claire to the bed, lowering her down into the soft bed covers and set about lighting a number of candles around the room.

She watched him move noiselessly, the flicker of the candles sending the room into a whirl of shimmering warmth. Her patience strained to bursting point until he finally approached her. With deft hands he undid her jeans and pulled them from her waist, and only when he had slipped her lace undergarments from her tingling skin did he begin to strip himself.

Claire trembled at the sight of him. The light from the candles danced along his body's contours and she heard a quiet moan escape her own lips when he finally lowered himself onto the bed with her.

"I love you, Claire," Michael said again. But he needn't have told her; she already knew. She already felt it in her heart.

His kisses blazed down her throat to her breasts, his lips sweetly caressing her firm nipples and then flowing along her dampening skin, past the hollow of her stomach to the velvety heat of her inner thighs. Claire opened herself to him, luxuriating in his tenderness and his deep love for her. She wove her fingers through his hair, wanting this to last forever, but wanting more at the same time.

When he had covered every inch of her body with his thirsty kisses, he returned to her lips, swallowing her hunger, devouring her passion, muffling her cries of ecstasy.

This time was different from the rest, she realized. This time she was giving herself entirely to Michael. Nothing beyond him mattered. Nothing was more vital than the circle of their love. He was the only reality she needed now.

Damp with sweat, she twisted, arched, strained her body against his in a delirium of pleasure as he drove her to a depth of passion and desire that she had never before experienced.

Michael, too, felt the change in Claire and within himself. They reached out to each other as if for the first time and he found in Claire's arms an intimacy that he had not thought possible.

As she moved with him, bringing him to the crest of his passion and holding him there until he could withstand the delirious pain no longer, he knew that she had, at last, given herself entirely to him. And he knew, in his heart, that he could never be separated from Claire again.

CHAPTER EIGHTEEN

CLAIRE HAD NO IDEA what time it was when she finally awoke. Sunshine flooded in through the wide slats of the oak shutters, and outside, in the stand of fir trees that bordered the view of the ocean, sparrows chattered incessantly.

Her gaze scanned Michael's bedroom—the polished white-oak flooring echoing the tone of the shutters, the eighteenth-century dressers and chests, the ample duvet covering the bed of the same cream-and-beige material as that draped over the tops of the broad window frames. Everything was so bright and fresh. She felt comfortable here, in the light of Michael's bedroom. But then, she'd felt comfortable in the candlelight as well, Claire thought, smiling to herself.

She didn't move, only pressed her back deeper into the curves of Michael's chest as she felt his arms tighten around her. As if by instinct, he drew her closer to him. Claire wondered if he was still asleep.

They had made love several times through the night, their previous lack of sleep having done little to diminish their renewed hunger for one another. And as the candles had sputtered and died, one by one, they had finally found sleep within the intimacy of their embrace.

"I love you, Claire," Michael whispered.

Love. Could she define it now? Now that she had found the exquisite warmth of Michael's embrace?

If love meant wanting to be with the other person every minute of the day; if it meant feeling whole again, and at the same time rediscovering a self that had been lost; if love meant yearning to be held in his arms forever, then, yes, she did love Michael.

Within their circle of passion, Claire had once again found a special place for herself. She belonged with Michael and he with her. She knew that now. The tenderness and caring he had displayed through their lovemaking last night had reaffirmed what she had been trying to deny for the past few weeks. Now she couldn't imagine what life had been like without him.

As she lay, spent but refreshed, beside him, Claire was reevaluating the plans she had made. She would not take a vacation with her father after the opening of her show, and perhaps she wouldn't return to the Soho apartment and pick up her life from there. And, certainly, she wouldn't be in a rush to forget about Westport, after all.

She ran a finger lazily along Michael's arm and stared at the blue sky past the French doors that led out onto a wraparound balcony. In fact, she thought, maybe she would even talk to Alec about subletting her apartment for a while. Maybe she would put it on the market. It wouldn't be hard to get rid of. And she was already imagining the work that would have to go into packing the place up.

Claire felt the tender brush of Michael's lips against the nape of her neck just before he shifted his body so that his lips were next to her ear. "What are you thinking?" he asked, his breath tickling her lobe.

She lifted his hand to her mouth and placed a gentle kiss in his palm. "I was just thinking that I could really get used to this."

"Hmm, I know what you mean." He groaned, nuzzling her ear until she turned toward him. Using his arm as a pillow, she looked at him, her face only a breath away from his. She ran a finger across his lips, along his jaw and then back through his hair before finally pulling his mouth to hers so that she could kiss him, the heat of his lips igniting pangs of desire throughout her body.

"Well, I suppose that you'd better start getting used to it then, hadn't you?"

"Hmm." He nodded, tasting her lips again. "I don't think it's going to be difficult to learn." He lifted his hand from her waist and brushed back a stray wisp of hair from her forehead. With his fingertips he traced her silky skin and then wandered back to spiral through her hair, while he let his eyes follow the contours of her face until they met hers. He held her gaze with a gentle intensity and she reached out to touch his cheek.

"What is it?" she asked finally, a smile curving her lips.

"Have I ever told you how beautiful you are?"

"Yes, you did. Several times last night."

"Well, then, I'm saying it again. You're beautiful, Claire Madden." He rolled over on top of her, supporting his weight on his elbows as he lowered his mouth to hers. "And you know something else?"

"What's that?"

"I think we should stay right here all day. In fact, what do you say about all week?"

"I think you know my answer."

He looked down at her while she traced his smile with her fingers. "So prove it to me."

"We can't, Michael." Claire heard disappointment in her own voice, and felt it in her heart. "Estelle's journal, remember? We have to look for the last journal. At least you should read the one I brought over. Then I think you'll agree that we really have to find the next one."

He stared down at her as if considering his options and the possibility of even forgetting the journal's existence. "Yes," he said finally, "you're right. I should take a look at it."

Easing himself away from her, Michael draped his legs over the side of the bed and gave her one lingering kiss before standing up. "You'll still be here when I get back?" he asked, pulling on a pair of pajama bottoms.

"Trust me, I'm not going anywhere."

Five minutes later, Claire looked up as Michael padded back into the bedroom. Decker was at his heels, tail wagging, and the journal was open in Michael's hands. He, too, had turned to the back of the book, Claire noticed as he sank onto the bed beside her. He was silent as he flipped through the same passages Claire had read the other night. His only movement was the gentle stroking of her hair while he read.

In time he closed the black book and looked across the bedroom through the French doors. Claire studied his profile, the shadow of his beard lending a rugged quality to the strong angles of his features. And yet there was a remarkable gentleness in his face that made her wonder how anyone could possibly consider him a suspect in a murder investigation.

Her fingers trailed down the muscles in his back. "So, what do you think?"

Michael took a deep breath, set the journal aside and turned to her. His eyes had hardened with a steely determination that Claire hadn't recalled seeing there before and his voice lowered with resolve. "I think you're right. We have to find the next journal."

BANNON LOOKED UP from his desk when Wesley entered
the station accompanied by a gust of cold air. The young
deputy stomped his feet several times on the front mat,
knocking snow from his boots, then removed his uniform parka and hung it on one of the hooks behind the
door. His face was bright red when he turned to Bannon.

"Cold enough out there for you, kid?" The sheriff
smiled as Wesley nodded and blew on his hands.

"And she's only going to get worse, they say. I hear
we're in for a blast by this afternoon. Ice showers and
blizzards. Been one hell of a season, hasn't it?"

"Yeah." Bannon nodded. "I'm not going to be missing this next winter when I'm retired down in Florida, I
can promise you that."

Wesley folded his gloves as he passed Bannon's paper-
strewn desk on the way to his own. File folders and pro-
cedural manuals neatly bordered the deputy's own meticulous desktop. Even his gloves seemed to have a
designated place when he set them next to the "In" tray.
Removing his holster, Wesley sat back in his chair and
began cleaning his gun.

"Well, if you ask me, it's not just the weather that's
gone wicked," he said eventually.

Bannon looked up from his paperwork again to eye his
youngest deputy.

"What do you mean by that, Wes?"

"I mean Westport. Things aren't what they used to be.
It's getting tense, you know? It's not just a matter of
handing out a few speeding tickets to the tourists anymore. It's more than checking vandalism of cottages along
the shore or chasing down some bored delinquents from
Westport High."

"What are you getting at?"

"Nothing, really. Just all of the stuff going on around here lately. What with those two robberies on Main Street last week, and the Hobson girl." He picked up his buffing rag. "You getting anywhere with that, Frank?" Wesley looked over at his fellow deputy, who had been trying to ignore the conversation.

For the better part of the morning, Bannon had watched Frank go through two more of the Bramley journals from the box they had brought down from the house several weeks earlier. The officer had moved from the desk only once, to get a cup of burned coffee. Now, as Wesley prompted him for information, he reluctantly withdrew his nose from the black book.

"What?" He squinted toward Wesley over the top of the journal.

"I was just asking if you'd gotten anywhere with the Hobson thing."

Frank shook his head and closed the book, tossing it back into the box by his desk. "No, Wes. I haven't," he answered coldly, then turned to Bannon. "Ray? You went through some of these before me, didn't you?"

Bannon nodded, his eyes never leaving the papers on his desk.

"And you didn't find anything in them either, did you?"

The sheriff cleared his throat and took another gulp of coffee. "I only glanced at 'em, Frank. I told you before, they're probably not even all there."

"Well, then, maybe we should start thinking about finding the rest of them."

Bannon put down his pen at last and looked across to Frank. "You really think you're going to find something in them?"

Shrugging his shoulders, Frank stood up and started pacing. "I don't know, Ray. But what if you got me another warrant? I could go up there and take a look around, make sure, you know?"

"You think that's going to help matters?"

He shrugged again. "It's worth a try. I just want to make sure we haven't left any loose ends, you know what I mean?"

CLAIRE AND MICHAEL HAD taken Greta up on her offer of a late breakfast, and at noon they had gone over to Claire's house to launch their search. At first they looked together, rummaging through dusty closets and forgotten cabinets, dragging out boxes of Estelle's belongings. By three o'clock they had separated, and Claire had started pulling out cushions from the sheet-draped collection of old furniture that had been moved up to the rooms of the second floor.

But, after several sneezing fits from the clouds of dust that stirred with each sheet, she had given up any hope of finding more journals there and had gone upstairs to the turret room.

Now, as she lugged even more boxes out from one of the corner closets of the studio, Claire was beginning to wonder if they would come up with anything at all. They'd found several older journals stashed away in the bottom drawers of forgotten desks, and one that had been mistakenly placed in a box with some paperbacks. But there was nothing more recent than the one Claire had found the other night.

If nothing else, their exploration of the old house allowed Claire a more thorough look at the individual rooms and their contents. Weeks and months could be spent restoring pieces of furniture that were tucked away so inconspicuously, and certainly work on the house it-self could take months of labor. She wondered if Michael was up to it.

As she sorted through the next dust-covered box, Claire made a mental note to see Lubinsky sometime soon to discuss the current status of the Bramley accounts and holdings. If there was enough money available, she could complete work on restoration of the first and third floors and perhaps even begin on the second. Michael couldn't very well do it all himself. She'd have to hire help, even roll up her own sleeves after the paintings for the show were completed.

In the back of her mind, Claire couldn't help wondering if Michael might one day consider living in this relic of a house with her.

"Anything?"

Claire jumped at the sound of his voice and stood up from her squatting position in front of the open box. Michael lingered in the doorway, leaning against the frame, his arms folded across his chest, and Claire was reminded of an afternoon only a few weeks ago, which now seemed like months. An afternoon when she had looked at him for almost the first time and found herself, even then, mysteriously and undeniably drawn to him.

She shook her head, closed the box and carried it back to the closet. "Nothing," she answered him as he crossed the studio.

Her back was still turned when Michael stopped in front of her latest painting. The canvas had to be at least eight by ten feet and was probably one of her largest pieces. He studied the daring swirls of color, the bold brush strokes, and found himself admiring her courage at tackling such large pieces.

"How far have you gotten?" Claire asked him, still half-buried in the closet.

"I don't know," he answered as she turned and dusted her hands on her jeans. "We just don't seem to be coming up with anything. Where haven't we looked?"

Claire shook her head and pulled back her hair with one hand. "That's it for this room. Unless I'm overlooking a loose floorboard."

"I don't think there's any likelihood of that. I would have come across it when I sanded them a couple of months ago."

"So, that's it then. I give up." With her own sigh of disappointment, Claire sank down onto the drop cloth, crossing her slender legs, and rubbed her face with her hands. "I mean, maybe there *isn't* even another journal, and we've just spent the past three and a half hours searching the house for an answer that isn't even here."

Michael joined her on the floor, sitting behind her so that he could rub her shoulders. "I don't think so, Claire. You can tell by the last journal that Estelle was trying to convince herself to write about the murder. I think that by the time she got to the end of the one you found last night she had persuaded herself that if she could write it down, she could also speak out about it. She had to have written it down somewhere."

"Maybe she didn't get around to doing that, Michael." He could feel the tension building in her shoulders again and worked at the knots of stress with his fingers. "Or maybe she *did* write about it and then threw it away, thinking that someone might find it."

"No, Claire, she wrote more. I know it. She must have. The last morning I saw her I got the feeling she wanted to tell me about what she had seen. She was nervous, on edge. And she'd made a call to Bannon."

"Bannon?" Claire turned her head to face him.

"Well, I'm quite certain that it was Bannon. She was really flustered when she realized that I'd heard the last bit of the phone call, and when I questioned her about it, she swore it was nothing."

"So what was it that you heard?"

Michael shrugged. "It sounded like she was trying to arrange for him to come up to the house. She wanted to talk to him about something. I don't know. I assumed at the time she was concerned about her safety. They had found Annette's body a couple of days before, and I know that she had concerns about staying in the house alone."

"But you think now that she was calling Bannon to tell him what she had seen?"

"I suppose she might have been, yes."

"Well, did Bannon ever show up?"

He shook his head and then rested his chin on her shoulder once again. "Not that I'm aware of. I didn't see her again until the following morning and by then . . . she was dead."

A silence fell over the studio. As Michael held Claire in his arms, feeling the rise and fall of her chest as she breathed, he tried to shut out the memory of finding Estelle's body. Perhaps Claire was right. Maybe Estelle never had written anything else after the last journal. There really was no way of knowing. Strangely, she had never dated the entries in her journals. Michael had blamed this on the fact that Estelle had never seemed to know what day of the year it was.

"Maybe you're right," he said finally, turning her face and placing a kiss on her lips. "Maybe she didn't write anything down and what you found last night really is the final journal."

But Claire didn't seem to have Estelle's diaries on her mind anymore. She twisted around in his arms and wound her fingers through his hair, responding deeply to his kiss.

Michael didn't say anything, only followed her lead. When he felt the heat of her hand press against his thigh through the thick denim of his jeans, he let his own hands wander to her waist and then up beneath her loose cotton shirt. He ran his fingers over the gentle definition of her ribs, then slid them upward until they reached her nipples, erect buds beneath thin lace.

If it hadn't been for Decker's soft whine only inches from his ear, Michael knew that in a matter of moments they would have been stretched out on the drop cloths, their bodies entwined in the intimate cadence of lovemaking.

Reluctantly, he pulled away from Claire, the heat of her lips clinging to his, and they both turned to glare at the intrusive retriever. He sat down beside them, his tail beating a slow rhythm against the floor beneath the drop cloth. In his mouth, with a thin trickle of drool running down its black cover, was another journal.

"No way," Claire exclaimed as she pulled herself into an upright position. Reaching past Michael, she took the journal from the dog's mouth and wiped it on the cloth between her legs.

"If this is what I think it is . . ." Michael could hear the hope in her voice as she opened the cover, but it didn't take him more than a second look to realize what it was that Decker had found.

"Don't get your hopes up, sweetheart. It's blank. I found that one in a desk drawer in the lounge."

"Thanks anyway, Decker," Claire said wryly, scratching the dog's ears for a moment before turning back to Michael.

"So," he murmured against her lips, "where were we?" And they took up their kiss where it had left off. With a growing desire to feel her body against his, moving with his, Michael pulled her even closer against him. He ran his hands across the contours of her back, cradling her, until he felt her own hand on his chest, pushing him back.

"Claire? What is it?"

"The desk," she gasped as she pulled herself up from the floor.

"The desk?"

"In the lounge. When I first got here it was covered with papers—bills and invoices and stuff."

"Yes?" Michael prompted, taking the hand Claire offered. She pulled him to his feet.

"Don't you remember? Henry Lubinsky came over the first week I was here." Michael nodded. "He collected all that stuff and took it away with him to his office. Said he'd get his secretary to go through it sometime. Michael, there was a journal with it. I had it in my hand. A black book. And it had Estelle's name written inside the cover."

THEY HAD GONE downstairs to double-check the desk, but had come up empty-handed. By the time Claire had made tea and joined Michael at the kitchen table, she was willing to accept any suggestions he might have.

"Where do we go from here, then?"

Michael looked at Claire through the steam rising from his tea. "I'm not sure," he said. "The journal you saw Lubinsky take may have been the one we're looking for, or it might just be another old one. But if it is her most recent, then we have to get it. Somehow."

Claire let out a long sigh and pulled her knees up to her chest, propping her feet on the edge of the chair. "I could just ask him for it, Michael. After all, I did inherit Estelle's estate and her journals are part of it.''

"Claire, you said yourself that we can't trust anyone. Look, Estelle knew who Annette's killer was, recognized him and was afraid of him. That can mean only one thing—that he's local. If anyone, including Lubinsky, gets wind of our snooping around…all I'm saying is, it could be dangerous."

Claire sipped her tea, letting the warm brew ease her nerves. She wondered at the fact that, even though they were on the verge of possibly discovering the last of Estelle's journals, the thought of being with Michael was at the front of her mind, not the journal. Not the murder of Annette Hobson. Not the possibility that Estelle's killer was still in Westport.

"What we have to decide now," he continued, bringing his eyes back to hers, "is whether it's worth the possible risk of getting the journal from Lubinsky's office."

There was no question in Claire's mind about that. She set her mug down and leaned across the table. "I'm getting that journal, Michael. I don't care about the risks at this point. I'm sick of being afraid in my own house. I'm not exactly thrilled with the idea of someone deliberately trying to kill my dog, or of you being a suspect in a murder investigation. I don't care what it's going to take to get that journal back, I'm going to get it, period."

Michael was silent for a long time after that, sipping his tea, staring past Claire, and even though she wasn't sure what was going through his mind just then, she could see determination begin to furrow his brow. Finally he looked at her and spoke again. "All right then, Claire Madden. Since something tells me that you're going ahead with this whether I'm with you or not, I suppose that we'd better organize ourselves."

"So how do you propose we get this journal from Lubinsky's office?"

"Don't worry." Michael stood up, leaving his cup of tea on the table. "I've got a plan. Come on, get your coat."

CHAPTER NINETEEN

THE WEATHER WAS TAKING a turn for the worse. The ice storm that the local weather forecaster had cautioned travelers about had launched its assault on the coastal strip by four o'clock that afternoon. When Claire pulled the Volvo around to the front of the Lubinsky and Ames law offices at 4:25, the large station wagon slid clumsily into the parking spot.

She had left Decker at the house and, according to their plan, had dropped Michael off at the doughnut shop on the edge of town. Now, as she picked her way carefully across the sidewalk and through the front door to the suite of offices, Claire only prayed that the rest of Michael's scheme would fall into place.

They had driven past the offices only a few minutes earlier to check for Henry Lubinsky's car. The dark blue Bonneville still sat out front in the unmetered slot designated as "Lubinsky and Ames Parking Only." As Claire closed the office door behind her, she heard the lawyer's voice from the back office.

"Oh, Ms. Madden. Are you here to see Mr. Lubinsky? He wasn't expecting you, was he?" His secretary snapped a piece of chewing gum between her lips.

"No." Claire unwrapped her scarf and glanced toward the far office. "No, Mr. Lubinsky isn't expecting me. But I won't be needing more than a moment of his time."

Claire checked her watch. Four twenty-eight. With the icy conditions, it had taken her longer than she and Michael had anticipated to cross town.

"Is he free?" she asked, edging her way toward the open door.

When the secretary looked away for a moment, Claire used the opportunity to close the distance between herself and Lubinsky's droning voice.

"Ms. Madden," the woman called after her. "He'll be through in just a moment. If you'd like to—"

But Claire had already turned the corner into Lubinsky's office. When the portly lawyer saw her, he slipped his short legs from the edge of the desk and sat up in his chair.

"Uh...yes, that would be fine...no...look, I have to go...yes, I've just had a client walk in. Um-hmm. Yes, I will be in touch...right...okay...I'll talk to you tomorrow then. Right, goodbye." He replaced the receiver in its cradle, his eyes never leaving Claire. "Ms. Madden. I wasn't expecting you."

Claire gave him a cursory smile and scanned the office. "Yes, well, I'm sorry for showing up unannounced. But I promise this will take only a moment."

He waved his hand at the chairs in front of his desk. "Please, make yourself comfortable. Can I have my secretary bring you a coffee?"

"No, thank you, Mr. Lubinsky. I really can't stay long." She looked at her watch again. She had a lot to say before Michael called.

"So," he mumbled, "what is it I can do for you today?"

"I want to sell the house."

He looked puzzled, but covered his reaction quickly as he leaned forward in his chair. "I'm sorry, you want to sell the Bramley house?"

"Yes." Claire nodded. "And I'd like you to prepare me a summary of the estate's holdings and assets." She looked around the office again, trying to appear casual in her scrutiny. "Nothing personal, Mr. Lubinsky, let me assure you, but Westport just isn't for me. If you know what I mean."

The lawyer nodded. "Yes, I suppose I can understand that. A young woman like yourself, used to the city and all. Can I ask what brought about this sudden change of heart? I thought your notion was to finish the restorations and—"

"As I already told you, Mr. Lubinsky, I'm not interested in living in the house, only selling it. I don't think—"

The phone on Henry Lubinsky's desk buzzed, and even though she'd been expecting the call, Claire jumped as well.

"Excuse me one moment." He held up a fleshy index finger and turned to the phone.

Claire casually looked away. She scanned the bookshelves along one wall and then the uneven row of filing cabinets that lined the back. Then she saw it, the box marked "Burnes Art Supplies"—the same box she had given Henry Lubinsky five weeks ago when he'd packed up the contents of Estelle's desk. It had been shoved back between two oak cabinets. Quickly, Claire ran through a mental list of what she had to do.

"Henry Lubinsky here."

The box that rested on top of it would have to be moved before the art-supplies box could be opened.

"I'm afraid you're a little late. Could you hold on for just a moment?"

It had to be Michael.

Lubinsky stabbed at the red "Hold" button on his telephone console and looked across the desk at Claire.

"Could you excuse me for a moment? I, uh, I have to get something from the other office. I won't be a moment. Excuse me, please."

Claire nodded, trying to appear calm as he shuffled to the door.

This was it.

She looked at the two boxes nestled between the cabinets and then back at the door of the office. The lawyer was already wandering down the corridor to the front desk, his leather loafers scuffing against the short-piled carpet. He had left the door open a crack, and through it Claire heard him pick up the phone at his secretary's desk.

She had to move quickly. Michael had promised that he would try to keep Lubinsky on the phone for one minute. But with the lawyer only a few feet down the corridor, sixty seconds didn't seem like enough.

She scrambled from her chair and raced to the cabinets across the room. On Lubinsky's desk, a lit button on the telephone's console glared at her. As long as that light was on, Claire thought, she was safe. *Just keep him talking, Michael,* she repeated over and over in her mind as she squatted down and tugged at the first box.

Though her lips never moved, Claire could hear herself counting out the seconds. *One thousand twelve, one thousand thirteen.*

The top box was heavier than she had thought it would be and she wrestled with it awkwardly. The cardboard sides stuck to the wooden cabinets, and only after wrenching it with a final yank was she able to dislodge it.

One thousand twenty-one, one thousand twenty-two.

For a split second she stopped. The light on the telephone still glowed encouragingly and she could just make out snippets of Lubinsky's conversation from down the hall.

"Mr. Dalton . . . really don't know what you expect me to tell her . . . no . . . can't see that it's any concern of yours. . . ."

Claire moved faster now. She knew the script of Michael's spiel and she knew there wasn't much left to it. She was running out of time. She struggled against the restricted movement imposed by her heavy winter coat. Sweat beaded on her forehead.

The lid of the art-supplies box lifted off easily, and as she riffled through the tangle of papers, she prayed that the journal would still be there, that Lubinsky hadn't had a chance to go through the contents yet. She realized that if the lawyer understood the importance of the book, she wouldn't find it buried among the other papers.

" . . . Mr. Dalton, I don't think that what Ms. Madden decides . . . yes, I understand that. . . ."

Just when she was about to abandon hope, Claire's fingers brushed against the pebbled surface of the journal. It was buried at the bottom of the box. She twisted it out from between other papers, spilling several of them to the floor.

Claire threw a panicked glance at the phone on Lubinsky's desk. The light was still on and she strained to hear his voice.

" . . . don't think we need to continue this conversation any longer. . . ."

She jammed the journal inside her coat. With shaking fingers, she snatched up the bills and receipts that had escaped and stuffed them back into the box. She threw on the lid and wedged it back in place between the cabinets. With a final rush of adrenaline, she picked up the other box and forced it back into its former position.

When she looked back at the telephone, the button was dark.

Above the hammering of her heart, Claire could hear Lubinsky shuffling down the corridor. Giving the top box one more shove and hoping that it didn't appear disturbed, Claire zipped up her coat to conceal the journal.

At the sound of Lubinsky's asthmatic breathing at the doorway, she hurled herself back into the chair.

"Sorry about the interruption, Ms. Madden," he wheezed, crossing the room and lowering himself into the wide chair behind his desk. "But you should probably know that that was Mr. Dalton calling. Apparently he intended to get in touch with me before you did."

She hoped he couldn't see the beads of sweat that she felt on her forehead beneath her bangs. "Oh yes? And what did Mr. Dalton have to say?"

"He wanted me to persuade you not to sell the Bramley house. I guess he has the same sentimental attachment to that house as your aunt did. But I'm certain you'll agree that it's just another house, right? Now, where were we?"

"I'm sorry, Mr. Lubinsky, but we'll have to discuss this in greater detail at a later date. I'm afraid I've made arrangements to meet with someone else right now." Claire stood up, pulling the drawstrings of her coat tighter around her waist. "Once again, I apologize for my unannounced visit," she told him, giving him a smile and extending her hand across the desk.

"Shall I draft a statement of your current assets then?"

"Yes, please. Perhaps I can come to see you next week sometime. I still have to make some final decisions regarding the house, and by then I might have been able to address some of Mr. Dalton's concerns.''

CLAIRE DIDN'T REMOVE the journal from her coat. As she started her car and drove to the far end of town, the book jabbed against her ribs. She drove slowly, as the freezing rain had glazed the streets with a slick crust of ice. When she pulled into the doughnut shop's parking lot, the station wagon slid a couple of times before she was able to bring it to a stop in front of the glass entranceway.

Michael was waiting at the door when she drove up. With a gust of cold air, he got in and shut the door.

"Did you get it?" he asked, and then put out a hand to stop Claire when she started to unzip her coat. "No, not here. Bannon and Turner are in there." He nodded toward the doughnut shop. "I'm sure they're watching. Let's just get out of here."

Claire put the car in gear and pulled cautiously out of the parking lot.

"No problems?"

She shook her head and smiled. "Not a hitch. I'm only grateful that Lubinsky actually had the box in his office and not out front with his secretary."

"So you did get it!"

Claire nodded, smiling at the amazement in Michael's voice. Setting down his cooling cup of coffee in the holder on the dash, he leaned across to give her a quick kiss.

"Don't sound so astonished. What, you didn't think I could pull it off?"

"Obviously my doubts were entirely unwarranted. Ever consider a change of career?" Michael laughed and gave her another kiss before he unzipped her coat and pulled out the black book.

"Now all we have to do is find out if it was worth the risk."

Claire watched him out of the corner of her eye as she steered the Volvo along the icy roads toward home. He leafed through the journal, and all she could see was more blank pages. Then she caught a glimpse of handwriting.

For what seemed like an eternity, Michael remained silent. He turned the page only once.

Claire struggled to concentrate on the treacherous conditions of the road ahead of her. "Is it the right one, Michael?"

He didn't answer.

"At least tell me that we didn't go through all of this for the wrong volume."

She waited for his response. Her hands clenched the steering wheel even tighter and, when he finally spoke, Michael's voice was low and flat.

"Yes, it's the right one."

She felt her heart pounding again, her head beginning to throb. "So what does it say?"

In the hush of the car's interior, even as Claire felt the grip of fear clutching at her racing heart, Michael's voice suddenly became very cold. "I think you'd better pull over, Claire."

CHAPTER TWENTY

THE STATION WAGON swerved once and slid to a stop.

It was Michael who reached across to turn the key in the ignition and cut the engine.

"Michael, what is it?"

He didn't answer her. Instead, he handed her the book and continued to stare out the windshield at the freezing rain that melted and trickled down the blurred glass.

Claire felt the familiar pebbled surface of the journal's cover against her cold fingers and looked over at Michael. His face had turned to stone and a quiet rage blazed in his eyes.

Fearfully, she opened the journal.

It contained a single entry in shaky blue ink, scrawled over three pages. The handwriting was jagged and irregular, with long segments slipping off the ruled lines.

Claire's eyes quickly scanned the writing, taking in only partial sentences in her haste. What she did glean from these hastily read snippets was enough to send the same sense of horror charging through her as she had seen in Michael's eyes.

"...can only pray that this diary does not find its way into the wrong hands, at least not until this ordeal is over.... I know now that I must confess my knowledge...will not tell Michael, for I will not put his life at risk...can only thank the Lord that I did not witness the poor girl's death. But I cannot deny the fact that I saw him bring her limp body here to the bluffs at the edge of the forest. I watched him as he covered her with snow to hide her. And once, when he looked up, my heart stopped. I do not think he saw me looking out the window... too far away to tell, exactly... but I saw the uniform... never forget the black-blue against the white snow... the bright yellow piping... I know that uniform."

Claire cradled the book in her hands, her wrists limp with disbelief. The tapping of the icy rain against the car roof threatened to lull her into a false sense of security, but she could not ignore the uneasy feeling that came from within. She stared down at the pages in her lap, the writing blurring before her eyes.

Eventually she cleared her throat and turned to look at Michael. "She doesn't say who it is."

He shook his head. "I know. I don't think she knew herself, really. She was nearsighted. But I think she had a pretty good idea. Read the next page."

She flipped over the page, hesitant to read further, uncertain whether she could handle the next revelation her aunt's writing might bring.

"...I do not know who else to call...Joey Adams...he will know what to do. He's a good boy. I can trust him. But it is nighttime now. I will call him first thing tomorrow. If anyone can put an end to this nightmare, I know he will."

"Joey Adams?" Claire's voice broke through the monotony of pelting rain and Michael finally turned to look at her. "So she wasn't talking to Bannon, after all? When you heard her on the phone the day before she died...you thought it was Bannon, but it was this Joey Adams person. She was calling to tell him what she knew." And then Claire heard her own voice uttering the very suspicion that had been hammering through her mind from the moment she had read the word *uniform* in Estelle's journal. "You think she was calling him about Bannon?"

Michael shifted in his seat, loosening the seat belt across his chest and running his hand through his damp hair. "I don't know what to think, Claire. There's no way of telling from the journal. Yes, she may have been calling Joey about Bannon. Or she might have been calling him about Frank or Wesley."

"You know this Joey Adams, then?"

Claire followed Michael's gaze past the hood of the car. The last of the day's gray light glistened on the sleek surface of the road and on the glazed branches of the trees that bordered it. The fields on either side rolled back into a dismal haze that made her shiver as she waited for Michael's response.

He reached over and took the journal from her, closing it and laying it in his own lap. "Joey Adams. Yes, I know him. You met his mother at The Laughing Lobster, remember? Ruth was friends with Estelle. I think Estelle used to take care of Joey sometimes when he was a kid. Anyway, she knew him."

"But what authority would he have over someone like Bannon?"

"He used to be a deputy under Bannon. Up until a couple of years ago. Before Frank came on. I don't know what went on between Joey and Bannon—if there was a disagreement or if Joey simply had the ambition to move on. He applied for a position on the Bangor police force. Last I heard, he'd made lieutenant."

"So, if he was the person Estelle was speaking with the morning you overheard her on the phone, why didn't he come? Why wasn't something done?"

Michael shrugged and looked away again. "Obviously Bannon or Turner or Wesley got to Estelle first."

Seeing the turmoil of Michael's thoughts reflected in his face, Claire reached out to take his hand. He returned her gesture with equal uneasiness, but she felt a renewed strength with his touch.

"So where do we go from here?" she asked. "Obviously we can't go to the Westport authorities. Even if we knew for certain that it was Bannon, we don't know that Frank or Wesley or both aren't somehow connected as well. And we can't exactly go running off with the journals and hope that someone's going to believe them. Estelle's writing doesn't really prove anything concrete."

"No, you're right," Michael said, resolve once again edging into his voice. "But they're a start. At least we have an idea now who it is we're looking for."

"Michael, you're not implying that we—"

"No, Claire, there's nothing we can do right now. Not against the authorities, anyway. But I'm also not going to sit around and wait for Bannon's next victim." He leaned over, planted another kiss on Claire's lips and looked into her eyes for a long moment before speaking again. When he did, it sent a chill through Claire. "I'm not going to let him hurt you, too, Claire."

"Michael, don't. It's not going to come to that. Trust me. Bannon doesn't know about this journal. He can't know about it, otherwise he would have already destroyed it." This time it was Claire who leaned over to kiss Michael, a lingering kiss that reminded them both of the love they shared, the love that would give them the strength to see this through.

Claire turned the key in the ignition. "So, what do we do now?"

Michael checked his watch as she eased the car onto the slippery road. "It's five-fifty. I say we get home and give Joey Adams a call. See what he can do for us."

WHEN THE PHONE on Lieutenant Joe Adams's desk buzzed, he didn't intend on answering it. In fact, he would have let it go on ringing if he hadn't thought that it might have been his wife calling.

He'd been home late every night for two weeks, and this morning he had given his wife a scout's-honor promise that it wouldn't happen tonight. She was probably calling to remind him to bring home the paper and another box of diapers, he thought as he picked up the phone.

"Adams here."

"Hello, Joey? Joey Adams?"

The line hissed. Joe paused. No one had called him Joey in over two years, not since he'd been in Bangor, not since he'd left his boyhood behind in Westport.

"Yes, this is Lieutenant Adams. What can I do for you?"

"This is Michael Dalton. From Westport?"

He thought for a moment. "Oh, yeah. You bought the Farnsworth place, right? Yeah. What can I help you with?"

"Well, it looks like we've got a problem out here in Westport that—"

"Yeah, yeah, the Hobson girl, right? I heard about that. Listen, I hate to brush you off, Mr. Dalton, but you really have caught me at a bad time, and besides, you've got to understand, Westport and Manan County are way out of my jurisdiction."

"I do realize that, Lieutenant Adams, and I wouldn't bother you unless I had to. It's just that, well, I understand Estelle Bramley tried to contact you shortly before her death."

Joe leaned heavily against the corner of his desk and checked his watch. Six-fifteen. He had intended to get out of the building at six sharp to be home in time for dinner. Balancing the telephone handset between his cheek and shoulder, he slipped one arm into the sleeve of his coat.

"And I'm going to tell you the same thing I told her, Mr. Dalton. It's not my jurisdiction. There's nothing the Bangor authorities can help you with. The only thing I can do for you is call Sheriff Raymond Bannon and let him know that—"

"Wait a minute, Lieutenant Adams. After Estelle spoke with you, did you also call Bannon?"

"What else was I supposed to do?" He slipped his other arm into the coat, hoping that in a matter of seconds he would be out the door and on his way home. Marsha was going to kill him.

"Did Estelle happen to tell you anything about what's going on up here?"

"I'm sorry, Mr. Dalton. I honestly didn't let her get as far as that. As I said, it's not my jurisdiction. That's Sheriff Bannon's territory. You really should be talking to him if you know something."

"Wait a second, Joe. I don't think you understand what I'm trying to get at. Trust me, I wouldn't be bothering you if I could talk to Sheriff Bannon about this. But it could be Bannon I'm referring to here."

"In connection with the Hobson murder?"

"And Estelle Bramley's."

"Mr. Dalton, do you realize what it is you're implying?"

He heard an affirmative grunt across the line, followed by another crackle and a hiss.

"I take it that you have some kind of proof to back up this suspicion of yours?"

"You could say that, yes."

Joe wiped his forehead with the back of his hand and looked around the office. Everyone from the day shift had cleared out long ago. Letting out a long sigh, he yanked open the top drawer of his desk and pulled out his address book. He knew he should have followed his instincts and left at six.

"All right, Mr. Dalton. Look, there's nothing I can do for you as far as my authority goes. But, as much as I think you're barking up the wrong tree, I'm going to give you a number to call. You got a pen?"

He waited, listening to the other man scramble for one.

"Yeah, go ahead."

Joe's finger followed the number scrawled in his book as he read it out over the phone and then listened to Michael Dalton repeat it for verification. "Yeah, that's it. Now, that's the number of someone I know over at the DA's office—Andrew Marlowe. He's with the special-investigations unit. You can give him a call about this, tell him what you know. But let me warn you, Mr. Dalton, you'd better be pretty sure before you go dragging the DA's office in on something like this."

He heard another grunt across the line.

"Maybe Marlowe can help you out. I don't know. But you'll have to wait until tomorrow anyway. It's after six. He'll be long gone by now." As he should be himself, Joe felt like adding.

"Thank you, Lieutenant. I really do appreciate your time."

"No problem," Joe lied, and he mumbled a quick goodbye before hanging up.

Six twenty-two. What difference was another two minutes going to make? Marsha had probably already burned the pot roast.

Joe flipped through his address book and hovered over the phone. He was doing the right thing, he told himself, by warning his old buddy. He listened to the rings until the phone was picked up and another crackle spit across the line.

"Westport Sheriff's Station."

Joe Adams cleared his throat. "Yeah, Frank? This is Joe Adams in Bangor. You got a minute?"

CLAIRE HAD HEARD all of Michael's side of the conversation, standing right beside him as he spoke to the lieutenant in Bangor. After he'd hung up the phone, he could see his own shock reflected in her dark eyes.

"So, after Estelle talked to him, he called Bannon?"

Michael nodded.

"Well, that about proves it then, doesn't it? Estelle called Joey Adams, hoping that he could help her. He turns around and gives Bannon a ring, and Bannon just sidles up here and kills her. She was a sitting duck, Michael. The woman didn't stand a chance."

"Claire, calm down for a second." He reached out to take her hands in his, but she backed away.

"No, Michael, no. It's all making sense now."

"What is, Claire?"

"Everything. The second break-in. When we called the sheriff's office to report it, Bannon wasn't there. Didn't Wesley say that he *thought* he'd gone home?"

"He might have, Claire."

"And the brakes of the car. He'd gotten to that mechanic before I did. Who's to say that he didn't set something up with the guy so I would be led to believe it was nothing more than an accident?"

"Or they might have just been faulty brakes," he offered, trying to calm her. He didn't want possible coincidences to cloud the very real implications of what they had just discovered.

"And Decker. Bannon said he couldn't prove anything about the trap. Said that it couldn't be traced. He even suggested that it was an old trap, yet you and I both saw that the bait was fresh." She turned at the kitchen counter and looked out the window above the sink, out across the gloomy fields toward the darkening woods, and Michael guessed that she was remembering the bitterness of that stormy night when they had found Decker in the trap.

"Claire, we can't jump to conclusions. We've got to think about this a bit more."

She turned from the window, anger in her eyes as she glared at him across the room. "So what are you saying, Michael? That these were all simply coincidences?"

"No, Claire, what I said was that I don't think we should jump to any conclusions. We don't know that it was Bannon. Estelle herself didn't sound entirely certain about what she had seen out there in the field that day."

"Fine, then." She turned her back and leaned up against the counter, staring out the window again. "I guess it's just my imagination."

"Claire, I'm sorry. I didn't mean anything by it." He edged up behind her, feeling the tension along her shoulders as he rubbed them. Feeling her warmth, smelling the trace of her perfume, Michael was immediately overcome by the desire to be with her, to lie with her, to drown their fears and suspicions in the love they shared for each other. And for one crazy moment, he wanted nothing more than to take Claire away from this. Away from Westport and the danger it might ultimately present.

Instead, he wrapped his arms around her, crossing them over her chest, and pulled her back against him. "I'm as confused as you are right now, Claire. Believe me, I want to get to the bottom of this, too." He leaned over and kissed her cheek. She didn't pull away. "I just don't want us to lose perspective on this." After a pause, he added, "I don't want anything to happen to you, Claire."

He wasn't sure how long they stood there—Claire leaning back against him, staring out into the cold dusk, listening to the freezing rain scratch against the window. In time he felt her breathe deeply and could sense the lessening of her tension.

But he couldn't take her away from this. As much as he wanted to, they couldn't turn their backs on what had happened. Not when they finally had the power to do something about it.

"What about Lubinsky?" Claire asked quietly.

"What about him?"

"He's a lawyer. Maybe there's something he can do. I mean, he's not my favorite person, but I think it's pretty obvious that he's not a threat. He would have destroyed the journal if he was in with Bannon, wouldn't he?"

Michael considered Claire's suggestion. She was right in the sense that Lubinsky could not have been aware of the journal's significance. But, at the same time, there wasn't anything the weaselly lawyer could help them with at this point.

"Look, Claire, there's nothing he can do. He's only a small-town lawyer. All we can do right now is wait. We'll give this guy Marlowe a call first thing tomorrow morning. Joey said he might be able to help. If nothing else, we'll at least have opened an inquiry into Annette's and Estelle's deaths. Maybe we can leave after that. I'm not sure we'd have to stay here during the investigation. I don't know how safe it would be."

Claire nodded, but remained silent as Michael stroked her hair.

"It's going to be all right, Claire. We're doing the right thing."

She turned within the circle of his arms then, looking at him, and Michael suppressed his urge to kiss her.

"Will you stay the night, Michael?"

He brushed her cheek with one finger, hoping that his smile would soothe her. "I hadn't thought otherwise." And then he bent his head to hers. There was more than longing behind her kiss—more like a thirst for reassurance that they were safe, that they could do something about this and that they had each other.

"But listen, sweetheart," he said, reluctantly ending their kiss, "I have to go to my place for a couple of minutes. I still have some phone calls to make today."

"You can make them from here," Claire offered.

"I will. But I need a couple of folders off of my desk before I make them. Are you going to come with me?"

She shook her head. "No, I could use the time to get some of my stuff cleared up in the studio. I left my things in a mess the other day."

"Claire, I don't want you here alone."

"Michael, I'll be fine." She smiled to prove her confidence to him. "Besides, you said you'll only be a minute or two."

"All right then," he said, slipping on his jacket. "But you've got your gun, right?"

"My gun? Michael, don't scare me."

"You have your gun, right?" he repeated, hoping that the stern look he gave her would convey his concern.

"Yes, Michael, I have my gun. It's on the table in the studio. You saw it there yourself, remember? And that's exactly where I'm going as soon as you get out of here, okay?"

"All right, then. I'll be right back."

As Michael started down the steps to the car, he slipped a little on the crust of ice left by the freezing rain and the dropping temperatures. It would be a slow crawl back to his place, he realized.

In a streak of gold, Decker bolted out the door behind him, and when Michael tried to call him back, the retriever only bounced around on the slippery ground in front of the Land Rover, anxious for a drive. "Decker, come here," he yelled again, but the dog only wagged his tail and ran once around the vehicle, thinking it was some amusing game.

"Take him with you," Claire suggested as she shivered in the doorway.

"Claire, he should stay here with you."

But she reached out and pulled up his collar. "I'll be fine, Michael," she whispered. "Take the mutt with you. He's been cooped up all afternoon. Besides, *I* don't want to stand around in the freezing rain while he does his business."

"All right, then," he finally agreed, slipping his gloves on and zipping up his jacket. "Lock up behind me."

CHAPTER TWENTY-ONE

RAYMOND BANNON DIDN'T leave the doughnut shop when Frank did. Caught up in a conversation with Burt Gifford and Jed Henderson, the sheriff didn't get out of the One Stop Donut Shop until almost six-thirty, and by the time he stomped into the Westport station, Frank was already gone.

He wiped his boots on the mat and crossed the front office to his desk. On top of his pile of folders and paperwork were several scrawled telephone messages that Wesley had taken over the course of the afternoon. But Bannon wasn't interested. The last thing he needed was a call-out on a night like this.

The roads had been treacherous just crossing town. In spite of the sanders that were apparently working overtime on all of the roads in and surrounding Westport, Bannon imagined that no one would be driving anywhere unless absolutely necessary. He certainly wouldn't.

"What's it been like around here, Wes?" he asked his deputy, taking off his holster and setting his gun down on top of the telephone messages.

Wes leaned back in his chair, his feet up on the desk as he cleaned his revolver.

"Quiet." He shrugged and watched Bannon fill his mug with day-old coffee. "I figured I'd just wrap up a couple more things and head on home before this storm gets even worse."

"Not a bad idea," Bannon replied, lifting his mug toward the window. "It's none too pretty out there tonight."

He returned to his desk again and sat back in his chair, unzipping his parka. He didn't really feel like doing any paperwork, didn't even feel like looking at the phone messages Wes had taken. They couldn't be urgent. Wes would have radioed him if they had been. All he really wanted to do was go home, stick a TV dinner in the microwave and fall asleep in front of the television.

Even now, he was beginning to wonder why he hadn't gone straight home from the doughnut shop.

"Where's Frank? I thought he'd be here by now."

Wes shook his head and nodded to the phone on Frank's empty desk. "He's been and gone. Got a call and raced out of here."

"A phone call? You know who it was?"

"Joe Adams, I think."

"He got a call from Joey?"

Wesley's feet dropped from the desk and he nodded his head. "Yup, that's what it sounded like. He didn't tell me. Why?"

"What was he calling about?"

"Like I said, Frank didn't tell me anything. I got the impression he might have been talking about the Bramley house, from the sound of it, but—"

Bannon snatched up his revolver and holster from the desk with such speed that the telephone messages fluttered to the floor. "Did he say where he was going?"

The young deputy shook his head. "Just said he had to check on something and flew outta here."

But Bannon had already crossed the station house.

Despite the weather and the chance that his hunch might be wrong, Bannon knew that he had to at least check up on it.

He remembered the last time Joey Adams had called. It was Frank's case and Bannon hadn't wanted to step on any toes, so he'd given the information to Frank. It had been storming that afternoon as well, and Frank had told him that he wouldn't be able get to it until the following morning.

By that time, Estelle Bramley was dead.

Bannon was playing on hunches now, and nothing more. He'd been having a lot of hunches lately, and he couldn't keep on ignoring them. If this call from Joey meant what he thought it did, he might already be too late.

"You want me to radio Frank?" Wesley called after him as the sheriff started out the door into the icy rain.

"No, Wes." He shot him one last steely glance. "No, there won't be time for that. Besides, I think I know where he's gone. Hold down the fort. I'll radio in if there's anything."

CLAIRE HAD WATCHED Michael get into the Land Rover and then had stood in the doorway, her gaze following the beams of the vehicle's headlights as they inched along the road to the next concession and disappeared from view.

Tension still played in the muscles along her shoulders and back. But knowing that Michael would be back shortly comforted her somewhat as she paced the floor of the studio. She checked her watch and gazed across the dark fields. The freezing rain had turned to snow, and through it Claire could just see the warm glow of lights in Michael's house.

The minutes ticked away like hours.

Claire turned back to the canvas she had begun to dabble at, but she was too tense, too distracted. After rinsing her brush in the jar of turpentine, she started to pace the studio again. Floorboards squeaked softly underfoot. The house was quiet. Without Decker padding from room to room and without Michael hammering downstairs, it was almost too quiet.

A chill ran through her and she knew it wasn't from the cold.

Heeding some intuitive inner voice, Claire crossed the room to the telephone and picked up the receiver. The harsh buzz of the dial tone blared in her ear. At least the phone was working, she thought as she returned to the worktable. Gathering up some of the spare rags, she uncovered the gun. She picked it up, the metal cool against her skin. She could still remember the day Alec had forced her to go out with him to buy the weapon. Not that he'd ever owned a gun, and not that she could ever imagine him buying one for himself. But he had been adamant. It had been only two or three weeks after Greg's death, and perhaps because the incident was still so immediate in her mind at the time, Claire had submitted to Alec's unyielding request. But even after firing several dozen rounds with the compact semiautomatic at the shooting range, Claire still couldn't imagine ever turning the deadly weapon on a person. Even Bannon, she thought as another chill twisted up from the pit of her stomach.

She set the gun back on the table. It wouldn't come to that. That's what she'd promised Michael. They would call the DA's office in the morning and that would be the end of it. She and Michael could leave Westport for a few days, a few weeks even—however long it would take for the authorities to wrap up their investigation. However long it would take before Westport felt safe again.

She had enough paintings finished now that, if need be, Alec *could* put a show together. He wouldn't be happy about it, if it did come to that. On the other hand, she certainly wasn't going to get any satisfactory work done here—not with the tension and the fear that came along with knowing that someone in Westport was getting away with murder.

Claire glanced at the gun again. It looked so out of place there, nestled among the tubes of paints and the vivid colors of her palette.

No, she thought again, it wouldn't come to that.

She finished cleaning the studio table and looked out once more to the lights across the field. Michael couldn't be much longer now. And when he returned, she wanted to hold him, to lose herself in the haven of his embrace.

She wanted to forget about what they had discovered. She wanted to feel the absolute abandon that had swelled within her only this morning when she'd woken up in his bed.

She wanted that feeling for the rest of her life, Claire realized now. She wanted to be with Michael, needed to be with him, more than anything she had ever wanted before. And no one, not even Raymond Bannon, was going to stand in the way of that.

Claire moved away from the window, warmed by both the memories of Michael and thoughts of the future they might share. She crossed the studio and turned down the hall to the master bedroom. She would light a fire. Maybe even run a bath, she decided as she lit some candles and started the kindling.

With the cold weather they had experienced over the past few weeks, Claire had become proficient at starting fires in the bedroom hearth, and soon a small blaze sputtered and licked at the logs. She turned from the hearth eventually, satisfied with her handiwork, and clicked on the ministereo in the corner, hoping to take the edge off the unnerving silence that shrouded the house. She paused to light another candle on the bedside table. Blowing out the match, she saw the photograph through the spiral of smoke. Greg smiled back at her, and instead of the pull she usually felt deep in her chest, Claire smiled quietly back at him.

It was time now. Alec had been right, she thought as she picked up the brass picture frame. It had taken time—time and Michael—but now she looked at Greg's photograph with nothing more than a warm fondness. No longer did she feel the wrench of pain, the dark memories, the emptiness.

Now Claire could put his picture away. Now she could go on, carrying the fondness of his memory in her heart as a warm reminder of who he had been, not what she had lost. And his memory would give her a newfound strength and vitality for life that she could not have conceived without having known him.

Greg would be with her forever. She wasn't saying goodbye. Even as she tucked his picture in the top drawer of her dresser, Claire knew he would always be with her in spirit, living on through her.

Touching the face behind the glass one last time, Claire closed the drawer.

She checked her watch. Michael would be back any minute now. She crossed the room to the connecting bathroom and switched on the light. Turning the taps, she emptied a packet of bubble bath powder into the swirling water and watched the steam rise from the wide tub. It would take awhile to fill, Claire thought as she turned from the tub and walked back through the door to the bedroom.

She worked at the clasp of her watch as she moved through the bedroom. When she finally looked up, Claire froze.

She heard her own gasp even as her heart lurched.

He stood motionless, just inside the doorway of the bedroom. She almost didn't recognize him at first in the dim light from the bathroom. His hair was soaked, its sandy brown color almost black as it lay matted against his head. His head was lowered slightly, and beneath the wet hair covering his forehead his burning eyes raged with an intensity that drove a hot knife of terror through Claire's chest.

It was his eyes, the brutality of his eyes, that purged all doubt in Claire's mind as to what his intentions were.

She struggled to breathe and for a fleeting moment feared that she might pass out.

This wasn't right. It was supposed to be Bannon, not him.

Claire took a step forward, determined not to let him recognize her fear.

"Frank." She fought to control the panic in her voice. "What are you doing here?"

Her thoughts raced madly. The gun. It was in the studio. In her mind, she could see the corner of the table where she'd left it.

But she had to get past Frank first.

The idea of locking herself in the bathroom flashed through Claire's minds. But the image of Michael coming back to face Frank, unwarned and unarmed, drove her another step forward.

She needed the gun.

Frank's eyes held hers with a malevolence that Claire could never, in her worst nightmares, have imagined. And then, with cool confidence in his power, he started to cross the room. His footsteps were purposeful, his stance assured.

"Sorry, Claire—I did knock." He looked around the bedroom and ran a finger along one of the bedposts as he steadily approached her. "Guess you didn't hear me. You were probably in the bathroom."

Claire threw a desperate glance around the room. There had to be something that she could grab as a weapon.

Frank was still in uniform. Drops of melted snow on his parka glistened in the flickering candlelight. The yellow piping of his uniform pants warned her. If he was still in uniform, he'd have his gun on him. And he'd be far quicker with it than she could possibly be with something like a fire iron from the hearth.

No, she had to get the gun from the studio.

Somehow...

"The door was open," he said coldly.

But she had double-checked the door when Michael left. She knew she had. Frank circled to the armchair and Claire saw his hand as it gripped the top of the chair, his fingers sinking into the soft fabric with a strength that Claire had to heed.

"You're nervous, Claire," he murmured.

"You surprised me." She forced an uncertain smile, hoping to convince him that she didn't suspect anything, hoping that he would believe her fear was based solely on being startled.

"Hmm." He took another step closer, his eyes still scanning the bedroom, his hand following the line of the mantelpiece. Claire watched him as he lifted a framed picture, turned it to catch the pale light from the bathroom and then carefully replaced it.

She took a step back from him, edging toward the doorway.

"You're not afraid of me, are you, Claire?"

She shook her head. Swallowing hard, she took another step. In the periphery of her vision, she could see the light from the studio spilling out into the hallway. It seemed impossibly far away. Still, she took another step.

"Hate to think you were afraid of me. I just dropped by for a visit. That's all. Just wanted to talk."

"You, uh, you could have called first, Frank." Claire edged closer still to the doorway. As long as she kept him talking, as long as she kept a distance between them . . .

"Had a chat with my buddy over in Bangor, Joe Adams."

Claire felt long trails of perspiration down her back. She felt droplets of sweat beading her forehead, but refused the urge to wipe them away. Any sudden moves might set him off.

"He told me you might have something on the Hobson case. So I told him I'd look into it. And here I am." He spread out his arms and smiled. Claire wanted to run then. To break away from Frank's stare, to flee from him and the house.

But she knew she'd never make it. She stood her ground. "What do you want from me, Frank?"

For every step Claire took back, Frank took another two toward her. And as he closed the gap between them, something behind his eyes, something desperate and vicious, triggered Claire's anger. A cold anger that swallowed her fear.

This was the same man who had assaulted and killed a seventeen-year-old girl. Then left her body in the fields. But he hadn't stopped there. He'd gone on to kill Estelle when he realized her knowledge of his crime.

And, now, there was herself.

Why should Frank stop at Estelle? Why should it end there?

"Are you going to kill me too, Frank? Like you killed Annette?"

He didn't respond. His progress was steady, his steps sure as he advanced upon her. She could see the cold determination in his gaze.

Claire knew then that Frank Turner had come here for only one purpose. And, as she stared into those eyes of savage hatred, a resolve stronger than she had ever known swept through her.

It *was* going to end here.

She was not going to let Frank Turner get in the way of the happiness she had found at last in Michael. She was not going to let him destroy her dreams—dreams that had been destroyed once before with a single gunshot.

"Why did you do it, Frank? Did you kill Annette because she knew something, too? Or did you just kill her because she wouldn't do what you wanted?"

Claire would never forget the speed with which Frank's hands shot out and seized her at that moment.

She had neither the time to pull away nor the chance to even flinch as his strong fingers dug into the soft flesh of her arms and shoved her back against the bedroom wall.

She was only six feet away from the door now, but the gun in the studio was the farthest thing from her mind.

MICHAEL EASED OFF of the gas, letting the Land Rover's weight propel it down the slight gradient in the road. Although the freezing rain had given way to wet snow some time ago, the temperatures were dropping and some sections of the roads were virtual skating rinks.

He had passed a sander on the way over to his house after leaving Claire, and had figured that he would have no problems getting back to her house. But now, with Decker whining softly beside him in the passenger seat, Michael was taking it easy. Even the Land Rover was barely a match for the treachery of the roads.

He glanced at the speedometer. Ten miles an hour. He could have cut across the fields and walked in less time than this.

In spite of the concentration required, the drive over to his house and back had allowed Michael the opportunity to contemplate his next moves. It had given him the time, finally, to go over the thoughts that had been lingering in the back of his mind for several days now. Thoughts that had utterly consumed him from the moment Claire had come to see him last night.

What he and Claire had shared last night, the love and affection that they had rediscovered in one another's arms, had been all that Michael needed to make his final decision.

Imagining life without her was impossible. Claire Madden had walked into his life and had touched a chord deep within him that he hadn't known still existed. He knew now, with a certainty that amazed him, that he could not be without Claire. That he needed her in his life. That without her he would be lost.

Last night, when they had made love and he had held her next to him, wanting to hold her forever, he had resolved that he would ask Claire to marry him.

As he turned into the drive, Michael was going over what he would say to her, the words he would use to ask her. But his musings came to a shuddering halt when he saw the patrol car.

Michael hit the brakes, ignoring the road conditions. The Land Rover swerved sharply and buried its front end in a bank of snow. Decker yelped once but clawed his way back onto the passenger seat unscathed. His back bristled and a low growl erupted from deep in his throat when Michael turned the engine off.

He didn't hear the dog. As he battled with the clasp of his seat belt and groped for the door handle, the only sound he heard was the thundering of his own heart.

Leaving Decker in the car, he half ran, half skated across the icy walk toward the door. It was unlocked. Fear gripped his insides and wrenched at them with a brute force.

Claire.

His own safety never once crossed his mind as he rushed headlong through the dark rooms. And when he reached the bottom of the staircase, his impulse was to race up to the third story, to find Claire, to ensure that she was all right. But instinct called out to him now, warned him that rushing blindly up the stairs would not save her. Instead, he crept forward slowly, cautiously, edging through the thick darkness.

The silence of the house pulsated in his ears. He strained to hear movement, voices, anything that might betray Claire's location in the old house.

Nothing.

Panic surged through him and he felt the heat of tears stinging his eyes at the thought of any harm coming to Claire.

Stealthily, he moved forward. And then, as he passed the second floor and started up to the third, Michael heard their voices. Above one of Claire's tapes on the stereo, he could hear her speaking. And then . . . Frank Turner.

Quickly, he slipped out of his jacket and continued to climb toward the third floor, trying desperately to remember which steps creaked.

When he reached the top step, his heart was racing.

The lights in the studio were still on, and farther down the hall he could see a soft glow from the bedroom. Closer to where he stood, he saw the shaft of light from beneath the hall door to the bathroom, and he heard the water running in the tub.

He could barely make out their voices as he crept along the hall to the studio. Frank was saying something about Annette Hobson. Then he heard Claire's muffled voice, but he couldn't make out the words.

Something fell to the floor and shattered. Michael heard what sounded like glass grinding underneath the hard sole of a boot.

Rage drove him on. The thought of Frank Turner harming Claire forced him into action. Without a moment of hesitation, Michael ducked into the studio and grabbed the Beretta that Claire had left on the worktable.

The cold, hard steel of the weapon in his hand was all the reassurance Michael needed now. He released the safety and edged toward the bathroom door.

BANNON CURSED AGAIN. He cursed himself for driving too fast and he cursed the road crew for not putting down enough sand. Then he cursed the patrol car as he kicked more dead branches into the icy rut his back wheel had created.

He was only five minutes away from the Bramley house. He could even see a light from one of the turret windows shimmering out through the falling snow. And he swore to himself that, if this didn't work, he'd walk the rest of the way to the house.

He eased down into the car and slammed the door.

He had tried to reach Frank by radio about five minutes ago but had gotten no response. In fact, that was how he'd slid into the ice trap he was in now. If he had paid more attention to the road than to the radio, he would have been at the Bramley house ten minutes ago.

With numb fingers, Bannon slipped the gearshift into Drive and eased his foot from the brake to the accelerator. The vehicle shimmied forward, slid again, threatened to veer off the road and finally straightened out.

The headlights glared off of the surface of the road, revealing wide patches of sheer ice. Bannon took it slow now. If he didn't get stuck again, he could be at the Bramley house in a matter of minutes.

CHAPTER TWENTY-TWO

CLAIRE DIDN'T MOVE. She didn't dare.

Frank had released her from his iron grip, but he still hovered over her. His left arm was extended, his hand braced against the wall only inches from her face, preventing her from moving any closer to the bedroom door.

When she did shift her weight, Claire felt shards of glass crack beneath her slippers. A rose-colored bowl had exploded across the hardwood floor in what seemed like a million splinters—testimony of her failed attempt at an escape.

He wasn't as tall as Michael, she thought absurdly as she looked up at Frank. But he still towered over her slight, five-foot-three frame. He leaned his weight into the arm that blocked her, bringing his body within inches of hers, and Claire could feel the heat of his breath against her face.

For one desperate moment, she wondered if this was how Annette Hobson had felt.

"What is it you want from me, Frank?" she asked, fighting to keep her voice steady.

He wouldn't answer her. He simply stood over her, his eyes seeming to bore right through her.

"Is it the journals you're after? Is that it?" Claire saw a brief flicker of interest sweep across his face.

"So you know about the journals, then."

"Is that why you broke into the house? And tried to kill my dog? So that you could look for Estelle's journals? To find the one that had your name in it?"

"The break-in was only meant to scare you, Claire. Nothing more. I needed to get into the house and look for them. But I knew I wouldn't have the chance until you decided to leave. You were always here, though. You and Dalton."

Frank's eyes never left Claire's as he spoke. "I needed you gone. Dalton, too. But you don't scare too easily, do you? I guess you're regretting that now, right?" He reached out for her cheek.

Claire instinctively jerked back.

"Just relax, Claire. I'm not going to hurt you, honest."

She shuddered as the trace of a smile twisted his lips. But it wasn't a shudder of fear any longer. Claire had gone beyond that point now. This time it was contempt.

"Is that what you told Annette just before you killed her?"

A low sigh escaped Frank's lips as he hung his head and closed his eyes. For a fleeting moment, Claire considered ducking beneath his arm and running to the studio for the gun. No, he would be too fast. She'd already witnessed that.

Her eyes had adjusted to the limited lighting and she could see Frank's face clearly. Every line, every mark, every twitching muscle would be etched in her memory.

"Annette has nothing to do with you and me, Claire," he said slowly.

Claire took a ragged breath. "I think you're wrong, Frank. I think she has everything to do with us. If you hadn't killed Annette, you wouldn't have had to kill Estelle, right? Without Estelle out of the way, I would never have shown up. And without me, Frank," she added, attempting a tone of confidence that took every fiber of her remaining strength, "without me, you wouldn't be facing an investigation from the district attorney's office tomorrow morning."

She watched his lips purse, his eyebrows crease together with renewed anger, and Claire thought that he might hit her.

He didn't. Instead he took a deep breath and leaned even closer to her.

"Annette got herself killed. You hear me? If she hadn't been so stubborn..." He seemed to fade away for a moment, lost in some memory, perhaps the memory of Annette's murder. "But maybe you won't be so stubborn, hmm? Maybe you're smarter."

Claire turned her face from the sour heat of his breath as he came even closer to her. She pressed herself tighter still against the wall, wishing she could fade back into it. She felt his cheek against hers, the day's growth of his beard burning against her skin as he tried to kiss her.

When she turned from him, Frank reached out and took her face in his hands. Rough fingers dug into the soft flesh of her cheeks as he yanked her around to face him.

It was then, as he forced her to look at him, that Claire noticed the movement in the bathroom.

In a flash she saw Michael edge up to the door. He held her gun in both hands and braced his shoulder against the doorframe.

Her gaze barely shifted, but it was enough to alert Frank. And, in that sickening instant, Claire knew that she had betrayed Michael.

She watched in horror as the deputy reached under his parka for his gun. It had already been unclipped and he was pulling it out before Michael even called out his name.

With Frank's arm pinning her to the wall, Claire struggled to free herself, trying to reach for his gun. But the glint of steel came up relentlessly, as if in slow motion.

She turned to look at Michael. He had taken another step into the bedroom and was raising the small semiautomatic toward Frank. And then, as she collected her remaining strength to hurl herself against Frank's weight, she heard the shot ring out.

Her own scream followed it. She cried Michael's name at the same time that she saw him thrown backward by the force of the bullet. The gun slid from his hand across the white ceramic bathroom floor and came to rest in a pool of water.

She twisted and pulled desperately, trying to break free from Frank's powerful grasp.

Claire heard her own voice cry out Michael's name one last time as she watched him sink to the floor.

WITH A FINAL SWERVE on the ice, Bannon's patrol car came to a stop outside the Bramley house. The sheriff was surprised to see Dalton's car in the drive as well. The Land Rover sat at an awkward angle, and when Bannon walked farther up the drive, he saw that its front end was buried in snow.

He edged closer to the vehicle. Considering the force that must have propelled the car into the bank, Bannon's immediate concern was for the possible passengers.

He sidled up to the Land Rover and reached out a hand to support his weight on the ice, when suddenly a canine face sprang to the window. Bannon jumped back, nearly falling over onto the ice, and watched as the dog's breath fogged the window and trickles of saliva ran down the glass.

He stared at the retriever for a second, hating it now even more than he had the first time he'd seen Claire Madden gripping its collar in this very same driveway a few weeks ago.

And then Bannon heard the gunshot.

Ringing out over the silent fields, its echo blasted a hole through the stillness of the night and sent his adrenaline pumping.

He unclipped his revolver and raced for the door.

FOR CLAIRE, time meant nothing.

She was back in the Soho apartment again. She heard the heart-wrenching crack of the gunshot. She ran the same length of corridor she had run over and over again in her nightmares. She saw the red blood splashed across her bright yellow slicker, on the walls and the carpet.

Frank's hands were like steel clamps digging into her arms as she wrestled to free herself. Every time she gained some ground, Frank pulled her back even farther. Farther away from Michael.

Through eyes blurred with tears, Claire watched Michael. In the shadows where he lay, she couldn't tell where he had been hit. She only knew that he wasn't moving.

And she knew then, as the familiar cloak of shock wrapped itself around her again, that if Michael died, she could not go on. She'd tried to before. When Greg had left her, when her world had fallen to pieces around her, she had struggled to continue. But now, without Michael . . . she knew she couldn't go through it again.

When her last effort to escape from Frank's clutches failed, Claire turned on him with all of her anger, with all the intensity of her pent-up sorrow and bitterness. She ceased her struggles and turned to look squarely at him. She couldn't remember if she had ever hated anyone or anything as much as she did Frank Turner at that moment.

Her voice was a ragged whisper as her muscles tensed for her final attack. "You son of a—"

Frank let out a short grunt as she collided with his chest, and in a flash she clamped her hand over his. She could feel the solid handle of the revolver in his broad hand. With her index finger, she followed the curve of his own as it wrapped around the trigger.

With her love for Michael driving her, Claire fought blindly against Frank's overpowering force. And as she struggled with him, feeling herself steadily slipping beneath his superior strength, she realized that she didn't care what happened to her.

They staggered and reeled, grappling with the gun in their hands. Its muzzle was wedged dangerously between them, but neither would slacken their grip. Claire's free hand slid across the slick surface of Frank's wet parka, groping for something to hang on to, anything to allow her a tighter hold.

But she was losing—she could feel it.

As Frank crushed her arm in his strong fingers, Claire could feel her own will diminishing.

Then Raymond Bannon stood in the doorway.

"Frank." His voice boomed a warning across the bedroom.

Out of the corner of her eye, Claire saw Bannon's great bulk filling the doorframe. She saw his gun raised, trained at the deputy. At the same moment, she felt Frank's grip on the revolver loosen momentarily.

And then, in horror, she felt his finger move beneath hers.

Nothing could have prepared her for the blast of the bullet's discharge. Her grip on the weapon weakened and she felt it slip out of Frank's hand as well. For one numbing moment, Claire wasn't certain if she had been hit or not. But when she looked at Frank again, she realized it wasn't her blood that was warming her hand.

Eyes wide, Claire watched him slump to the floor in front of her. She backed away, blinking, as if to drive the sight from her memory.

And then, a small cry escaping her throat, Claire staggered across the room to Michael.

She fell to the floor beside him, the heat from the blazing hearth burning against her skin as she reached out to touch him. Underneath one hand, she could feel the slow rise and fall of his chest. Her breath caught. He was still alive.

With trembling fingertips, she traced the outline of his face, fluttering down from his closed eyes to his lips, following the line of his jaw and finally along his neck, where several strands of his hair were matted with blood.

The shoulder and sleeve of his sweater were soaked in blood. The dark gash of his wound glistened in the flickering light of the fire. With a surge of relief, Claire saw that the bullet had struck a safe distance from his heart.

She folded her legs beneath her and gently lifted Michael, cradling him in her arms, feeling his warmth against her chest. When his eyes fluttered open, she felt a tremor shake her body as another sob escaped her. A tear rolled from her cheek and dropped onto her hand as she brushed his hair from his face.

"I'm not dead, Claire," he whispered, his voice tainted with pain as he struggled to give her a reassuring smile.

A shaky smile crept across her own lips as she looked down through her tears into the calm gray of his eyes, touching his lips again with her fingers, marveling in the life she held in her arms. She bent down and kissed him gently. "I know you're not, Michael."

"So why are you crying?" He blinked and stared up into her eyes.

Claire leaned over then to press her cheek against his, rocking him gently, feeling the warmth of his life pulsing with hers. "Because I love you, Michael. Because I love you."

And Claire cried even harder now, knowing that Michael had not left her, knowing that they would be together and nothing could come between them again.

EPILOGUE

CLAIRE SQUINTED against the glare of gallery lights. With a fixed smile, she glided through the crush of people mingling in the main area, sipping champagne, buzzing with enthusiasm.

She wasn't naive enough to think that they were all discussing her work, but she had been able to catch some snippets of conversations: observations, comments, scattered compliments and the customary remarks of how these works were going to refashion the New York artworld. She recognized the rehearsed speeches that many gallery goers carried with them to every show opening, and kept on smiling.

"You look fantastic," Alec whispered in her ear, sliding an arm around her slender waist and pulling her to him so he could plant a kiss on her cheek.

"Thanks." Claire flashed him an appreciative smile.

She had slipped into the tight, low-cut black dress less than an hour ago, and had pulled her hair back into an elegant sweep off her neck. She felt the heat of the gallery lamps glaring down on her bare shoulders as Alec ushered her past one of her paintings and away from the crowd.

"This is great," he said in an excited whisper. He nodded to several onlookers and continued to scan the room. The arm around Claire's waist tightened its grip. "Do you realize who is here tonight? I mean, *everyone's* here. Oh, and look, there's Walters. And even Breckner's here. You can bet you're going to be reading about this tomorrow, darling.''

Claire grinned. Alec lived for nights such as this. All the pressure, all the stress he put himself through was well worth it if it ended like this.

"I have to tell you, Claire, I really had my doubts this time around.''

"Oh, come on. Don't I always pull through for you, Alec?''

He nodded. "Um-hmm. But this time . . . no, this time, darling, you cut it down to the wire. You really had me guessing.''

Claire had to admit, as she studied the canvases that lined the walls of the gallery, that she, too, had had her share of doubts. She could still see the damp paint glistening on several canvases she'd touched up at the last minute.

While Michael was recovering in the Westport hospital, Claire had forged ahead with her work. And, as she had promised Alec, she had given him plenty to choose from. Now, two weeks later, with the show underway and the paints packed up for the time being, Claire could finally savor the sense of accomplishment.

"Well, you can relax now, Alec. It's all finished.'' She nodded across the gallery to the whirlwind of people and lights. "There you have it. Now, go on, bask in your glory. It only lasts one night.''

With another quick kiss, he left her side and Claire watched him as he disappeared into the crowd. She took a deep breath, letting it out slowly as she scanned the room. Another two hours and this would be over. Another two hours and she could put up her feet and forget all of the formal protocol and the stuffy art-world etiquette.

Realizing that her champagne glass was empty, Claire set it down on the nearest table and was about to turn when she felt a strong hand on her bare shoulder. A smile was already breaking her pensive expression as she looked up.

"I hardly recognized you," Michael whispered through his own soft smile, and he pressed a lingering kiss to her lips.

Claire pointed to the black shimmer of her dress. "No paint."

"That must be it." He nodded and ushered her behind one of the gallery partitions. "Not that I don't think you're the sexiest woman alive in your paint-covered shirts, but I have to admit that tonight you look absolutely incredible."

"Well, thank you." She let her eyes skim over his suit, noting the thin black sling over his good shoulder, and finally met his beaming smile again. "I could say the same about you," she admitted as she slipped her hands around his waist. "I do like the jacket but, you know, jeans and sawdust really do have a special effect on me."

With the buzz of the crowd curtained off by the partition, Claire lost herself to Michael's kiss, and only when one of the waiters wandered by with a tray of champagne glasses did they pull away from each other. Michael reached over and lifted two glasses in his free hand, nodding a thank-you to the departing waiter.

"So, tell me, do you always draw such a crowd, Ms. Madden?"

She peeked around the partition and surveyed the roomful of people one more time. She nodded and gave him a satisfied smile. "Usually. But I could have sworn that a certain someone told me he couldn't make it to-night?''

He grinned and handed her a glass of champagne. ''I lied. You didn't think I could possibly stay away, did you? Besides, I had to ask you something, and I knew you'd be getting home late after the opening and you wouldn't feel like talking on the phone and—''

''What is it, Michael?'' But Claire already knew what he was about to ask. She had seen it in his eyes all last week. She could see it written across his face even now.

He set down his glass and looked squarely at her. ''I want you to move to Westport.''

''You want me to move to Westport?''

Claire felt his good arm wrap around her waist, drawing her to him. She could feel his breath brush against her lips, and was about to fall into the fever of his kiss again when he added, ''Yes...right after you marry me.''

And then Claire kissed him. With all the passion and love she felt for Michael, she answered his devotion, knowing that she could, at last, dare to live fully again.

''Can I take that as a yes?'' he murmured as he pulled reluctantly away from her, searching her eyes for her answer.

''No,'' she whispered, ''it's far more than a yes. It's a forever.''

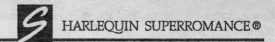

HARLEQUIN SUPERROMANCE®

COMING NEXT MONTH

#594 THE PRINCESS AND THE PAUPER • Tracy Hughes
Jessica Hartman's beloved father was gone, leaving maddening
instructions in his will. In order to inherit her share of the ailing
company that bore her name, she would have to work side by side
with her estranged half-brother. Like it or not, she would have to
confront the forbidden feelings Cade ignited in her.

#595 NOT QUITE AN ANGEL • Bobby Hutchinson
Sometimes private investigator Adam Hawkins thought
Sameh Smith was from another planet. In her endearingly clumsy
way she helped derelicts, street kids and prostitutes. But she was
also a mystery. She had no personal history prior to April 1994,
and Adam was determined to find out why.

#596 DANCING IN THE DARK • Lynn Erickson
Alexandra St. Clair Costidos wanted her son back. His influential
father had spirited him away to an impregnable Greek island to
punish her for leaving him, and the law could do nothing. It was
time for drastic measures. Alex hired mercenary John Smith to
help her, but even if she regained her son, she was in danger of losing her heart.

#597 THE YANQUI PRINCE • Janice Kaiser
Reporter Michaela Emory thought it was time to take some risks.
How else could she have wild adventures and meet the man of her
dreams? Suddenly, she got the chance to do both when she flew to
South America to interview the legendary Yanqui Prince. A mod-
ern-day Robin Hood, Reed Lakesly was renowned for his courage
and charisma. Suddenly Michaela had more adventure and passion
than she'd bargained for....

AVAILABLE NOW:

#590 KEEPING KATIE
Patricia Keelyn

#591 TWILIGHT WHISPERS
Morgan Hayes

#592 BRIDGE OVER TIME
Brenda Hiatt

#593 GHOST TIGER
Janice Carter

Fifty red-blooded, white-hot, true-blue hunks
from every State in the Union!

Look for MEN MADE IN AMERICA! Written by some
of our most popular authors, these stories feature fifty
of the strongest, sexiest men, each from a different state
in the union!

Two titles available every other month at your favorite
retail outlet.

In April, look for:

LOVE BY PROXY by Diana Palmer (Illinois)
POSSIBLES by Lass Small (Indiana)

In May, look for:

KISS YESTERDAY GOODBYE by Leigh Michaels (Iowa)
A TIME TO KEEP by Curtiss Ann Matlock (Kansas)

You won't be able to resist MEN MADE IN AMERICA!

HARLEQUIN SUPERROMANCE®

A DARING NEW CONCEPT
FROM SUPERROMANCE

WOMEN WHO DARE
Bright, bold, beautiful...
Brave and caring, strong and passionate...
They're women who know their own minds
and will dare anything...for love!

#594 THE PRINCESS AND THE PAUPER by Tracy Hughes

Jessica Hartman thinks it's grossly unfair that she has to share her inheritance with Cade, her no-good bum of a stepbrother. Cade was adopted, and Jessica hasn't seen him since she was a small child. Why should *he* be sharing her wealth?

Even more disturbing for Jessica, her feelings for Cade aren't sisterly *at all*....

AVAILABLE IN MAY, WHEREVER
HARLEQUIN BOOKS ARE SOLD.

WWD94-1

INDULGE A LITTLE 6947 SWEEPSTAKES
NO PURCHASE NECESSARY

HERE'S HOW THE SWEEPSTAKES WORKS:
The Harlequin Reader Service shipments for January, February and March 1994 will contain, respectively, coupons for entry into three prize drawings: a trip for two to San Francisco, an Alaskan cruise for two and a trip for two to Hawaii. To be eligible for any drawing using an Entry Coupon, simply complete and mail according to directions.

There is no obligation to continue as a Reader Service subscriber to enter and be eligible for any prize drawing. You may also enter any drawing by hand printing your name and address on a 3" x 5" card and the destination of the prize you wish that entry to be considered for (i.e., San Francisco trip, Alaskan cruise or Hawaiian trip). Send your 3" x 5" entries to: Indulge a Little 6947 Sweepstakes, c/o Prize Destination you wish that entry to be considered for, P.O. Box 1315, Buffalo, NY 14269-1315, U.S.A. or Indulge a Little 6947 Sweepstakes, P.O. Box 610, Fort Erie, Ontario L2A 5X3, Canada.

To be eligible for the San Francisco trip, entries must be received by 4/30/94; for the Alaskan cruise, 5/31/94; and the Hawaiian trip, 6/30/94. No responsibility is assumed for lost, late or misdirected mail. Sweepstakes open to residents of the U.S. (except Puerto Rico) and Canada, 18 years of age or older. All applicable laws and regulations apply. Sweepstakes void wherever prohibited.

For a copy of the Official Rules, send a self-addressed, stamped envelope (WA residents need not affix return postage) to: Indulge a Little 6947 Rules, P.O. Box 4631, Blair, NE 68009, U.S.A.

INDR93

INDULGE A LITTLE 6947 SWEEPSTAKES
NO PURCHASE NECESSARY

HERE'S HOW THE SWEEPSTAKES WORKS:
The Harlequin Reader Service shipments for January, February and March 1994 will contain, respectively, coupons for entry into three prize drawings: a trip for two to San Francisco, an Alaskan cruise for two and a trip for two to Hawaii. To be eligible for any drawing using an Entry Coupon, simply complete and mail according to directions.

There is no obligation to continue as a Reader Service subscriber to enter and be eligible for any prize drawing. You may also enter any drawing by hand printing your name and address on a 3" x 5" card and the destination of the prize you wish that entry to be considered for (i.e., San Francisco trip, Alaskan cruise or Hawaiian trip). Send your 3" x 5" entries to: Indulge a Little 6947 Sweepstakes, c/o Prize Destination you wish that entry to be considered for, P.O. Box 1315, Buffalo, NY 14269-1315, U.S.A. or Indulge a Little 6947 Sweepstakes, P.O. Box 610, Fort Erie, Ontario L2A 5X3, Canada.

To be eligible for the San Francisco trip, entries must be received by 4/30/94; for the Alaskan cruise, 5/31/94; and the Hawaiian trip, 6/30/94. No responsibility is assumed for lost, late or misdirected mail. Sweepstakes open to residents of the U.S. (except Puerto Rico) and Canada, 18 years of age or older. All applicable laws and regulations apply. Sweepstakes void wherever prohibited.

For a copy of the Official Rules, send a self-addressed, stamped envelope (WA residents need not affix return postage) to: Indulge a Little 6947 Rules, P.O. Box 4631, Blair, NE 68009, U.S.A.

INDR93 .

INDULGE A LITTLE
SWEEPSTAKES

OFFICIAL ENTRY COUPON

This entry must be received by: MAY 31, 1994
This month's winner will be notified by: JUNE 15, 1994
Trip must be taken between: JULY 31, 1994-JULY 31, 1995

YES, I want to win the Alaskan Cruise vacation for two. I understand that the prize includes round-trip airfare, one-week cruise including private cabin, all meals and pocket money as revealed on the "wallet" scratch-off card.

Name_____

Address _____ Apt. _____

City_____

State/Prov._____ Zip/Postal Code_____

Daytime phone number_____
(Area Code)

Account #_____

Return entries with invoice in envelope provided. Each book in this shipment has two entry coupons—and the more coupons you enter, the better your chances of winning!
© 1993 HARLEQUIN ENTERPRISES LTD.   MONTH2

INDULGE A LITTLE
SWEEPSTAKES

OFFICIAL ENTRY COUPON

This entry must be received by: MAY 31, 1994
This month's winner will be notified by: JUNE 15, 1994
Trip must be taken between: JULY 31, 1994-JULY 31, 1995

YES, I want to win the Alaskan Cruise vacation for two. I understand that the prize includes round-trip airfare, one-week cruise including private cabin, all meals and pocket money as revealed on the "wallet" scratch-off card.

Name_____

Address _____ Apt. _____

City_____

State/Prov._____ Zip/Postal Code_____

Daytime phone number_____
(Area Code)

Account #_____

Return entries with invoice in envelope provided. Each book in this shipment has two entry coupons—and the more coupons you enter, the better your chances of winning!
© 1993 HARLEQUIN ENTERPRISES LTD.   MONTH2